BAD MEN

John Connolly

In 1693, the settlers on the small Maine island of Sanctuary were betrayed to their enemies and slaughtered. Since then, the island has known only peace — until now. For men are descending on Sanctuary to hunt down and kill the wife of their leader and retrieve the money that she stole from him. All that stands in their way are a young rookie officer, Sharon Macy, and the island's strange, troubled policeman, the giant known as Melancholy Joe Dupree. But Dupree is no ordinary policeman. He is the guardian of the island's secrets. He knows that Sanctuary has been steeped in blood once; it will tolerate the shedding of innocent blood no longer. All hell is about to break loose . . .

SHUTTER ISLAND

Dennis Lehane

Summer, 1954. US Marshal Teddy Daniels has come to Shutter Island, home of Ashecliffe Hospital for the Criminally Insane. Along with his partner, Chuck Aule, he sets out to find an escaped patient — a murderess — as a hurricane bears down upon them. But nothing at Ashecliffe Hospital is what it seems. And neither is Teddy Daniels. Is he there to find a missing patient, or to look into rumours of drug experimentation, hideous surgical trials, and lethal countermoves against Soviet brainwashing? Or is there another, more personal reason he has come here? As the investigation deepens and the questions mount, Teddy and Chuck begin to believe that they may never leave Shutter Island — because someone is trying to drive them insane . . .

NOBODY TRUE

James Herbert

I wasn't there when I died. I was having one of those out-of-body dreams, the kind where you feel your spirit has left your body and it isn't really a dream. But somebody murdered me while I was away. Mutilated me. Left nothing for me to come back to. Who did it? The serial killer who was terrorizing the whole city? Or someone closer, someone known to me? But I had no enemies. At least, I didn't think I had. Then I began to discover things about myself. Funny what people say about you when they think you're dead. And it's scary when you meet the serial killer, when horror is followed by even greater horror, when your own family is threatened and only you can stop the killings . . .

FOREVER ODD

Dean Koontz

In the town of Pico Mundo, a friend of Odd's has disappeared. It's feared he is dead. But as Odd applies his unique talents to finding the missing person, he discovers something worse than a dead body. Odd Thomas had never asked to communicate with the dead — the dead sought him out. As the goodwill ambassador between our world and theirs, he must do the right thing; for Odd lives between two worlds in a town he can never leave. Now Odd faces new enemies, some living and some not. But the adversary he encounters is unspeakably cunning. Every sacrifice is needed now, as a life-changing revelation rushes towards us, and Odd Thomas must stand between us and our worst fears.

THE DEVIL YOU KNOW

Mike Carey

Felix Castor is a freelance exorcist in London. At a time when the supernatural world is in upheaval, spilling over into the reality of the living, his skills are in demand. A good exorcist can charge what he likes — but there's always the risk of taking on a spirit that's too strong. Then it's game over . . . Though Castor has been officially 'retired' since a close encounter that he only just survived, he accepts a seemingly simple exorcism. But what should have been a straightforward job is turning into the Who Can Kill Castor First Show, with demons, were-beings and ghosts lining up to claim the big prize. But that's OK: Felix Castor knows how to deal with the dead. It's the living who piss him off . . .

TWISTED SOULS

Shaun Hutson

Imagine your worst fear. A fear that eats away at you. The people in the Derbyshire town of Roxton know what it's like to live with fear. In London, Emma Tate's parents have been killed in a car crash and her husband's business is failing. Emma, her husband and two of their friends hope to find some peace in a luxury house near Roxton. But Emma and her companions uncover secrets about themselves that bring undreamed-of horrors . . . Roxton, too, is a place of secrets. What was the reason for the closure of the mine? What mysterious force is at large? . . . Emma and her companions are led into a nightmare and to a meeting with their own most twisted and vile desires.

Shaun Hutson is a bestselling author of horror fiction and has written novels under nine different pseudonyms. He was one of eight bestselling authors taking part in the BBC's *End of Story* competition. Shaun lives and writes in Buckinghamshire with his wife and daughter.

DYING WORDS

Giacomo Cassano, a thirteenth-century writer, believed that creative people, with great gifts given by God, have to pay a terrible price for them. Bestselling biographer Megan Hunter's new book about Cassano promises to be a success. But when Megan's editor is horrifically murdered, Detective Inspector David Birch finds no evidence to link another human being with the death. The crime scene divulges destroyed copies of Megan's book about Cassano, and pulverised pages from horror writer John Paxton's latest blockbuster. Links between the two writers are investigated, but as DI Birch sifts through the evidence he begins to suspect that the answer lies elsewhere. As the death toll mounts, he discovers links he could never have imagined, and answers beyond not just belief, but sanity itself . . .

Books by Shaun Hutson
Published by The House of Ulverscroft:

TWISTED SOULS

SHAUN HUTSON

DYING WORDS

Complete and Unabridged

CHARNWOOD
Leicester

First published in Great Britain in 2006 by
Orbit, an imprint of
Little, Brown Book Group
London

First Charnwood Edition
published 2007
by arrangement with
Little, Brown Book Group
London

The moral right of the author has been asserted

British Library CIP Data

Hutson, Shaun, *1958 –*
   Dying words.—Large print ed.—
Charnwood library series
1. Authors—Fiction
2. Murder—Investigation—Fiction
3. Horror tales
4. Large type books
I. Title
823.9′14 [F]

ISBN 978–1–84617–841–2

Published by
F. A. Thorpe (Publishing)
Anstey, Leicestershire

Set by Words & Graphics Ltd.
Anstey, Leicestershire
Printed and bound in Great Britain by
T. J. International Ltd., Padstow, Cornwall

This book is printed on acid-free paper

This novel is dedicated to my wife, Belinda. I don't deserve her but I thank God I've got her.

Acknowledgements

Right, here we go again. Another list of people, places and things that have featured in some way, shape or form before, during or after the writing of this novel.

Once again, if there's anyone missing from this list who I've forgotten, I apologise. I'll get you next time . . .

My first thank you is and always will be, to my publishers. Especially to Barbara Daniel, Andy Edwards, Clara Womersley, Sheena-Margot Lavelle, Carol Donnelly and everyone else who puts up with me on a frighteningly frequent basis.

Extra special thanks to my 'Wild Bunch' — my superb sales team. Just a little extra mention for one of them in particular: Mr Andrew Hally. It was, in some small measure, thanks to him that this book came about. I was suffering from appalling writer's block at the time, and it was during a conversation we had (no, not the one about Spurs finishing above Liverpool, Andy . . .) that something sparked in this feeble brain of mine and eventually gave birth to this novel.

Huge, immeasurable thanks to my fantastic agent, Brie Burkeman. I know I joke about our occasionally volatile working relationship, but she really has taught me more in the last two years than I care to mention. Thanks, Brie.

Back with publishers, I'd like to thank David

Crombie and Catriona Jardine for allowing me to have such a great time working with them. Let's hope there're plenty more to come.

The same goes for everyone at Working Partners who endure my phone calls and God knows what else, but allow me to indulge in some of my most enjoyable journeys in writing. Thanks folks.

Thanks also to Stephane Marsan.

This next bit is going to sound like name-dropping but you should all know me better than that by now so here goes.

Many thanks, as usual, to Mr James Whale and Melinda. And, of course, to Ash.

Special thanks to Bruce Jones. A man who consumes haggis at a rate unlike anyone I've ever seen. A man whose heart is as big as his talent (but not quite as big as his dog . . .). Cheers, mate.

Thank you also to Mr Shane Richie, whose appalling taste in football teams is balanced, thank God, by him being such a decent human being. No phone calls after that cup game I notice, you bastard . . . Take care, mate.

Many thanks to October 11 Pictures. Especially the 'Irish Coen Brothers'; Jason and Jonathan Figgis. As always, it's a pleasure to work with you, fellas. Thanks to Maria also (yes, that English bloke is still on the bloody phone . . .).

Thanks also to Jo Roberts (I don't think you're leaden, mate) and Gatlin Pictures. And by the way, I don't ★★★★★★★ swear that much, Jo.

Thanks, as ever, to Sanctuary Music, especially Mr Rod Smallwood, Val Janes and Dave Pattenden and, of course, to the six noisy sods who continue to delight me with their music. I speak of course of Steve, Dave, Bruce, Adrian, Janick and Nicko. All the best, lads.

A very big thanks to Marc Shemmans, a man of incredible patience among other things.

On a more personal level, I'd like to thank Brian at the bank. Everyone at Chancery, and Leslie and Sue Tebbs.

Even though I never seem to answer her e-mails, I'd also like to thank Meaghan Delahunt.

Thanks to my very good friend Martin 'Gooner' Phillips. We've known each other forty-odd years yet he still talks to me . . .

To Ian Austin, Zena, Hailey, Terri, Becky and Rachel, Nicky and to Sandi at Waterstone's in Birmingham.

Thanks seems a bit inadequate a word to say to Graeme Sayer and Callum Hughes who continue to run, organise and expand www.shaunhutson-.com so brilliantly. Once more, to everyone who has ever visited the site, contacted me through it or keeps coming back, thank you. Or thanks to those two guys more to the point.

Thank you, as ever, to Claire and everyone at Centurion who take care of me when I have to travel.

I know I say this every time but my thanks to the two greatest influences on my life and work go to the sadly departed Sam Peckinpah and Bill Hicks. I still feel their loss all too keenly, as should anyone who recognises true genius.

A huge thank you to Cineworld UK, especially Mr Al Alvarez and, of course, to everyone at Cineworld Milton Keynes, especially Debbie, Paula, Mark, Martin, Sharon, Mel, James, Terry, Nick and everyone else I've forgotten or who's left by now. I seem to spend most of my waking hours at the pictures but then again, do you blame me . . . ? Thanks to all of you from me and my sandwiches . . .

I have to thank Liverpool Football Club, naturally. My love and admiration for that club goes so deep at times that it scares me, but (and yes, I know it seems like ages ago now) for *that* night in Istanbul alone, I will always be grateful. May 25th 2005 will live in my memory for ever as I'm sure it will every other Reds fan who was there (and yes, at half-time, I did think we were screwed. How wrong I was . . .). To all those in the Bob Paisley lounge and who sit around me at Anfield, thanks.

An incredible thank you to my mum and dad for everything.

My wife, Belinda. Well, what do I say? Thank you is never enough. Without her there would be nothing. It's as simple as that.

My other girl is the same. Who else would enjoy getting up at six-thirty to drive to Wigan with me? (Thank God we won . . .) To say I love her is an understatement beyond measure. She knows I'm crazy (she's told me enough times). I think she's taught me more than I've taught her about some things. This book is for my wonderful daughter.

Now, you lot. My readers. All ages. New and Old. If there's a more loyal, honest bunch I'd like to see them.

Time for another journey.

Let's go.

Shaun Hutson

'Where there is no imagination there is no horror.'
Sir Arthur Conan Doyle

1

The car missed the bus by inches.

There was a high-pitched scream of rubber on tarmac as the Renault skidded past. The driver of the bus sounded his horn angrily, the sound adding to the cacophony already filling the air.

Detective Inspector David Birch gripped the wheel of the car more tightly and drove on, pressing his foot down harder on the accelerator. Ahead of him, his eyes fixed like laser sights upon it, the silver-grey Nissan he was pursuing also speeded up, scraping the side of a Mini as it pushed and barged through the traffic on Jamaica Road.

More horns blared as the two cars hurtled along the thoroughfare, Birch keeping the Renault as close to the fleeing Nissan as he could. There was perspiration on his face. His shirt was sticking to his back.

'Where the fuck is he going?' Birch muttered, aware that they were approaching another set of traffic lights.

The Nissan showed no signs of slowing down and shot through the junction with the lights on red.

Birch followed without hesitation.

Beside him in the passenger seat, Detective Sergeant Stephen Johnson glanced at his watch.

1

'We've been chasing the bastard for thirty minutes,' he remarked.

Birch glanced down and saw that the fuel tank was half empty. He accelerated as he saw a short stretch of clear road.

'Maybe he'll run out of petrol,' Johnson offered, hopefully, nodding in the direction of the Nissan.

'Where's our fucking support?' Birch demanded. 'We've been on him all the way from Canning Town.'

'There're marked units moving parallel with us. Others up ahead.'

'Tell them to cut off all routes across the river.'

Johnson lifted the two-way to his mouth.

'This is Unit Seven,' he said, gripping the side of the seat as Birch sent the Renault veering around another car, the wheels slamming into the kerb. 'Heading up St Thomas Street towards Borough High Street. Suspect must be prevented from crossing the river. Close London Bridge.'

After a second or two a metallic voice rattled into the car. 'Closing A3 on approach to London Bridge,' it said before disappearing in a hiss of static.

More lights ahead. They were on green this time. Beyond them Birch could see a pedestrian crossing. There were people waiting on either side of the street.

'Shit,' he murmured, watching as the Nissan bore down on the black and white lines across the road.

A man stepped on to the crossing, jumping back hurriedly when he realised the Nissan

2

wasn't going to stop.

The silver-grey vehicle hurtled past him then turned sharply left and right, cutting across the path of several other cars. Up ahead of the Renault, two vehicles collided, momentarily blocking the street.

'Moving into Southwark Street,' Johnson said into the two-way.

Birch saw a police motorcycle swing out from a side street. It roared after the Nissan.

From above he heard another sound. The police helicopter swooped as low out of the sky as it dared and hung there like some massive metallic bird of prey. It followed the two speeding vehicles for a moment then once more rose high into the air.

Birch gripped the wheel more tightly and drove on.

2

There was an unedifying jolt as the Renault momentarily mounted the pavement to avoid the damaged cars blocking the thoroughfare. Both policemen grunted as Birch swung it wildly back on to the road again.

Up ahead, the uniformed motorcyclist was less than twenty feet from the rear of the speeding Nissan.

'Just stay with him,' Birch muttered under his breath.

The bike was gaining by the second.

'Moving down Stamford Street,' Johnson said into the two-way. 'All units converge.'

More traffic lights.

The Nissan shot through the next set, narrowly avoiding a collision with a Mercedes. There were more blaring horns and the shriek of tyres, and as the Renault sped onwards after its prey Birch could smell the stink of burning rubber strong in his nostrils.

The police motorbike was now within ten feet of the Nissan. The rider suddenly accelerated, coming up on the inside of the vehicle.

Birch shook his head. 'Tell him to stay back,' he snapped.

Johnson had the two-way to his mouth when the Nissan suddenly swung violently to the left. It hit the motorbike and sent it veering out of control.

The two wheels mounted the pavement, and the rider managed to control the bike long enough to guide it back on to the road.

'No,' snarled Birch.

The Nissan lurched left once more, its driver wrenching the wheel violently, slamming into the bike with even greater force.

This time, the motorbike was shunted towards a line of parked cars. It struck the side of a Vauxhall. The impact sent the bike rider flying from his seat. He hit the bonnet of the Vauxhall, skidded across it and landed on the other side. The bike crashed on to its side and ricocheted back into the road, tyres still spinning.

Birch twisted the steering wheel to avoid the obstacle, his offside tyre clipping the bike.

There was a sound of shattering glass. Pieces of the bike's windscreen and portions of one Renault headlight skittered across the tarmac like crystal shrapnel.

Somewhere behind he heard screams but his eyes never left the road. Never left the Nissan that he was still pursuing.

Johnson turned slightly in his seat and saw the injured police motorcyclist lying motionless on the pavement, people running towards him, some to help, others to merely gaze in bewildered fascination at his body.

On the right, the gaunt edifice of the National Theatre appeared.

Up ahead, traffic on the roundabout was heading straight for them.

'He's going for Waterloo Bridge,' Birch said.

'All units,' Johnson repeated into the two-way.

5

'Suspect is crossing the river at Waterloo Bridge.'

Birch twisted the wheel left and right, intent only on not hitting anything. In front of him, the Nissan wove in and out of the heavy traffic, ignoring the blaring horns, somehow finding a path through. It finally swung left on to the bridge.

Birch followed, narrowly avoiding a taxi whose driver gestured angrily at him.

'Get out of the road,' the DI roared as he drove on, his teeth gritted as he saw people ahead crossing.

Ahead, the Nissan ploughed on.

It hit a woman and sent her careering backwards on to the pavement. She flopped down on to the flagstones, cracking her head hard on the concrete.

'Close the far end of Waterloo Bridge,' Birch rasped.

The police helicopter, seeing the open space over the river, suddenly swooped down again, dropping to within a hundred feet of the fleeing Nissan.

'All units converge,' Johnson ordered. 'Strand and Aldwych.'

'Bastard's got nowhere to run now,' hissed Birch and pressed down harder on the accelerator.

3

The sunshine glinted on the dirty grey surface of the Thames as it snaked through London, but Birch cared nothing for the river beneath him as he sped over Waterloo Bridge. All that mattered to him was the Nissan and its occupant and he was closing on them with every second.

I've got you now, you bastard.

He guided the Renault round an Interflora van; nothing now between him and his prey but open road.

Look in the rear-view mirror, shithouse. Look and see. You're going nowhere, you murdering fuck.

The police helicopter wheeled away back up into the sky and Birch nodded to himself.

'Hang on,' he said, through clenched teeth.

Johnson did as he was instructed, and the Renault shot forward as Birch stamped on the gas pedal. The dark blue car slammed into the rear of the Nissan, the impact causing both cars to skid slightly.

Birch smiled thinly.

That's for the first of the five, you piece of shit. How long ago was it now? Eight months? That's how long we've been hunting you, isn't it? Eight long fucking months.

He hit the accelerator again and sent the Renault crashing into the back of the Nissan a

7

second time. The impact was so savage that part of the Nissan's rear bumper came free. Portions of shattered tail-light spilled into the road.

That's for the twelve-year-old you raped and murdered.

The Nissan swerved. Birch rammed it again.

That's for the one who was fourteen. The one you strangled with electrical flex after you'd raped her. The one you hung from the highest diving board at Southwark Park swimming pool. Just to taunt us, eh?

'Suspect's vehicle is in Lancaster Place,' Johnson said into the two-way, glancing briefly at his superior's blazing expression. 'Why wasn't the road blocked?'

A fourth time, Birch sent the Renault slamming into the Nissan's rear end.

And that's for the latest one. For the little nine-year-old. The one you buggered as well. Raping her wasn't quite enough this time, was it? Nor was blinding her with a soldering iron while you did it.

The traffic lights at the end of the road were on amber. Someone tried to cross but the Nissan drove through anyway, narrowly missing them.

'Turning left into the Strand,' Johnson continued.

Birch saw uniformed men on the street. The wail of sirens filled the air as more police cars came hurtling from the direction of the Aldwych.

End of the line, cunt.

'We've got him,' the DI breathed, eyes blazing.

He momentarily eased the pressure on the accelerator, cursing to himself as he saw the

8

Nissan heading directly for two police cars trying to block the road. It hit them with a thunderous crash, the impact enough to open a gap between them large enough for the Nissan to scrape through.

Uniformed men ran towards the stalled grey vehicle. Birch hit the brake and he and Johnson hauled themselves out of the Renault.

The driver of the Nissan, blood running from a cut just below his hairline, was already out and running towards Southampton Street.

Don't let him get away. Not now.

The DI saw him pull the long, sharp blade from inside his jacket as the first of the uniformed men came within reach of him.

'Watch it,' bellowed Birch.

The blade flashed. Wielded with a combination of effortless expertise and demonic force, it caught the constable across the right ear, sheared off part of the lobe and hacked into his neck deeply enough to sever a major artery. A fountain of blood erupted from the wound as the man fell to his knees shrieking helplessly, hands clutching at the yawning gash.

'Fuck,' snarled the DI and ran on, Johnson close beside him.

Some of the uniformed men were gathering around their fallen companion, others had already run to their cars. More were joining the two detectives in the chase.

'He's heading for Covent Garden,' Birch gasped as he and Johnson ran.

Ahead of them, the bloodied knife still

clutched in his fist, their quarry sprinted away with surprising speed for a man in his early fifties.

'If we don't stop him we'll lose him in the crowd,' panted Birch.

4

Birch sucked in a deep breath, feeling it rasp in his throat as he ran, Johnson pounding along beside him. Both men had their eyes fixed on their target.

He was less than fifty yards ahead of them but, Birch thought, if he managed to disappear into the maze that was Covent Garden Market he could vanish as easily as a puff of smoke in a high wind.

So many people to hurt. So many places to hide.

Behind him, Birch could hear sirens. Uniformed men were now joining the pursuit, but the two detectives were still the closest to the suspect.

Up ahead there were screams. Shouts of fear and shock as members of the public caught sight of the knife held by the running man, who sometimes crashed into them in his haste to get away.

Birch and Johnson did their best to avoid collisions with the hapless bystanders but it proved impossible. The DI hit a group of teenagers and sent two crashing to the ground. Some of their companions laughed, while others shouted abuse at the two policemen.

The suspect dashed through one of the stone archways leading into the market itself and Birch lost sight of him.

'Steve,' he shouted, still running, gesturing to his companion. Johnson understood and veered off to his left, taking a route that would lead him to the far side of the market.

Birch blundered on through the same arch, almost colliding with two women carrying large blue shopping bags. They looked in bewilderment at his sweat-stained face. The DI looked wildly to right and left.

No sign of the man he sought.

'Where are you, you bastard?' he whispered under his breath, walking now through the hordes of browsing shoppers gathered round the many stalls in the market, inspecting the wares on offer.

His quarry could be anywhere by now. He might even have run straight on, out through the other side of the market and up to Covent Garden Tube station. If the bastard had managed to get down on to the platforms and board a train, they hadn't got a hope in hell of finding him.

Birch walked up an aisle, checking the sea of faces that surrounded him, his heart thudding not from the exertion he'd just subjected it to but from nervousness. He swallowed hard and tried to control his breathing.

Come out, come out, wherever you are, you scumbag.

He passed a jewellery stall where two women were inspecting silver rings. Another vendor was selling framed photos of London. Potential buyers were perusing the selection. Birch reached the end of the aisle and peered out across the cobbled area beyond, scanning the faces there.

'We've lost him.'

He heard the voice close behind but didn't turn.

'I said — ' Johnson began again but Birch raised a hand to silence him.

'He's here,' the DI said quietly. 'I know he is.'

'How can you be sure? He could have made it to the Tube station or be hiding in any one of these shops,' Johnson insisted.

Birch took a step away from his companion, still raking his gaze back and forth over the crowd.

'He could have cut back towards Bow Street. I'll get the other units to seal off Long Acre.' The DS reached into his jacket pocket for his mobile phone. He was about to say something into the mouthpiece when Birch slapped him hard on the arm and pointed towards a figure moving briskly away from the market, looking furtively around him.

'I told you the bastard was still here,' he said triumphantly.

He set off running, his feet pounding across the cobbles. Johnson joined him. They were less than thirty yards from the man when he spotted them.

'Stop,' roared Birch, but the suspect was already running.

5

Along King Street they raced. Those walking towards them paused to allow them past. Some tried to sidestep, wondering why these men in suits were running so fast and so purposefully. Others glanced at the figure they were pursuing: the older man in the leather jacket who occasionally looked over his shoulder at those who followed him.

For Detective Inspector David Birch, the world had narrowed to just the twenty yards that separated him from his quarry. Faces of onlookers were indistinct as he passed them. All he was aware of was the thudding of his heart, the rasping of his breath and the growing ache in his muscles. But he pushed those feelings to the back of his mind and concentrated on the only thing that mattered to him. Catching up with the man he was chasing.

Ahead of him, his quarry dashed down Garrick Street then across St Martin's Lane, slamming into a man coming the other way. The man jumped to his feet and turned to grab at his assailant, but he hesitated when he saw the knife swing into view.

There were more screams as the blade cut through the air, missing the man by inches.

Those in the path of the runners dodged to escape the onrushing men, in particular the one wielding the knife. The blood on it was starting to congeal now.

Birch tried to force more speed from his pounding legs, and Johnson kept pace with him, shoving people aside if he had to in his eagerness to reach the quarry.

Off to his right he heard more sirens, but the sound drifted meaninglessly on the air with the shouts and screams of those on the pavements. Cars sounded their horns as the men ran into the road.

Birch sucked in another deep breath, telling himself that his prey was slowing down a little. He almost tripped as he rounded a pile of rubbish bags stacked on the pavement outside a café.

Getting tired, you bastard?

The older man looked back, almost stopped running for precious seconds.

Birch, encouraged by this show of weakness, found extra strength and ran on even faster.

There was now less than fifteen yards between himself and the suspect.

'Stop there,' he bellowed.

The man swayed uncertainly for a moment.

'Sanderson,' the DI roared.

Malcolm Sanderson wiped sweat from his face and spun round once more, determined to escape. Just ahead of him, he saw the means.

'He's going into the Tube,' Birch said, shooting out a hand and practically dragging Johnson along with him. Sanderson had already disappeared into the entrance.

Birch and Johnson rushed after him, buffeting

their way past people climbing up from the subterranean depths of Leicester Square station.

The policemen took the stairs two at a time, hurtling down the steps with little regard for their own safety.

'There,' Birch snapped, seeing Sanderson struggling over the automatic barriers.

A uniformed London Transport official was shouting angrily at Sanderson, trying to stop him from scrambling over.

'Get away from him,' Birch shouted as the older man landed on the far side and ran towards the escalators.

The uniformed man watched in bemusement as Birch also clambered over the barrier. 'What the hell are you doing?' he shouted, but the two policemen ran on.

Sanderson was already on his way down the moving stairway, knocking people out of his way where he had to, almost falling. Birch and Johnson followed, feet pounding on the metal slats. Those watching from the rising escalator looked on incredulously. Someone laughed. There was even a cheer.

Sanderson reached the bottom and tripped.

He rolled over, got to his feet with surprising agility and ducked into the archway that led through to the Northern Line.

Birch jumped the last three steps and landed heavily, also rolling over before scrambling to his feet to continue his pursuit.

Johnson was right behind him. But the DS misjudged the jump from the escalator and landed heavily on his left ankle. He cursed and felt red hot pain shoot through the joint and up his leg. However, he dragged himself back to his feet, trying to ignore the increasing pain, forcing himself on in spite of his injury.

They pounded down the short walkway and then the stairs that led to the platforms.

Birch recognised an all too familiar sound.

A train was pulling in.

'If he gets on that we've lost him,' he panted, skidding out on to one of the platforms.

He scanned the faces of the passengers waiting there.

No sign of Sanderson.

'Other platform,' Johnson gasped and spun round.

Southbound, a train was preparing to pull out. Johnson, wincing against the pain from his ankle, ran down the length of the six hundred ton transport, peering through windows, looking for their suspect and hoping to Christ that he didn't see him. If he did, that meant he was seconds from escaping.

He suddenly turned and hurtled back as fast as he could towards the driver's cab.

Stop him pulling out. Stop the fucking train.

From behind him there was a scream. Shrill. Terrified.

He stopped and headed back to the northbound side, where he saw Birch advancing slowly towards the far end of the platform.

Another scream echoed through the underground cavern, reverberating off the walls and curved ceiling.

The thunder of the approaching train was

growing louder but Birch seemed oblivious of it. His attention was fixed on something else. For a moment, Johnson almost forgot the pain from his ankle.

'Oh, Christ,' he murmured.

6

The woman Sanderson held captive was in her early thirties.

Smartly dressed. Pretty. She'd been carrying a briefcase but had dropped it when he'd grabbed her. It lay at her feet, some papers spilling from it. Something to do with her work, Birch thought as he advanced on her and the man who held a knife to her throat. All kinds of thoughts tumbled through his head as he walked to within a few feet of the woman.

Where was she going? Where had she come from? Was she married? Did she have kids? It was as if any of those thoughts were preferable to the one that stuck most stubbornly in his mind. The one that told him she was going to be dead in a minute or two.

'Stay back,' Sanderson hissed, pressing the bloodied blade more urgently against the woman's neck. 'Or I'll cut her throat.'

'I don't doubt it,' Birch said evenly, looking past the terrified woman's face.

Johnson moved up alongside his companion, his breath still coming in gasps. By now it felt as if someone had stuck an air pump into his ankle and inflated it. The joint was throbbing fiercely.

'I'm going to get on that train,' Sanderson said, nodding in the direction of the carriage now rolling to a halt along-side him. 'And you're not going to stop me. If you try, I'll kill her.'

'Then kill her now,' Birch rasped. 'Because there's no fucking way you're getting off this platform except in cuffs. Got that?'

A look of uncertainty flickered momentarily across Sanderson's face, then he seemed to shake off the threat, pressing the knife more firmly against the soft flesh of his captive's throat.

'Don't open the doors,' Birch roared towards the tunnel mouth, his eyes never leaving Sanderson. 'Driver. Can you hear me?'

'I'll kill her,' the older man insisted. 'Don't play games with me.' He tugged harder on the woman's hair, dragging her head sharply backwards to expose her neck even more.

'Driver,' Birch shouted again. 'Can you hear me? I'm a policeman. Use your radio. Check with your controller if you don't believe me. He'll tell you what's going on.'

There was a moment of interminable silence, punctuated only by the terrified woman's sobs.

'I can hear you,' a voice from just inside the tunnel called.

'Don't open the doors. Don't let anyone on or off. Take the train out of the station now,' Birch commanded. 'Do it.'

'Do you want her death on your conscience?' Sanderson said quietly. 'Because it'll be your fault when she dies.'

'I'll live with it,' Birch said flatly, his blazing gaze never leaving Sanderson's.

Johnson looked at his superior briefly, then turned to see uniformed officers spilling on to the platform at the far end.

'Keep them back,' Sanderson rasped, some of the bravado now missing from his tone. 'If one of them comes any nearer I'll kill this bitch.'

Johnson, leaning against the wall to take some pressure off his injured ankle, held up a hand to halt the advance of the uniformed men. 'Clear the platform,' he shouted. 'Get everyone out of here.'

'Driver,' Birch shouted. 'Take this train out of the station now. Move.'

There was a loud hydraulic hiss and the train began to pull slowly away. From inside the carriages, people stared out at the drama being enacted before them. At the far end of the platform, the uniformed men were hustling the last of the waiting passengers to the exit.

'You bastard,' snapped Sanderson.

Birch smiled almost imperceptibly. 'I can't see from here,' he said quietly. 'But I'm guessing that the policemen who've just arrived on this platform are from an ARU. That means they're carrying guns and it means they're very good shots.' He ignored the sweat that ran down his face in rivulets. His eyes never left Sanderson's. 'Now usually in a hostage situation if some mad bastard's got a gun to someone's head or a knife to somebody's throat, then the marksmen have to be careful that they've got a clear shot. Because if they shoot and the bullet hits the wrong area of the body they run the risk of some kind of muscular spasm when the bad guy dies. Then maybe his finger'll tighten on the trigger and blow the fucking hostage's brains out anyway. But down here, they haven't got that

21

problem. They've got a clean shot at you. They'll put one through the base of your skull and sever your spinal cord, and it'll all happen so quick that knife will just drop to the ground.'

Sanderson swallowed hard.

'It's up to you. If I give them the signal they'll shoot now. Kill you and her. If you cut her throat they'll shoot you anyway. However you look at it, the only way you're going to walk off this platform is if you let her go.'

The woman was sobbing almost uncontrollably now.

'Let her go and you live,' the DI continued. 'Anything else, you're a dead man.'

Sanderson gripped the knife handle so tightly his knuckles turned white. He looked from Birch to Johnson then beyond to the uniformed men clogging the far end of the platform.

'Let her go and you live,' the DI repeated evenly.

Sanderson was breathing heavily. He tried to swallow but his mouth was chalk-dry.

'Just drop the knife,' Birch murmured.

The woman was crying softly, her body shaking.

'It's your decision,' said the DI, raising his hand.

'What are you doing?' Sanderson demanded.

'Giving them the signal,' the policeman told him. 'When I drop my hand, they start shooting.'

7

The woman tried to pull away from Sanderson, now suddenly as afraid of the possible hail of bullets as she was of the blade at her throat.

She was breathing quickly. Hyperventilating.

Sanderson held her more tightly.

'I'm going to count to five,' Birch said, his arm still in the air. 'Then they open fire. Got that?'

Sanderson shook his head, a smile distorting his face. There was no humour in it. The expression looked like some twisted sneer.

'You won't let her die,' he chided.

'You're going to kill her anyway, aren't you?' the DI breathed. 'Knife or bullet. What's the difference? I'm counting. One.'

Sanderson looked down the platform at the uniformed men gathered there.

'You're bluffing,' he hissed.

'Do I look like I'm bluffing? Two.'

Johnson took a step back, closer to the wall.

'You can't do this,' Sanderson blurted. 'You can't endanger the life of a member of the public. You're not allowed to.'

'I can do whatever I fucking like if it means getting rid of a piece of shit like you. Three.'

'They won't shoot,' Sanderson insisted, nodding in the direction of the uniformed men.

'They'll follow orders. Four.'

The woman sniffed loudly, her ragged breathing echoing round the platform.

'Please don't,' she gasped.

Birch didn't even look at her. His gaze never left Sanderson.

'Last chance,' he said quietly. 'Drop the knife.' He lowered his hand slightly, ready to sweep it downwards. 'Five.'

Sanderson glared at the policeman, the blade still pressed against the woman's throat.

Only then did Birch look at the woman.

'I'm sorry,' he murmured.

Sanderson dropped the knife.

The blade landed with a loud clang on the concrete platform.

No sooner had the metal struck the ground than Johnson stepped stiffly forward and pulled the woman away from Sanderson, who took a step backwards. Johnson and the woman headed off down the platform, the DS keeping his arm around the woman both to comfort her and also to relieve the pressure on his ankle.

'Good choice,' Birch said, grabbing Sanderson by the arm. He slipped his hand inside his jacket and pulled out a pair of handcuffs, which he fastened quickly round the older man's wrists, pressing his face close to his quarry. 'Scary, isn't it?' he hissed. 'Having time to think about your own death? Do you think that's what the girls you killed felt like before you finished them off, you cunt?'

He gripped Sanderson by one shoulder and made to walk him down the platform towards the waiting uniformed men.

'I'll be out in ten years,' Sanderson said

smugly. 'Maybe less. An insanity plea. Diminished responsibility. Wait until the jury hear about my terrible childhood. The abuse I suffered. They'll understand why I killed those bitches.' He turned and looked at Birch. 'Even if it's a longer sentence it won't be too bad. I'll have my own cell. Privacy. I'll have a better life than you.' He smiled triumphantly.

Birch held his gaze for a second then nodded slowly.

'You know what,' he muttered. 'You're probably right.'

Even if he'd seen the movement coming, Sanderson would have been powerless to stop it.

With a strength fuelled by rage, Birch grabbed the other shoulder, almost lifting Sanderson off the ground. Then, with a grunt of disgust, he shoved him over the platform edge.

The older man screamed loudly. He seemed to hang in the air for precious seconds, then he dropped on to the live rail with a thud.

His body jerked uncontrollably as the massive surge of electricity shot through it. His screams filled the station. Smoke began to rise from his ears and his nostrils. Even his eyes.

Several of the uniformed men dashed to the edge of the platform and stared down.

Birch looked on impassively.

'A better life than me?' he murmured, eyes never straying from Sanderson's still contorting body. 'I don't think so.'

8

It was early evening by the time Birch got to the Middlesex Hospital.

He'd spent most of the intervening period back at New Scotland Yard. Firmly ensconced in his office trying to complete what had felt like reams of paperwork. By the time he'd walked out he hadn't even finished a quarter of it. However, the prospect of continuing the following day and, as far as he could see, for a few more days to come didn't bother him. Malcolm Sanderson was off the streets. Better than that. The bastard was dead.

As Birch walked through the hospital and stepped into the lift he smiled to himself. It had taken eight months to nail him but it had been worth the wait. Worth the sleepless nights. The constant examination and re-examination of evidence. The surveillance. Everything.

There would be no more of that now. Not even the worry that some senile fucking judge was going to end up spoiling all his hard work by admitting a plea of insanity. None of that mattered any more. Now there would be other cases. New cases.

Birch got out at his chosen floor and walked down the corridor, looking for the room number he sought. He smiled at a nurse who passed him carrying a bedpan. He even nodded a greeting to a man in a wheelchair who emerged from one of

26

the other side rooms. He was dressed only in underpants, his bare torso displaying a large variety of tattoos.

The DI found the room he wanted but paused outside when he heard voices coming from within. He waited until he'd identified them both, then knocked and walked in without waiting for an invitation.

'Typical,' Birch said, smiling. 'I should have known. Always lying around.'

Detective Sergeant Stephen Johnson sat up in bed and grinned at his superior. Beside him, his wife turned and also smiled at Birch, who crossed to her and kissed her tenderly on the cheek.

'Are you all right, Natalie?' he said. 'Long time no see.'

She touched his arm, then sat back on the plastic chair beside her husband once again.

'Where's the chocolates and flowers then?' Johnson smiled. 'That's what you're supposed to bring when you visit someone in hospital. That or a bottle of Lucozade.'

'Fuck off.' Birch smiled. He looked down at Johnson's left ankle, which was heavily bandaged. 'What's the news?' he wanted to know, nodding in the direction of the ankle. 'Break? Sprain?'

'They took an X-ray when I got here,' Johnson explained. 'Kept me waiting for two hours first but finally got round to it. I twisted it. The doctor said he thought there might have been ligament damage but there wasn't. It's nothing that a bit of rest won't cure. It's just badly

27

swollen, but that should have gone down by the morning.'

'How long are you in for?'

'I can go home tonight if I want to. They need the bed.'

'You should get them to keep him in, Nat,' Birch said, squeezing the younger woman's shoulder. 'Get a bit of peace and quiet at home for a night.'

Natalie Johnson grinned. 'I'm just glad he's all right,' she said, pressing her husband's hand.

'He's had worse and he will do in the future,' Birch told her.

'That's what I'm afraid of,' she murmured. 'Steve said the policeman that Sanderson stabbed died before they could get him to hospital.'

'Yeah, I heard.'

'That could have been one of you two.'

Birch nodded. 'But it wasn't,' he reminded her. 'That's what matters.'

'Was the dead policeman married?' she asked.

'With two kids,' Birch said. 'His wife was told this afternoon.'

A heavy silence descended, finally broken by Birch.

'So, when are you back?' he asked Johnson.

'A week, tops.'

Birch nodded. 'Listen, I'm going to leave you two alone,' he said. 'I just wanted to nip in, see if you were all right. Find out how long I was going to be working on my own.' He smiled. 'And to say thanks for helping me get Sanderson.' He put out his right hand. Johnson shook it warmly. The

DI squeezed Natalie's shoulder again. 'You take care of him, Nat, but don't put up with too much whining from him. You know what he's like.'

'Dave, can I talk to you for a minute?' she said, getting to her feet.

'Of course you can.'

'Nat, leave it, will you?' Johnson sighed.

'There's a café on the ground floor,' Natalie went on. 'I wondered if you wanted to get a coffee or something, if you're not in a hurry? I'm staying here until Steve's ready to go then I'll drive him home.'

'You don't mind me buying your missis a drink, do you, Steve?' Birch said. 'I'll bring her back in one piece, I promise.'

They turned and headed for the door. Johnson heard their footsteps echo away down the corridor.

9

As Natalie Johnson sipped at her coffee she watched Birch take a bite from his biscuit. The three from the small packet he'd purchased at the counter were laid out before him on the table top.

He chewed and pointed to the biscuits, but Natalie shook her head.

'Thank God for that,' he joked. 'This is my dinner.'

She frowned.

'I'm only kidding,' he reassured her. 'I'll get a takeaway on the way home.'

Again Natalie took a mouthful of coffee, sometimes glancing round the café at the three other customers. A man with heavy bandaging round his stomach was seated near a tall pot plant with a woman opposite him and a small child seated on his lap. The little girl was giggling sporadically and, every so often, she would turn and stroke the man's face.

Natalie looked away, her gaze turning more intently on Birch.

'You heard what he said, Nat,' Birch told her. 'He'll be back at work in a week.'

'That's what I'm afraid of,' she confessed.

Birch reached for another biscuit.

'It was his ankle today,' she reminded the DI. 'I could just as easily be visiting him in here again next week only then he could have been shot or stabbed or anything else ... ' She allowed the sentence to trail off.

'What do you expect me to say? You're right. Steve could end up shot or stabbed. Any of us could. We all know that. You knew that when you married him. You and the wife of every copper on this or any other force.'

'Occupational hazard?'

'Yeah, if that's what you want to call it. Nat, if you want Steve to resign then you talk to him about it. It's not my place to do that. Besides, he's bloody good at what he does. I've worked with him for the last six years. I trust him and that goes a long way in this game.'

'But if anything happens to him I'm the one who's left a widow. You just walk away, Dave. Get yourself another partner.'

'You want him behind a desk that's fine. Just don't expect any help from me getting him there.'

She regarded Birch irritably over the rim of her cup.

'He's a big boy, Nat,' the DI continued. 'He knows the score. He has done from the beginning. We all do. The reward is worth the risk.'

'Reward? What reward?'

'Getting scumbags like Malcolm Sanderson off the fucking streets for good,' snapped Birch.

'I hope the wife of the policeman who was killed this afternoon agrees with you.'

'The families of the girls Sanderson raped, tortured and murdered will.'

Natalie drained what was left in her cup. Birch

31

reached across the table and refilled it from the stainless steel jug next to her.

She nodded her thanks and tipped in some milk.

'How did your wife cope with this lifestyle, Dave?' she wanted to know. 'With what you do?'

'Which wife?' He smiled. 'First or second?'

She shrugged. 'Either?'

'My first wife died just after I was made a detective sergeant.'

'I'm sorry. I didn't know.'

'It's OK. I like talking about her. The memories are all good ones.' He looked down at his left hand. 'I suppose it'd stop the confusion if I took my wedding ring off.' Birch turned the silver band between his thumb and forefinger.

'How did she die, if you don't mind me asking?'

'Cancer. I used to wonder if it was my fault in some way. You know, the stress that came with my job. Her having to put up with me coming home in foul fucking moods. I tried to keep it from her as much as I could but things don't always work out the way you want them to, do they?' He picked up his coffee cup and looked into its depths for a moment, then the spell seemed to break and he was looking at Natalie once more. 'My second wife just got bored with coming second to the job. That was one of the things she said to me as she walked out. The guy she'd been fucking around with behind my back for eighteen months was sitting outside the flat waiting to pick her up.' He leaned forward and lowered his voice to a conspiratorial whisper. 'I can only assume he talked about his work. Perhaps that was the attraction.'

'I'm sorry to pry,' Natalie said apologetically.

'Feel free. I've got nothing to hide.'

'Was your second wife right? Did she come second to your job?'

'Yeah. I told her she would before we got married but she couldn't accept it. She told me I kept her at a distance. Wouldn't let her be a part of my work. And she was right.'

'Why did you do that?'

'Does Steve come home every night and talk about what he's done during the day?'

'Not unless I ask him.'

'Well, I wouldn't tell even when I was asked.' Birch smiled. 'Why do you want to know what he does?'

'Because I'm his wife. I love him. I want to support him.'

'All the more reason for him to protect you from it. That's what I was doing.' The DI sucked in a deep breath. 'What we do and the stuff we see, it's not for sharing over a cosy dinner, Nat.' His tone darkened. 'What was I supposed to do? Go home and say, 'I was called to a house today where a body had been discovered. He'd been beaten to death with a claw hammer then cut up with a circular saw. He must have been there a while because there were maggots in the wounds'? Or 'You should have seen the state of the nine-year-old we found murdered today. Strangled with cheese wire then raped. By the way, what kind of day did you have, darling?'?' He shook his head. 'Stuff like that belongs here.'

He tapped his temple with one index finger. 'And it should stay here.'

'How long have you been divorced now?' Natalie enquired. 'Fifteen months, isn't it?'

'Something like that,' he told her. 'I've been busy, Nat. Other things on my mind.'

'Do you still see your second wife?'

'Why should I? There were no kids. I never wanted them. No custody battles to be fought. None of that.'

'Would you get married again?'

'If the right woman came along.' He raised his eyebrows, a slight smile creasing his lips. 'Between cases, naturally.'

Natalie sat back in her seat and let out a weary breath.

'Is this what I can expect from Steve in years to come?' she sighed. 'Am I going to get pushed out? Stepped on for the sake of the job?'

'You'd know better than me, Nat. You're the one married to him. It depends how he feels. For me, the job's the only thing. Steve might change his mind as he gets older. Some guys do. They lose their edge. Their desire to do the work. It just grinds them down. You either thrive on what you do or it crushes you. Breaks you. There's not much in the middle.'

'So you're never giving up?'

'Like the man said, 'Everything I am is what I'm chasing.' ' He shrugged. 'And to tell you the truth, I wouldn't have it any other way.'

The Gift of Life

She had prayed there would be no pain.

Ever since an elective Caesarian had been decided on, she'd been grateful. But as the doctors and nurses worked around her she still feared, somewhere in the back of her mind, that the epidural would wear off. That something would go wrong.

She had voiced these concerns many times and, on each occasion, her fears had been soothed somewhat by the medical staff.

Now she lay on the gurney, the green canvas screen across her lower body preventing her from watching the work of the surgeon and his team. She felt some movement. Powerful movement. Tugging. More than once, the gurney moved. She realised that the initial incision and those that followed had been completed. They had opened her up. Eviscerated her

(there was no other word she could think of that so aptly described the procedure she was undergoing)

to get to the child she was carrying.

She looked to her left where her companion was swathed from head to foot in a green smock and trousers over his own clothes. A green hat hid his hair, and a surgical mask of the same colour and material covered all but his eyes.

He held her hand tightly. Supportively.

She swallowed hard while the surgical staff spoke comforting words. A nurse who passed by touched her cheek gently then squeezed her other hand.

Everything was fine, they told her. She had nothing to worry about, they repeated, as if it was some kind of litany.

Almost finished, the surgeon had said on a number of occasions.

Machines all around her in the operating room sent out a symphony of different sounds as they measured various vital signs.

She glanced to her left once more and the man who held her hand gripped it more tightly, then leaned forward and kissed her forehead.

He tasted sweat upon the flesh there.

The chief surgeon said that it would be another five minutes and then the baby would be free.

The woman on the gurney closed her eyes, but a vision of a scalpel cutting into her womb filled her mind. Images of hands reaching into her body to pull the child free. She opened her eyes again, trying to control her breathing.

The man holding her hand so tightly wiped her forehead with a piece of sterile gauze. He made no attempt to look in the direction of the surgeon and nurses working on the other side of the canvas partition. His attention was fixed on the woman on the gurney. He touched her cheek tenderly, spoke words of encouragement to her.

She wondered why the words didn't make her feel safe.

There was more movement from the other

side of the screen. She caught a brief glimpse of a bloodstained scalpel. And above the mask the surgeon wore she saw something register in his eyes that made her heart beat faster. The blips on the oscilloscope accelerated to match her new-found concern.

He called for help from one of his colleagues and the woman saw the same look in the newcomer's eyes.

From the gurney, she asked what was wrong but no one answered her.

The man holding her hand told her not to worry, but that emotion was pouring through her veins as quickly as the fear had clutched at her heart.

Again she asked what was wrong and once more received no answer.

She wanted to get to her feet, to pull the canvas screen down. She wanted to see what the doctors were gaping at.

There was no crying.

For terrifying seconds, she thought the baby might be dead. Was that why the medical staff were looking aghast? Although, as she studied their expressions (or at least as much of their expressions as she could glean above the surgical masks) she began to realise that what she saw in their eyes was something other than sadness. Beside her, the man clutching her left hand was also looking towards the foot of the gurney. He too was perplexed by the reactions of those delivering the baby, his view, like hers, restricted by the partition.

The woman called out to them, demanding to

know if the child was alive, wanting to know why it wasn't crying, needing to be told why it was silent.

Then it made a sound. A sound that seemed to fill the operating room and drummed in her ears.

And, when she heard that sound, she understood the expression in their eyes and she prayed for the silence again.

10

The red stain on the paper tablecloth looked like blood.

Megan Hunter looked down at the spilled wine and moved her seat back slightly as the waiter swiftly and expertly removed the toppled glass then set about re-laying the table, apologising profusely as he worked.

'It wasn't your fault,' Megan told him. 'Please, don't worry about it.'

'There is none on your clothes?' he asked, with something akin to terror in his eyes.

Megan looked down at the matching light brown linen jacket and trousers she wore and shook her head.

'No harm done,' she told him. 'Honestly. It's fine.'

The waiter apologised again despite her entreaties then retreated to the kitchen to fetch their desserts.

'You just can't get the staff these days, can you?' said Frank Denton, sipping at his own drink.

'He couldn't help it, Frank,' Megan insisted.

'At least the book's safe,' Maria Figgis proclaimed, lifting the hefty tome into the air.

All three of them laughed, the sound mingling with the cacophony created by the other diners in Joe Allen's restaurant.

Maria drank some of her wine, accepting a

refill when Denton offered. He took the opportunity to top up his own glass.

The waiter returned with a replacement glass for Megan.

'I've got some cuttings here if you want to see them, Megan,' Denton said, reaching into the inside pocket of his jacket.

'I'll look later, when we have our coffee,' Megan told him. 'They might put me off my dessert.'

'I doubt it. There isn't a bad one among them,' Denton assured her. 'The one from *The Times* is positively glowing. I don't know what you said to him during that interview but he's smitten. Read it.' He pushed the piece of paper across the table towards her.

'Later,' Megan repeated, refusing to look at the cutting. She held Denton's gaze for a moment then sipped at her drink.

'I don't know why you get worried about reviews, Megan,' Maria offered in her attractive Irish accent.

'I always have been, Maria. You know that.'

'As your agent I will always shelter you from the most hurtful ones.' Maria smiled.

'So, there have been bad ones.' Megan chuckled. 'I knew it.'

'Only at the beginning,' Maria told her. 'And then only from a blinkered minority.'

There was more laughter round the table.

'Your biographies have always been well received,' Denton reminded her. 'And they've always sold very well.'

'The bottom line,' Megan added.

'Well, much as we'd all like to say that we're in the publishing business purely for the enlightenment of readers, we all know that's not true,' Denton said with something like disappointment in his voice. 'Fortunately the sales figures for the last two books, the biographies of Dante and Caravaggio, have been better than most of the fiction we published in the last two years. And, as you know, advance orders are excellent.'

'Dante and Caravaggio are much better known than Cassano,' Megan said. 'I mean, if you stopped ten people in the street now and asked them if they'd even heard of Giacomo Cassano how many would say yes? Very few. If any.'

'Well, thanks to this,' Denton tapped the jacket of the book, 'if you stopped ten people in the street in two weeks' time and asked them who Giacomo Cassano was I'd be willing to bet most of them would at least recognise his name. And if you read these reviews you'll understand why.'

'I told you,' Megan said. 'After dessert.'

'Speaking of which,' Maria added, smiling.

The waiter returned and put their plates down in front of them. He apologised once more for having knocked over the glass of wine, then scuttled off to fetch the bill for a table on the far side of the dining room.

Megan looked at the book lying on the table close to Frank Denton's arm. It had a dark blue jacket, the white bas-relief letters on the front standing out vividly against it.

Megan glanced at them as she began to eat. *The Seeds of the Soul*, and, at the bottom of the jacket, the author's name: *Megan Hunter*.

41

11

Detective Inspector David Birch spat the cold coffee back into its plastic cup.

'Shit,' he murmured, wiping his mouth with the back of one hand. He dropped the vending machine receptacle into the waste bin beside his desk and exhaled wearily. There was a clear plastic container and the remnants of a half-eaten sandwich in there too.

He looked down at the pile of papers before him. Reports he'd written, statements he'd read. He blinked hard and massaged the back of his neck with one hand, feeling the beginnings of a headache.

He got to his feet and crossed to the window of his office. It was on the seventh floor of New Scotland Yard and he had a wonderful panoramic view of the city from his vantage point. A shimmering heat haze hung like a translucent blanket over the capital. The city was baking in temperatures that were threatening to hit ninety degrees Fahrenheit.

Dog days the Americans called them. Unbearably hot summer days when there was little or no respite from the unforgiving heat. Tempers frayed more easily. Arguments erupted with greater frequency. It was a fact. More crime during the summer.

More crime. More work.

Birch was about to get himself a hot coffee

from the machine just down the corridor when his office phone rang.

'Birch,' he said into the mouthpiece, still gazing out over London.

He recognised the voice at the other end immediately.

'Yes, sir,' he said. 'I'm still working on it.' He paused, listening intently to the voice. 'Yes, sir, I know. Well, it's all in my report — 'The voice cut him short and Birch rolled his eyes as he listened. 'Now?' he asked in answer to the question directed at him. 'Yes, sir.'

He put down the phone and headed for his office door, turning right into the corridor and wandering towards the lifts. He jabbed the 'Call' button and waited.

When the doors finally slid open a bald man with a pencil moustache and closely trimmed beard stepped out. His face was shiny with sweat, droplets of it glistening on his hairless head. He was carrying his suit jacket over his shoulder and there were large circles of sweat radiating from both his armpits, staining his light blue shirt. He nodded and smiled at Birch, who returned the greeting and prepared to step into the lift.

'Hang on a minute, Dave, I've got something for you,' said the other plain clothes detective. He reached into his jacket pocket and pulled out a small piece of paper that he handed to Birch. 'It's a map of the Underground. I thought you might find it handy next time you're chasing a suspect.' He laughed. 'It's got all the train times on it, so next time you can chuck them under a train instead of just frying them on the tracks.'

'Yeah, very funny,' Birch said as his colleague started off up the corridor towards his own office. 'Hey, when are you going to shave that moustache and beard off? You look like a fanny with teeth.'

'Takes a cunt to know a cunt, Dave,' the other man called as the lift doors slid shut.

Birch smiled, shook his head and punched the button on the panel for the floor he wanted.

The lift began to rise.

As it did, his smile began to fade.

12

'So, the promotional tour starts in Glasgow,' Maria Figgis mused, watching as Denton refilled her wine glass.

The editor nodded. 'I've got a provisional itinerary back at the office,' he said. 'I'll e-mail it to you when I get back and I'll get the publicity department to call you later today.'

'There were some extra bookshops in Dublin I wanted Megan to do signings at,' Maria said. 'We Irish are more fond of our books than you guys over here. Never forget that. And I need to talk to Margaret Daly about the interviews she's organised in Ireland.'

Megan rummaged through the small bowl on the table for some sweetener, ripped open the paper envelope and dropped a Canderel into her cappuccino.

'I've worked with Margaret before,' she said. 'She's brilliant. Although I always get the feeling she's trying to kill me by working me to death. Last time I was there I did fifteen interviews in one day.'

'The price of fame,' Denton murmured, raising his eyebrows.

Megan eyed him over the rim of her cup.

'I was speaking to RTE the other day. They loved the book and they're very interested in making a documentary about Cassano. They're ready to commission a company called October

Eleven Pictures to do it,' Maria continued. 'They all think he's a fascinating character.'

'I agree with them,' Megan said. 'That's why I wrote the book. I think people should know about him and what he did and thought. After all, if not for him Dante might well never have written the *Divine Comedy*.'

'There's probably a few hundred thousand kids doing exams right now who'd be happy if there never had been a *Divine Comedy*,' Denton grinned. 'Or a Dante for that matter.'

'In years to come, maybe *The Seeds of the Soul* will be on the syllabus,' Maria interjected. 'Cassano could become as famous as Dante or Cavalcanti thanks to your book, Megan.'

'I think he had a few too many skeletons in his closet for that,' Megan remarked.

'That's what makes him so interesting,' Denton offered. 'Everyone loves unravelling a mystery. Finding out secrets.'

'Even Cassano's secrets?' Megan pondered. 'I don't think some of his teachings are suitable for study by teenagers, do you?'

'You maintain in your book he was fundamentally a good man,' Denton said, a note of defiance in his voice.

'He wasn't the monster the Church at the time made him out to be,' Megan countered. 'Right up until his execution he maintained his love of God and that his preachings and beliefs praised God, not demeaned Him. You should know that, Frank. You've read the book.'

'Wasn't it difficult to remain objective about

46

him while you were writing it?' Denton wanted to know.

'You asked me that the first time you read the manuscript.'

'I'm asking again.' There was a slight edge to Denton's tone that Megan wasn't slow to pick up. 'You said yourself that you agreed with many of the things that Cassano wrote and preached. Even the more extreme doctrines. Do you still feel the same way?'

Megan was about to answer him when Maria suddenly stood up, gazing across the restaurant in the direction of a table on the far side of the dining room.

'Will you two just excuse me for a minute, please?' She beamed. 'I've just noticed someone I have to speak to.'

'One of the perils of eating somewhere frequented by so many people from the publishing business,' Megan observed as her agent bustled across to the table she sought and embraced each of the women seated there in turn. There was a great whoop of laughter from them that drew the attention of most of the other diners. Megan smiled indulgently. 'Maria loves her work,' she said.

'And what about you, Megan?' Denton asked. 'Do you still love your work? Every aspect of it?'

'I'm looking forward to the publication of the book if that's what you mean, Frank.'

'And the promotional tour? Different city every day. One radio and TV station after another. The same inane questions asked by idiots who've only scanned the press hand-outs

47

about the book and wouldn't dream of actually reading the bloody thing.' He gazed at her over the rim of his wine glass. 'Lonely nights in hotels.'

'I like my own company,' she told him flatly. 'Besides, someone from the publicity department will be travelling with me as usual. I won't be lonely.' She finished her coffee.

There was another great whoop of laughter from the far side of the dining room but Megan didn't look round.

'Maria's still doing her stuff by the sound of it,' she said. 'What time do you have to be back in the office?'

'Not for a while,' he told her, glancing at his watch. 'Would you like another coffee?'

'Why not?' Megan murmured.

Denton regarded her for a moment longer then turned to look for a waiter.

13

Christ, he wanted a cigarette.

Birch hesitated for a moment as he stepped out of the lift, digging his hand into his jacket pocket. He fished out a disposable lighter and a pack of SuperKings, looked longingly at them for a second then pushed them back out of sight and made his way along the corridor until he found the door he sought.

He straightened his tie, ran a hand through his short brown hair and walked in.

The outer office was bigger than his own, he noted. It hadn't changed much since the last time he'd been in it over a year ago. Same paintings on the walls. Same carpet. Same secretary.

She looked up at him and smiled efficiently. A woman in her fifties. Immaculately dressed and with a pinched face and hooked nose that reminded Birch of a bird of prey, surveying its next meal with detached indifference. The office was air-conditioned but the DI had the feeling that the woman would have looked just as immaculate had she been working next to a blast furnace.

'Detective Inspector Birch to see the Commissioner,' he said.

For fuck's sake. It's like waiting to see the headmaster after you've just put bricks through his study windows and written 'wanker' on his desk in bright yellow marker.

'Take a seat, Detective Inspector,' she said, heading for an oak-panelled door to her right. 'I'll let Commissioner Stowe know you're here.'

Birch nodded but ignored her offer of a chair. Instead he glanced in the direction of the oak-panelled door, slid one hand over the cigarettes in his pocket and wished even more that he could spark up.

He heard muffled voices from within, and then the immaculately dressed secretary re-emerged, opened the oak-panelled door a little more and ushered him in.

Birch nodded in thanks and entered the office beyond.

If the outer office was well cooled by the air-conditioning, the temperature inside this inner sanctum was positively glacial. Birch almost shivered as he stepped across the threshold, and wouldn't have been surprised to see icicles hanging from the anglepoise lamp on the desk before him.

Seated behind it was a man in his mid-fifties. Solidly built, with hands like ham-hocks. Short, greying hair clung defiantly to his head, and his bull neck looked as if it had struggled to fit inside the collar of his white shirt.

Metropolitan Police Commissioner Adrian Stowe glanced at Birch, nodded, and jabbed a finger in the direction of the high-backed leather chair in front of his desk.

'Sit down, Birch,' he said brusquely. The detective complied.

Stowe sat back in his seat and steepled his

fingers before him, regarding the younger man evenly.

'There are a number of reasons why I wanted to speak to you,' he said. 'Firstly, I wanted to congratulate you for your work on the Sanderson case. I'm well aware of the amount of time and effort that went into securing his arrest. Well done. What I'm not so keen on offering my congratulations for is what happened after his arrest.'

'Sir,' Birch began, sitting forward slightly. 'I understand what you're going to say — '

'You have no idea at all what I'm going to say,' Stowe cut across him, his voice rising slightly in volume. 'Now just shut up and listen.'

The DI sat back in his seat.

Shit. Here we go.

Stowe leaned forward, tapping a piece of paper on his desk.

'This is the cost of your little chase across London,' he said accusingly. 'At least twenty vehicles damaged, many of them written off completely. Numerous instances of property destroyed and at least twenty-seven people injured, five of whom are still in hospital. A grand total of almost one point two million pounds' worth of damage. And that doesn't include any civil actions that may be taken against you personally and the department as a whole. Not to mention the fact that you endangered the life of a hostage.' Stowe's tone was disarmingly even but Birch could see a vein throbbing angrily at his superior's left temple.

'There was no way I was letting Sanderson

escape,' the DI explained. 'And, as for the hostage, he was going to kill her, sir. I did the only thing I could to save her life.'

'Well, that woman whose life you saved is threatening to sue for everything from unreasonable behaviour to post-traumatic stress disorder.'

'Why? Because some fucking ambulance chaser's told her she can make a few bob?'

'After the way you behaved on that platform, Birch, she's lucky she's not in a bloody coffin, let alone an ambulance.'

'I wasn't the one trying to kill her, sir. The only reason she's alive now is because of me. Sanderson would have cut her throat.' Birch could feel his heart pounding hard against his ribs.

'That's something we'll never know, isn't it?' Stowe reminded the younger man. 'The fact remains that the chief suspect in a murder case will never come to trial because, according to the pathologist's report I have before me, he was thrown on to the live rail of a Tube track.'

'He fell, sir,' Birch said quietly.

Stowe stroked his chin thoughtfully. 'The evidence doesn't support a fall. It reinforces the belief that Malcolm Sanderson was pushed from that platform by you. My only option is to suspend you, pending further investigation. That suspension to be effective immediately.'

14

'It doesn't pose a threat to Megan.' Frank Denton shook his head and took another sip from his wine glass.

'I wish I could agree with you, Frank,' Maria Figgis answered. 'But I've had reservations from the beginning.'

'Why are you so worried about it, Maria?' Megan asked.

'Because the two books are published on the same day,' Maria continued. 'Yours and John Paxton's.'

'Paxton's is a horror novel,' Megan reminded her. 'The audiences for his book and mine are completely different.'

'I'm well aware of that, Megan. It's the fact that Paxton and his book will be receiving so much hype and coverage in the media at the same time as your book is being promoted. I voiced my concern at a lunch months ago when Frank told me that the publication dates coincided.'

'And I disagreed with you that publication of *The Seeds of the Soul* should be moved on account of Paxton's book,' said Denton. 'As Megan said, hers is non-fiction. Academic.'

'You know what it's like whenever a new book of his is released,' Maria persisted. 'There's a media circus around it and him. Every other book published at the same time

53

gets chewed up in the feeding frenzy irrespective of the subject. The film of his last book opens worldwide two weeks before publication day. The media will barely have finished crawling all over that before the new book appears. You won't be able to turn on a television or open a magazine or newspaper without seeing John Paxton somewhere.'

'That's understandable,' Megan countered. 'He's one of the biggest selling authors in the world.'

'He gives the public what they want,' Denton said. 'I suppose you have to admire him for that. He's been at the top of his game for more than fifteen years now. There isn't another horror writer who can hold a candle to him.'

'I was speaking to his agent the other day,' Maria said. 'She says this new book, *The Fairground Phantoms*, is the best thing he's ever written.'

'The usual offering, I would imagine,' Denton sneered. 'Violence, sex, horror and more violence?'

'It works for him and it works every time,' Maria pointed out. 'He's found a very successful formula and he sticks to it. He's not the only writer who does that.'

'So, he's been repeating himself for the last fifteen years. Am I meant to be impressed?' Denton asked.

'There's more to his writing than reworking the same ideas over and over again, Frank,' Megan said, running two hands through her shoulder-length blonde hair. 'You should know.

You worked with him at one of his publishers.'

'Yes. On three books. Not the most edifying experience I've ever enjoyed as an editor and I don't mean just the writing.' He drank some more wine. 'For some unknown reason he still sends me signed copies of all his new books. His latest opus arrived this morning.'

'And you still don't like him?' Megan queried.

'As a writer I suppose you can't deny his talent. But as a person he's opinionated, confrontational and aggressive,' Denton told her, holding up his hands. 'Shall I stop there or would you like me to go on?'

'And he swears a lot.' Megan chuckled. 'Don't forget that.' She finished what was left in her coffee cup. 'Well, I've always found him rather attractive. He says what he thinks and he doesn't care who he upsets. That's one of the things that makes him attractive. He genuinely doesn't give a fuck.'

'When you've got as much money as he has you don't have to give a fuck,' Maria added, smiling.

'Well, I'm glad you think so highly of him,' Denton muttered.

'Let's see if you still hold him in such high esteem if your own book gets lost in his slipstream,' Maria said.

'You're worrying needlessly,' Megan insisted. 'I expected better of you than that, Maria. A little more fighting spirit.' She grinned. 'I didn't expect the voice of doom.'

'We'll see,' the agent told her.

Denton looked at his two guests then held up a hand to summon a waiter. The rest of the dining room at Joe Allen's was empty. 'If you two ladies have finished I'll get the bill.'

15

For long moments, neither man spoke. The chill in the room generated by the air-conditioning seemed to deepen as they gazed unblinkingly at each other.

It was Commissioner Stowe who broke the silence.

'I would require your warrant card and your ID,' he said, holding Birch's gaze.

The DI reached into his pocket and pulled out a thin leather wallet. He slapped it down on his superior's desk top.

'I would require them if I was suspending you,' Stowe continued. 'Under the circumstances, that's not my intention.'

Birch looked puzzled. 'So, am I suspended or not, sir?'

'Did you push Sanderson off that platform?'

'No, sir.'

Stowe smiled. It was a gesture that Birch hadn't been expecting. One that lit up his superior's features for brief seconds.

'Of the seventeen men on that platform at the time, including your partner, Detective Sergeant Johnson, not one single man has reported seeing you push Sanderson on to the track. The hostage saw nothing; she was being helped away at the time. All I have that says Sanderson was pushed is a somewhat vague pathologist's report. I couldn't justify an investigation into what really happened on that platform. There'd be no point. There are no witnesses. I'd simply be wasting public money.'

The older man pushed the slim leather wallet back towards Birch, who nodded, picked it up and slid it into his jacket once again.

'Thank you, sir,' he said.

'Obviously, I can't be seen to condone what happened, but speaking as one copper to another, and not as the Metropolitan Police Commissioner to one of his detectives, if you were somehow responsible for Sanderson's death then that is, of course, reprehensible. Speaking as one man to another, I'd like to think I'd have done the same. I know what it's like on the streets, Birch. I worked them for eleven years, the same way you do now. I haven't always been insulated inside an office. I know what goes on day to day during investigations.'

'Sanderson said that he'd probably get off with an insanity plea.'

'Judging by the nature of his crimes, I'd say he was right. A good brief would have got him fifteen or twenty years in Rampton. Not really what you'd call justice. And I certainly don't think the families of Sanderson's victims would have been satisfied with a sentence like that, do you?'

'No, sir, I don't.'

There was another long silence, broken again by the older man.

'What are you working on at the moment?' he enquired.

'The Paedophile Unit were investigating what

looked like a trafficking ring. They think kids from Africa are being smuggled in and used as human sacrifices. Could be up to three hundred a year. They've had a suspect under surveillance for a couple of months. They think he might already have killed three kids himself. The others he's farming out to whoever pays the highest. They asked for my help.'

Stowe grimaced. 'You'd better get back to work then,' he said.

Birch nodded and got to his feet. He turned and headed for the door. As he reached it, the sound of Stowe's voice stopped him in his tracks.

'David?'

It was peculiar to hear his superior call him by his Christian name. Birch turned to face the other man.

'Yes, sir?' he said.

'Off the record. Man to man.' Stowe smiled. 'Did you push him?'

'Off the record?'

Stowe nodded.

'You know what it's like, sir,' the DI said, the faintest trace of a smile on his own lips. 'In the heat of the moment, sometimes little things slip your mind, and, for a copper, I've got a lousy memory.'

Stowe grinned. 'Get out.'

'Thank you, sir. It was good to talk to you.'

He closed the door behind him.

16

'You don't like him, do you?'

Maria Figgis spoke the words through a fixed grin as she waved in the direction of the taxi. The cab pulled away and Frank Denton glanced out of the rear window to wave back at the two women standing on the pavement outside the restaurant.

'He's a good editor,' Megan Hunter said, also watching as the cab turned the corner of Exeter Street and disappeared out of sight.

'That wasn't what I asked.'

'Maria, I don't have to like someone to work with them. Anyway, what makes you ask a question like that? Did I say or do something during lunch that made you think there was some kind of antagonism between me and Frank?'

'Is there?'

Megan cracked out laughing. 'You should be the writer.' She grinned. 'You're the one with the overactive imagination. Thinking I don't like Frank Denton. I work with him for a week or two on each of my books. I occasionally have lunch with him if he asks me.'

'I think he'd be happier if it was a little more than lunch.'

'What's that supposed to mean?'

'I haven't got time to be standing on street corners idly chatting. I've got clients to look after. I should be getting back to the office. Here comes a taxi now.'

'You're not going anywhere,' Megan told her, injecting as much mock indignation into her tone as she could muster. 'You're coming with me. You can explain yourself more fully.'

'Where are we going?'

'Round the corner to the Savoy. We can sit and chat over a pot of tea.'

'Go on then. The office can wait for another hour or two.'

The two women began walking, Megan's high heels clicking loudly on the pavement. She could feel the hot tarmac through the soles of her shoes. The sun was still beating down mercilessly. As the two of them emerged into the Strand it bathed them in the full fury of its heat.

They hurried across the road and into the welcoming shade of Savoy Court, the glittering edifice of the hotel towering above them. The flags above the main entrance fluttered slightly in the dismally ineffective breeze.

The doorman doffed his top hat and smiled a greeting at them as they passed through into the foyer of the hotel and onwards, down a flight of marble steps to an area just outside the dining room where a number of tables were draped with gleaming white tablecloths. The two women sat at the nearest unoccupied one.

Megan reached into her handbag and took out her cigarettes and lighter.

'So, tell me what you mean about Frank,' she said, blowing out a stream of smoke.

'You know as well as I do, Megan. The guy is

61

infatuated with you.'

Megan nodded slowly. 'I'm flattered,' she said. 'But not interested. He's nearly twenty years older than me for a start.'

'Age is no barrier to desire.'

'Very profound, Maria.'

'I've found that over the years my philosophy tends to fall on deaf ears. Just be careful.'

Megan looked at her agent with something close to irritation in her expression.

'Careful of what?' she wanted to know. 'How I conduct myself around him? How I speak to him? What's wrong, Maria? Are you afraid I'm giving off the wrong signals?'

'I didn't say that.'

Megan stubbed her cigarette out in the ashtray, watching the plume of smoke rising lazily into the air.

'I'm not a naive teenager, Maria,' she said. 'I'm thirty-five, and in case you've forgotten, I've already got one broken marriage behind me and more failed relationships than I care to remember.' She looked around her at the other people taking tea. 'Everyone seems to be in a couple,' she murmured distractedly. 'I'm beginning to think there's something wrong with me.'

'Perhaps you should give more thought to Frank Denton then.' Maria smiled.

Megan didn't return the gesture.

'No thanks,' she said. 'And if you're right about him being infatuated with me that's his problem. Not mine.'

Complications

When the woman woke she found her situation a little ironic. She'd been awake during the birth. She'd insisted upon that. Only afterwards had there been the need to sedate her.

Now she sat up in bed sipping from the plastic beaker of water the doctor had handed her.

The private room she was in was spacious and comfortable but as she looked from the doctor to the father of her child, comfort was the last thing occupying her mind.

There was a cot beside the bed but no child within.

She asked where her child was.

The doctor explained that there had been complications. That the child

(a boy)

was being cared for in another part of the hospital.

She asked him what kind of complications and he told her there were problems with the child's breathing.

The woman looked at her partner angrily and asked if he had seen the boy yet but he assured her that he wouldn't look at their son until he could do so with her at his side.

She asked the doctor if they could see their son but she was all too aware of the stitches now holding her stomach together after the Caesarian. Soon she would be encouraged to get up

63

and out of bed, but the doctor told her that he would prefer her not to over-exert herself just yet.

She wanted to know when she could see her child. She wanted to hold it like any other mother who has just given birth.

She didn't care for the expression on the doctor's face when she asked the question and she could feel herself becoming increasingly uneasy.

She wanted to know exactly how bad her son's breathing problems were. She demanded to know if she was being told everything. Her partner too was becoming more agitated by the doctor's vagueness.

If they could not visit their boy then why couldn't he be brought to them? They had a right to see him. The hospital couldn't keep their baby from them.

The doctor warned them that the child's breathing had yet to stabilise, and when the woman realised that more than four hours had passed since the birth her heart began to beat faster. She insisted on knowing the condition of her son. And she wanted to see him.

The doctor was silent for longer than either the woman or her partner was comfortable with.

Then, finally, he told them that it wasn't just the child's breathing that was causing concern.

Yes, there was fluid in its lungs that needed to be drained.

Yes, the nasal passages were malformed.

(The woman swallowed hard at the mention of the word.)

But there were other matters to be taken into consideration too.

The man demanded to know what those matters were. Was their son's life in danger? What was being kept from them?

The doctor said it would be simpler to explain once they'd seen the child. He suggested that it could be brought to the room in a portable incubator in an hour or two, and he would speak to them in more detail then. He would explain everything. They could see for themselves what was wrong with their son.

The woman and her partner wondered why the colour had drained from the doctor's face. Why his mouth had suddenly become dry and why his hands had begun to shake.

17

When Birch opened his front door he found five envelopes lying on the mat. Wearily he scooped them up, glancing out at the evening sky for a moment. The sun was bleeding to death in the sky, spilling its colour across the firmament, but despite the approach of night the heat that had been so unbearable all day was barely dissipating. The temperature was still high and a cloying mugginess now also filled the air.

Birch was grateful that at least the house was cool. He walked through from the hall, dropped the envelopes on the kitchen table and then filled the kettle. As he passed the radio on the worktop to his left he switched it to a news channel, then he made his way through to the sitting room where he flicked on the television.

The sound of voices filled the house. Birch hated silence. He had done ever since the death of his first wife. He wasn't listening to what was being said on the radio programme and he hadn't lingered in the sitting room long enough to see what was on the TV, but there were voices in the house and that was all he cared about.

He could hear next door's kids still playing out in the garden, bouncing around noisily on their large trampoline. Laughing and shouting. It was more welcome sound for the DI and he smiled to himself as he waited for the kettle to boil.

Once he'd had a cup of tea, he promised

himself, he'd wander round the corner to the Chinese and get himself something to eat. He'd had nothing since early afternoon and his stomach growled loudly as if to remind him of that fact.

Chinese or fish and chips?

Decisions, decisions.

There was also an Indian not far from Tooting Broadway Tube station. All were within five minutes' walking distance of his house.

He'd often considered that many of the major events that had shaped his life during the past fifteen years had taken place within a two or three mile radius of the house in which he now stood.

His first wife had been diagnosed with terminal cancer at St George's Hospital (a mile or so south of the house) and she now lay buried in Streatham cemetery (about a mile and half to the north).

His second wife had been a teacher at a school just off Burntwood Lane near Wandsworth Common (two miles north-west or less as the crow flew).

Funny old world.

Fucking hilarious, eh?

The kettle boiled and, still without switching on a light, Birch dropped a tea bag into a mug and topped it up with water before he fetched milk from the fridge. The light that came on when he opened the door was the first meagre illumination of the evening.

Almost out of milk.

He could nip into one of the shops nearby and

pick up some more when he went out to get his takeaway.

For now, he sipped at his tea, then finally flicked on the kitchen light and laid himself a single place at the table. He sat down and picked up the letters he'd retrieved from the mat when he arrived home.

Two were offering him loans. Another was trying to tempt him with a credit card. He binned them. The fourth was the phone bill. The fifth . . .

For fuck's sake. How many times did he have to tell them?

It was addressed to Mrs L. Birch. His first wife.

She had, it informed him, already won a prize in their draw.

'Fucking idiots,' rasped the policeman and tore the letter in half. He balled it up and hurled it in the direction of the waste bin. 'Stupid fucking idiots.' It wasn't the first time it had happened since she'd died but it was the first time for nearly six months.

And it hurt.

Birch got to his feet and moved away from the table.

Go and get your takeaway. Eat something.

He sucked in a weary breath and headed for the front door, leaving his jacket hanging in the hallway. The walk would do him good. Clear his head. He closed and locked the front door behind him and set off into the warm night.

18

Darkness had invaded the sky completely by the time Megan Hunter pushed open the French windows that led out on to her sitting room balcony. She closed her eyes for a moment, enjoying the cool breeze that greeted her. But it was all too fleeting and the cloying humidity that had followed the sweltering day soon returned to wrap itself around her.

She sipped her mineral water, the ice in the tall goblet clinking pleasingly against the Waterford crystal. Drops of condensation ran down the outside of the glass and she collected one on the end of a slender index finger and rubbed it across her forehead.

As she stood looking out over Norland Square, now so delicately lit by the street lamps and the lights from other houses and flats opposite, she could hear a mixture of sounds drifting around her from various different sources. The hum of traffic from Holland Park Avenue to her right. Occasional snatches of conversation as people passed by below her and the music that floated lazily from the speakers of her stereo in the sitting room behind her.

Her flat was one of six inside a large converted Victorian town house and it had been her home for the last four years. It was quiet, perfect for her work, and the location was ideal.

She leaned on the stone balustrade for a

moment longer, enjoying her drink, then she turned and headed back inside the flat, leaving the French windows open should any breeze spring up. The thick carpet felt luxurious beneath her bare feet and the room was welcoming, lit, as it was, only by the standard lamp behind her and the two wall lights on either side of the large television.

The wall to her right was dominated by a huge book-case that stretched from floor to high ceiling. In front of the staggering array of books was her desk with her computer perched on it. She'd checked her e-mails when she got home and been delighted to find, among several from friends and business associates, an invitation (forwarded to her by Maria Figgis) to speak at the British Museum. They were, she had discovered, running a series of lectures during the coming weeks on Italian writers. They had been struck by the advance publicity for her book about Giacomo Cassano and hoped she would accept their invitation. She had also been overjoyed to hear that *The Seeds of the Soul* had been short-listed for the International Literature Awards in the category of Best Biography, on the basis of an uncorrected reading copy submitted by the publishers in time to meet the deadline.

Perhaps, she wondered, it might be an appropriate time for her to crack open one of the bottles of Bollinger she had in her fridge but then again, celebrating alone was never very satisfying.

Alone. The word seemed to echo inside her head for a moment. It only seemed to be at times

70

like this that her single existence bothered her. Most of the time she enjoyed her independence and her freedom from emotional entanglements. But occasionally, in times of what should have been pure joy, she missed having someone close to help her luxuriate in her triumphs. She had many friends, even more acquaintances, but even friendship couldn't always fill the void left by the absence of a lover.

She had a wonderful career and a lifestyle that most would envy. With her new book due for publication in a couple of weeks her world, she decided, was a very pleasant place to be.

Why then the feelings of emptiness? And sometimes, in the dead of night, of such loneliness?

Megan refilled her glass with Perrier then changed the CD, lowering the volume. She glanced across at the phone.

A sudden breeze set the net curtains fluttering and Megan stood motionless for a moment gazing at the billowing, diaphanous material. Then she returned her gaze to the telephone.

She picked up the receiver, dialled and waited. It was answered on the third ring.

19

Frank Denton held the receiver in his hand for a moment longer then dropped it back on to the cradle. He looked down at the phone as if expecting it to ring again, but it didn't. The house remained silent.

He felt tired. It had been a long day, he'd drunk more than he normally did at lunchtime and the heat had a way of sapping the strength as effectively as the most strenuous exertion. Besides, he had work to do. He always had. Be it manuscripts from would-be authors or the work of those already fortunate enough to have found a publisher, there was always something to wade through. He had more of a new manuscript to read this very night. It was on his bedside table.

As he prepared to climb the stairs he thought about the script. What he'd read so far was encouraging. A story of abuse suffered by one girl at the hands of her father and her two brothers from the time she was eight until just after her sixteenth birthday. Books like that were always popular. Denton was gratified that the suffering of others was received with such unstinting enthusiasm by the book-buying public. Especially when he had been the one to unearth this particular gem. The author was twenty-three now. She was a very attractive young woman and that would certainly help with the promotion of the book.

Denton ensured that the doors and windows on the ground floor of the house were locked then made his way upstairs. Photographs of his family lined the wall all the way up to the landing. There was one of his older sister. Another of his parents, and one of his grandparents. After the death of his mother and father the day before his own eleventh birthday, Denton had come here to live with his grandparents. They had raised him with as much love as they could, trying their best to act as surrogate parents, especially when he was home from boarding school for his holidays.

He paused beside their photo and smiled at the recollection. They had willed this house to him upon their deaths. His grandfather had died of a heart attack fifteen years ago, and a stroke had taken his grandmother a little under four years later. Denton had lived alone in the house ever since. He'd often thought of selling it and moving into somewhere smaller. With property prices as they were he knew he could expect to make a huge amount of money, but there was a large part of him that was reluctant to leave the place. As if to sell it would be to betray the memory of the grandparents who had raised him.

Denton made his way into his bedroom and switched on the bedside light. He sat on his bed and looked around at the room he'd called his own for the last forty or more years. The air itself was thick with memories.

And everywhere there were books. On shelves on the stairs. In every room in the house. Many of them he'd had since he was a child. A love of reading had been instilled into him from an early age and that love had blossomed, to his parents' and grandparents' delight. The older works in his room were on the higher shelves, the new tomes occupied the lower tiers.

Denton closed his eyes briefly and it was as if that simple gesture dragged him out of his reminiscences and back to the real world. He glanced across at the small desk in one corner of the room where a number of hardback and paper-back volumes lay. One of them was *The Seeds of the Soul*. He crossed to it and picked it up, glancing at the inside back flap. A black and white photo of Megan Hunter smiled back at him. He replaced the book gently.

Close by was a copy of *The Fairground Phantoms*. Denton opened it at the title page. There was an inscription scrawled in black ink: *To Frank, all the best,* and, beneath it, in a sweeping hand, *John Paxton.*

Denton studied the signature for a moment longer then dropped the book back on to the desk.

He undressed, folded his clothes neatly and put on pyjama bottoms. Then he set his alarm clock for 6 a.m., settled down on the bed and picked up the manuscript from the bedside table.

The room was silent but for the turning of pages and the ticking of the clock.

It was 11.26 p.m.

20

As he parked the Renault, Birch saw that both ends of Merrivale Road had been closed off as he had instructed. He swung himself out of the car, ran a hand through his hair and walked towards the blue cordon where a uniformed constable stood sentinel.

Birch showed the man his ID and the policeman nodded, lifting the cordon for the detective to duck under.

There were a number of vehicles, including several marked police cars, parked in the street, blue lights turning silently. Some of the unmarked cars, Birch assumed, belonged to residents of the houses. Those that had been left rather more haphazardly he guessed were the property of other crime scene visitors. An ambulance was also in attendance, its back doors open wide. Two paramedics waited within.

There were lights on in the windows of some of the other houses in the street and Birch wondered what thoughts were going through the minds of these residents of Putney who had been woken to find their normally peaceful habitat invaded by the emergency services. He glanced at his watch and saw that it was 4.07 a.m.

As he drew near the front door of the house he sought he saw forensics men dusting for prints, the powdered graphite from the brushes they used standing out starkly against the brilliant white of the entryway.

Birch eased his way past the men and into the hallway of the house.

Instantly, the smell struck him.

The familiar coppery odour of blood was heavy in the air, but there was something else. A cloying stench that clogged his nostrils and made him cough.

'I should have stayed off for another week, shouldn't I?'

Birch recognised the voice and turned to his left. He smiled when he saw Detective Sergeant Stephen Johnson emerge from the sitting room.

The DI patted the younger man on the shoulder.

'It's good to have you back, Steve,' he said; then his expression changed. 'What have we got?'

'Come and have a look.'

Johnson led him up the staircase, moving slowly, glancing at some notes he'd made.

'The house belongs to a Frank Denton,' the DS told his superior. 'Fifty-four years old. Lived here alone. A neighbour heard a disturbance about half past two. Thought it was a burglary. A local mobile unit responded. As they were getting out of the car they heard screams from inside the house. They banged on the door but couldn't get an answer so they broke in.' The two detectives had reached the top of the stairs by now and Johnson gestured towards the open door of Denton's bedroom. 'This is what they found.'

Birch took a step into the room, his eyes fixed on the body of Frank Denton.

It was lying on its back across the bed, one hand trailing on the floor. The carpet, sheet and pillows were soaked with blood. More of the crimson fluid had spurted on to the walls. But, as he looked more intently at the corpse, Birch realised what that cloying stench was that he'd smelled when he first entered the house.

It was the noxious stink of internal organs.

Denton's body had been torn open from sternum to groin, exposing his intestines, pieces of which had been pulled from the gaping cavity. In addition, portions of the right ribcage had been ripped away, allowing a clear view of one lung.

The single eye that remained in its socket bulged insanely. The other dangled from the tendril of the optic nerve, hanging as far as the right ear which was itself barely attached to the side of the blood-drenched skull. Round the neck, strips of flesh had been stripped away like old wallpaper and now hung like translucent tendrils.

'Any idea on the murder weapon, Howard?' Birch asked a tall, grey-haired man in his mid-fifties who had a pair of half-moon glasses perched on the end of his nose.

Howard Richardson shook his head, then realised that the DI had addressed him without taking his eyes off the corpse.

'I can't say until I've examined him properly, David,' he admitted. 'But from the nature of the wounds I'd say a large, edged weapon. Possibly more than one.'

There was a second of blinding light as the

police photographer's camera recorded another angle of the crime.

Birch was still staring intently at the body, surveying every ruined inch of it.

'You said a neighbour heard a disturbance, Steve,' he commented. 'Did anyone see anything?'

'We've got statements from the people in the houses on either side of this one,' Johnson said, 'and from three opposite. None of them saw anyone entering or leaving the house. The other residents of the street are being interviewed now.'

'Any signs of forced entry?'

'No. That's another weird thing. All the doors and windows upstairs and down were locked from the inside. Like I said, the mobile unit that got here first had to break the front door down to get in.'

Birch frowned and leaned closer to the body, his eye caught by something on the torn thorax.

'What's that?' he asked, pulling a pen from his inside pocket and using the tip to point out what had attracted his attention.

'I'm not a hundred per cent sure yet,' Richardson told him. 'But it's on the bed and the floor around the desk too.' The pathologist motioned towards more of the matter that littered the area where the body lay.

'It looks like confetti,' Birch observed.

'Torn paper,' Richardson agreed. 'My thoughts exactly. I'm not surprised. Look.'

For the first time since he'd entered the room, Birch allowed his gaze to leave Denton's body. He followed the pathologist's pointing finger and saw that several books lay on the bedroom floor. The covers of some had been torn off but a number had been rent along the spine, the pages scattered around wildly. Even individual pages had been ripped, some of them so badly that they were little more than strips.

The manuscript on Denton's bedside table was untouched but there were splashes of blood on its A4 sheets.

'If those books were knocked off the shelves during the struggle,' Birch mused, 'they'd be scattered around the room, not torn to bits like some of these are.'

'Perhaps the killer hated books as well as Denton,' DS Johnson remarked. 'It could be symbolic. Denton was a book editor. Perhaps the killer was destroying Denton's work as well as him.' He shrugged.

'Find out if any of the damaged books were edited by Denton,' Birch said.

'One of them's the Bible,' Johnson said.

The other men in the room laughed.

'Check them anyway,' Birch insisted. He looked at Richardson. 'I want a full pathologist's report by ten this morning, please, Howard.'

Richardson nodded.

The room was again lit by the cold white flare of a camera flash.

'By the way,' the DI wanted to know. 'Was anything stolen?'

'Not that we can tell,' Johnson informed him. 'We even found fifty quid in cash in Denton's wallet. The downstairs rooms are immaculate.

Like I said, there isn't even any sign of forced entry.'

Birch nodded.

'All right,' he said. 'We'll let forensics finish what they're doing in here. Get the statements from the other people in the street. I'll have a look around the rest of the house.'

The brilliant white glare of the camera flash illuminated the room again. In that blinding whiteness, the blood that covered so much of the bed and the ruined body looked as black as pitch.

The flash glinted momentarily on the one open eye of Frank Denton and, for a fleeting second, it looked to Birch as if the dead man winked at him.

Poor bastard.

The DI turned and walked out of the room.

21

Birch looked up at Putney Bridge, glancing over the rim of his cup as he watched the traffic beginning to build up as people went about their daily business, happily oblivious of the fact that, less than half a mile away, a man had been brutally murdered.

What they don't know doesn't hurt them.

Of course it would be on the local news that evening. In the later editions of the *Standard*. But to those who heard about it or read of it, the incident would be no more significant than every other killing that blighted the capital or any other city, town or village in the country.

The café where Birch and Johnson now sat also gave them a view of the wharves. Beyond, the Thames looked black and forbidding in the half-light, choppier than normal.

'Nothing taken,' Birch said. 'So the motive wasn't burglary. Denton didn't catch someone in the act of robbing him and end up getting killed for his trouble. Somebody broke in specifically to butcher him.'

'No one broke in, guv,' Johnson reminded him. 'No forced entry, remember.'

Birch nodded. 'Then if no one broke in, Denton let them in,' he mused. 'Perhaps he knew his killer. That's the only explanation. But then again, if that mobile unit had to break his front door down to get in when they first arrived, what the fuck happened after he was killed? The murderer walked out and locked the door behind him? Could he have had a key?'

'If Denton knew him or her, maybe. Perhaps it was his girlfriend who topped him.'

'Maybe, but his injuries didn't look as if they were inflicted by a woman, did they?'

'Depends what she used on him. Hell hath no fury and all that shit.'

'You need strength to gut somebody the way he was opened up.'

'Strength or expertise. Maybe the killer knew where and how to cut. If it was a woman.'

'I want a list of all his friends, enemies, acquaintances, working associates, lovers, dogs, cats and fucking goldfish. Anyone he's been in contact with during the last five years that might have some reason for killing him.'

'That's going to take a while, guv.'

Birch merely nodded. 'You said that the mobile unit heard screams from inside the house and that was why they broke the door down in the first place,' he continued. 'So whoever killed him didn't leave the front way, did they?'

'The back door was deadlocked and bolted. They didn't leave that way either.'

Birch sipped his coffee and gazed thoughtfully at the bottom of the cup.

'So how did they get out of the house?' he mused. 'Never mind so fast. How long between the neighbour's call and the mobile unit arriving?'

'Ten minutes, tops.'

'So the murderer had the time to carve up

Denton and escape from the house before our guys arrived? Maybe the screams they heard were just the last sounds he made. The death throes.'

'That still doesn't explain how the killer got out of a locked house and managed to leave the doors and windows locked.'

Birch looked at his companion. 'Welcome back, Steve.' He smiled. 'You picked a hell of a fucking case to come back to.'

'Tell me about it.' The DS sighed, finishing his own coffee.

'So, what are you going to do tonight when you get home?' Birch asked. 'Tell Natalie what we found today? Describe the state of Denton's body?'

'Why should I do that?' Johnson wanted to know, his expression one of puzzlement.

'She might ask you.'

'Why bring that up, guv?'

'That little chat she and I had that night I came to visit you in hospital. She asked me about the job. How it had affected my relationships. So I told her. She seemed to think it was strange that I used to keep the details of the job from my wives. I told her that was the way it had to be. For me, anyway.'

'Is this going somewhere, guv?'

'Make sure you know your priorities, Steve. This kind of work isn't really a job, not if you want to be the best at it. It's an obsession. And it can destroy you. If not you, then sometimes those around you. I wouldn't want you to end up the same way as me. I wouldn't want you to lose

Natalie because of the job.'

'It won't come to that.'

'I wish I could have been that sure.' He got to his feet. 'Another coffee?'

Johnson nodded.

'Then I want another look inside Denton's house before we go back to the Yard,' Birch said, his face set in hard lines. 'There might be something we missed first time round.'

22

The message had taken her by surprise.

Megan Hunter had been working when the e-mail arrived. Usually she checked her electronic communications before she started writing at nine-thirty every morning, then waited until lunchtime before glancing at any more that might have arrived. For some reason, she had checked this particular one immediately.

It had shaken her. There was no other word to describe her reaction as she'd read the words on the screen. The sender had asked her to ring, which she had done with a hint of nervousness.

Was it nerves? Anxiety? There had been another feeling that caused her pulse to quicken slightly, one she couldn't put a name to. The same one she was feeling now in the back of the cab as it moved slowly through what seemed like unusually heavy traffic. The driver had his right arm propped on the open window as he drove, allowing the hot sun to beat down on his skin.

If there was any air-conditioning in the cab it wasn't working very efficiently. Megan was uncomfortably warm. She wondered if she'd have been better off driving her own car to the appointed rendezvous, but decided that would have been a bad idea. Her concentration tended to wander when she was nervous and then there was the problem of finding somewhere to park. Despite the fact that the journey from her own flat was relatively short she convinced herself that the decision to take a taxi had been the right one.

She glanced out of the window as the cab turned into Kensington Church Street. Her heart began beating a little faster. For a fleeting second she didn't want to get out of the taxi.

What are you going to do? Tell the driver to keep going? Go straight past the spot where you're supposed to stop?

She had surprised herself at how quickly she'd made a decision after the phone conversation she'd had. Even more surprised perhaps that she was now so close to her destination.

Too late to turn back?

The cab was slowing down.

'Just here on your right,' the driver told her cheerfully, bringing the vehicle to a halt.

'Thank you,' Megan said, easing herself out and scrabbling in her handbag for her purse. She gave the driver a ten pound note and didn't wait for the change.

As she stood on the pavement she could feel the rays of the sun bearing down upon her. People walking in either direction body-swerved to avoid her, one or two cursing the fact that she was merely standing immobile on the concrete.

Megan sucked in another deep breath then glanced at her watch.

She was a little late. She would apologise.

She ran a hand through her hair and checked her reflection in a shop window as she approached the building she sought.

She was wearing a lilac top beneath her linen

jacket and her diaphanous white skirt billowed as a particularly strong breeze caught it, blowing it up slightly to reveal a little more of her shapely legs. Megan swallowed hard, aware once more of the heat from the sun. She pulled off her jacket and draped it over her arm as she approached the main entrance of the restaurant.

A waiter came up to her and asked her if she required a table but she shook her head.

'I'm meeting someone, thank you,' she explained, glancing around.

At that moment, she spotted that someone at a table in the far corner.

Megan's heart thudded even harder against her ribs. She thanked the waiter and made her way towards the table she sought.

23

'You read my report. Everything I found was in there.'

Howard Richardson watched over the top of his half-moon glasses as Detective Inspector Birch walked slowly round the stainless steel slab, his gaze fixed on the savagely mutilated body of Frank Denton.

Detective Sergeant Johnson hung back slightly, allowing his superior to make a complete circuit of the corpse. The younger man noticed that there was still some blood in the shallow gutter round the rim of the slab. Richardson also noticed and washed it away with a few well-aimed jets of water.

The morgue was silent but for the dripping of a tap and Birch's footsteps as he prowled endlessly around like a carrion feeder waiting to begin its latest meal.

'I want to go through it again, Howard,' said the DI at last, his gaze still fixed on Denton's body.

'If you think it'll help,' the pathologist agreed.

'He was killed with a long knife, possibly with a curved blade,' Birch began.

'Butcher's knife of some kind?' Johnson suggested.

'Not a knife found in the house,' Birch stated.

'No.'

'So the killer brought his own weapon of

choice,' the DI continued.

'What about the sex of the killer?' Johnson interjected.

'I'm as sure as I can be that it was a man,' Richardson told him. 'A very strong man. Some of the cuts to the chest and abdomen were three or four inches deep. The actual killing stroke severed the aorta. Denton bled to death. That, combined with shock.'

'Defence cuts on the hands and arms,' Birch noted, pointing at one particularly savage gash on the inner left forearm.

'Yes, but not as many as I would have expected,' the pathologist told him.

'Meaning what?' Birch mused. 'That the attacker struck too fast for Denton to try and protect himself?'

'That's one explanation. Another is that he was so surprised by the appearance of the killer that he didn't react in time.'

'Well, if some guy with a bloody great curved knife appeared in your bedroom in the middle of the night it'd shock you, wouldn't it?' Birch said.

There was another moment of silence, then Johnson spoke. 'Was the knife used to remove Denton's eye as well?' he wanted to know.

'No,' Richardson said. 'The scratch marks around the socket were made by fingernails. The eye was . . . clawed out, for want of a better word. But not with the same frenzy that the knife wounds were inflicted. The reason I can say that with certainty is because the eye was still attached to the optic nerve. If it had been torn out by the killer while he was still in some kind of demented state the chances are the nerve would have been snapped when the eye was pulled from its socket.'

'So he cut Denton up with this curved knife then calmly popped his eye out?' Birch said, but it came out more as a statement than a question. 'Any fingerprints on the face from where he took out the eye? He must have left some latent prints behind when he did that. He couldn't gouge out an eye wearing gloves, could he?'

'Actually he could,' Richardson said. 'It's not as difficult as you might think to pop out an eyeball. You can do it with a thumb and index finger if you know what you're doing.'

'So, were there any prints?' Birch repeated.

'Not enough to identify anyone. I sent the fragments of the two prints I found to Hendon but I wouldn't expect them to get much. There were no prints anywhere else on the body.'

'You said that the eye was removed more . . . calmly than the way the stab wounds were inflicted,' Johnson cut in.

'There were over thirty wounds to Denton's face, neck, chest and abdomen,' Richardson explained. 'They were carried out quickly and with tremendous force. The classic signs of a frenzied attack. It's unusual for a killer to be able to bring his emotions under control so rapidly once he's fallen into such a frenzy.'

'How long did it take him to kill Denton?' Birch wanted to know.

'Less than two minutes,' the pathologist answered. 'If it's any consolation, he was probably dead when the killer removed his eye.'

'What about the fibres you found on the corpse?' Birch enquired. 'Can we identify the murderer from those?'

'There were very few, for some reason. Some woollen threads, presumably from his clothing, but that's it. I didn't even find any of his skin under Denton's fingernails. The only other fibre I found was wood pulp.'

'From the books in Denton's bedroom,' said Birch.

Richardson nodded. 'It was all over the body.'

'Why destroy the books?' Birch mused. 'Some kind of trademark? Like the popped-out eye? Is he trying to tell us something?'

'I wish he'd tell us how he got in and out of Denton's house,' Johnson interjected.

Birch raised his eyebrows. 'No prints on any of the doors or windows,' he said. 'How the fuck did he get in and out?' The DI began prowling round the slab once more. 'He kills in a rage but calms down quickly enough to take out one of his victim's eyes. He rips several of the victim's books to pieces and scatters the bits around the crime scene. He steals nothing. He enters and leaves the house without a trace and without any sign of forced entry or exit. So far we have no apparent motive, no witnesses and no clue as to whether this is a one-off or the beginning of something.' Birch crossed to the mutilated body of Frank Denton and leaned close to the face. 'What did you see?' he murmured. 'Who is he?'

24

Megan found that her hand was shaking slightly as she inserted the key in the door. She stepped into her flat, closed the door behind her and leaned against it for a moment, her head spinning.

So many thoughts were tumbling through her mind. She felt drunk. Not quite in control. It was a feeling she'd been experiencing ever since she left the restaurant more than an hour earlier.

She'd eaten little while she was there, unable or unwilling to force down too much food as she'd tried to cope with some of the things she had heard.

Now she sucked in a deep breath and walked through into the kitchen where she spun the cold tap at the sink, retrieved a glass from a nearby cupboard and filled it to the brim with the cool, clear liquid gushing from the tap. She gulped several large mouthfuls, took another deep breath then drank more.

After leaving the restaurant she'd walked up Kensington Church Street to Notting Hill, but her passage had been unsteady and on more than one occasion she'd had to stop and lean against the wall of a shop to recover her composure. She'd attracted some concerned glances from passers-by the second time but had shrugged off their good-natured enquiries about her well-being. Everything was fine. She was fine. There was nothing to worry about. She just needed the fresh air.

Nothing to worry about.

The phrase seemed to echo inside her head, competing for space with all the other words and images spinning around in her mind.

Eventually, she'd headed briskly home, hoping that the walk would clear her head, but it had been a forlorn hope. The relentless heat of the day had only served to make her feel worse and her feet were throbbing from having walked so far in her high heels.

Now, standing in the kitchen, she pulled off her shoes, feeling the cool tiles beneath her bare feet. She drank another glass of water and walked through into the sitting room, where she sat down at her desk.

Still Megan could not seem to clear her head. Like the early stages of inebriation, it felt as if someone had wrapped her brain in cotton wool. She didn't seem able to focus on anything clearly, or to control the myriad thoughts circling in her mind.

She felt her heart beating a little faster. As she caught sight of her reflection in the monitor screen of her computer she thought how dark she looked beneath the eyes. As if she hadn't slept for a week.

Megan sipped more slowly at the glass of water she'd carried through from the kitchen and tried to relax. Now, in the safety and familiarity of her own flat, that shouldn't be so difficult.

Take some deep breaths.

She smiled to herself.

Make yourself a cup of tea.

The universal cure-all.

Again she smiled, feeling her heart slow a little. The throbbing at the base of her skull was beginning to ease as well and for that she was grateful. Perhaps she'd take a couple of painkillers just to ensure it didn't get any worse.

She was still considering this option when the phone rang.

Megan briefly considered letting the call go on to the answering machine but finally decided to pick up the receiver.

She recognised Maria Figgis's voice immediately.

However, within a minute or two, as Megan clutched the phone more tightly, she was beginning to wish she hadn't taken the call.

Attrition

Every passing minute had felt like an hour. From the moment the doctor had left the room where the woman and her companion waited, time seemed to have slowed down.

The man, at least, had the luxury of being able to pace back and forth in the small hospital room, his irritation and concern surfacing every so often in the form of some verbal outburst.

The woman remained confined to her bed, her own impatience and frustration now almost intolerable.

A nurse had been in once or twice to check the woman's chart and both of them had asked questions about their baby but the nurse had told them that she knew nothing about the child. She didn't know if it was going to be brought to them, as promised, in a mobile incubator.

The man had raised his voice when she'd said that for the second time, barely able to control what was rapidly becoming a rage fuelled by fear.

In quieter moments, the two of them sat and looked at each other and talked in hushed tones of the son they had yet to see.

They had spoken of the severity of the breathing problems they had been told of, speculated on the nature of the 'other matters' the doctor had mentioned. Exactly how ill was their boy? The man had suggested that even if the child was dying

(the woman had begun to cry at this point)

then they still should have been told. Even more so, in fact. If their child was so critically ill, they might have only a short time to spend with it before it left them for ever.

Perhaps it had suffered some kind of brain damage, liver or kidney failure. Nature had a habit of playing cruel tricks and the two of them considered every one slowly and carefully even though that only added to their mental anguish.

And still the minutes crawled on so slowly.

The man had finally suggested finding the child himself. If it was as ill as they had been led to believe it would be in the Intensive Care Unit. He would go there and see for himself what was wrong with their son.

Despite her own desperation, the woman had managed to dissuade him from this course of action, although she herself felt she could wait no longer for news or sight of her child.

Her child.

The two words still resonated inside her head, as if she couldn't believe it. Couldn't come to terms with the fact that she had given birth.

Perhaps the full significance of the situation still eluded her because she had yet to see her son. And the way things had transpired, she was beginning to wonder if that was ever going to happen.

Her partner stood by the window of the room every so often, looking out over the hospital car park. More than once he watched ambulances arrive. And he saw visitors come and go. Men who were allowed to visit their newly born children. And the thought of those other men gazing upon and holding their offspring caused him pain and anger in equal measure.

When the door of the room finally opened and the doctor entered, the man's first instinct was to fly furiously at him. To vent his rage and his frustration at having been made to wait so long for the first sight of his son.

The woman felt the same way, but when a nurse pushed a small portable incubator into the room both of them found their attention turning away from the man in the white coat. All that mattered now was that they would see their son. Hold their son if they were lucky.

The man took a step towards the incubator but the doctor shook his head and raised a hand to stop him.

The child's breathing problems had stabilised, he told them, which was why the visit had been permitted. But it would be a short one.

For just a fleeting second, the woman wondered why the nurse pushing the incubator was not looking down at the child within it. Instead, she seemed to be doing her best to focus anywhere but on the tiny form inside the plastic.

The woman raised herself up against her pillows, her heart beating faster. All she wanted was to see her son. Momentarily, all the frustration and anger of the previous hours were forgotten.

The nurse wheeled the incubator closer to the bed.

As she did so, a single tear rolled down her cheek.

25

Birch didn't even look up when he heard the knock on his office door. He merely called for whoever was outside in the corridor to enter, keeping his gaze on the various reports, photographs and statements spread out before him.

'Am I interrupting?' Detective Sergeant Johnson asked, pausing momentarily at the threshold before stepping into the office and closing the door behind him.

Only then did Birch look up.

'No,' he said, shaking his head. 'I wish you were. If you were interrupting that'd imply there was something to interrupt.' He raised his hands and sat back in his chair. 'Like some fucking progress on this Denton case.' The DI took a deep breath, held it a moment and then exhaled. 'It's not like he didn't have any enemies; I mean to say who doesn't? If we go through all his friends and acquaintances I'm sure we can find two or three with reason enough for wanting him dead. That's one of the weird things about this case. Everything at the scene of the crime points to the fact that he was killed by someone who broke into his house. And yet there's no sign of forced entry so how's that possible? Evidence suggests the killer simply walked in, or was let in by Denton himself. But the doors and windows were still locked after Denton was killed, so who let the killer out? Also, if it'd been a burglar he'd disturbed, it's unlikely he would have been killed so brutally. And if it was a burglar, why was nothing taken?' Birch looked at his colleague. 'Did you check out the books that were found destroyed in his room?'

'Two of the eight that were torn up were edited by Denton,' the younger man announced. '*The Seeds of the Soul* and one called *Unmarked Graves*. But he had worked with one of the other writers too. John Paxton. His latest book was one of the ones we found destroyed. Denton had edited some of his stuff about five years ago.'

'But not this new one?'

'No.'

'What about the authors of the books he did edit? What kind of relationship did Denton have with them?'

'Strictly professional. He still edits the books of Megan Hunter, the woman who wrote *The Seeds of the Soul*. The guy who wrote *Unmarked Graves* lives in Ireland and we can place him there the night Denton was murdered. Like I said, Paxton hasn't worked with him for about five years. Apparently he sends him copies of all his books, though — that's why there was one there. But there's no bad blood between any of them. At least not that we know of, and certainly not enough to suggest that one of them butchered him like that.' Johnson looked at one of the crime scene photos laid out on his superior's desk.

Birch nodded. 'Nothing seems to have been taken,' he murmured. 'That doesn't mean there wasn't anything in the house that the killer wanted. Maybe Denton just disturbed him before he found what he was really looking for.'

'Which was?'

'At the moment I don't know. I'm going back there tonight to have a look round.'

'Do you want me to come with you?'

Birch shook his head. 'You go home, Steve. You've got something to go home for. It doesn't matter if I'm out all night every night.'

'Do you fancy coming back to our place for some dinner?'

'I appreciate the offer but no thanks. I don't think I'd be very good company tonight.' He smiled. 'Nothing new there though.' He hooked a thumb in the direction of the office door. 'Go on. Go home to your wife. If I find anything at Denton's house that looks promising I'll call you.'

Johnson nodded and got to his feet.

'I'll walk down with you,' Birch said, pulling on his jacket. He glanced out of his office window and saw the lights of London sparkling in the darkness.

He had reached the office door when his mobile phone rang. He reached into his jacket and pulled it free, flipping it open and pressing it to his ear.

'Birch,' he said, and listened to the voice at the other end of the line. Johnson saw his superior's face darken. 'When?' Birch nodded. 'Yeah, I got it.'

He snapped the phone shut.

'You'd better ring home, tell Natalie you'll be late,' he told the younger man. 'There's been another murder.'

26

The room looked like a slaughterhouse.

Broken furniture, shattered ornaments and even a smashed fish tank were all spattered with blood. The fish were scattered across the carpet, all dead apart from one that still flapped and gasped feebly for breath in a puddle of spilled water and blood. The walls of the flat too were streaked crimson, the result of arterial spray.

There was even blood on the television screen, smeared across it like a red curtain.

To the rear of the sitting room, framed by bookshelves that reached from floor to ceiling, double doors opened out on to a small balcony that offered a view of the Thames. The doors were also splashed with blood, as were many of the books. What remained of a glass-topped coffee table occupied the centre of the room, jagged, splintered shards scattered around it. Uniformed and plain clothes policemen moved slowly and methodically about the room, each performing their assigned task.

A flash exploded brightly, illuminating the contents of the flat.

The body lay in the middle of the floor.

It was a man, that much was evident. But little else, so badly mutilated was the corpse.

Both eyes were missing, torn from their sockets. One lay beside the body. Of the other there was no sign. The face and neck were lacerated by deep cuts, some down to the bone. A portion of the ribcage was visible, the bones gleaming whitely amidst the pulped and riven flesh. The torso had been split by several savage wounds that had exposed the intestines. The mouth was open, the bottom jaw cracked and bent to an impossible angle. Several teeth had been dislodged by what must have been thunderous blows and a portion of the tongue lay on the carpet like a bloated, corpulent leech.

Detective Inspector Birch stood motionless amidst the devastation, glancing around, attempting to take in every detail of what he saw.

'Donald Corben,' said a balding, plain clothes policeman, nodding towards the corpse. 'Forty-two. He lived alone. He was a restaurant critic for one of the broadsheets. A book reviewer for another newspaper and some magazines. He'd been on TV a few times. Public school. Daddy runs a magazine. One of these 'take the piss out of the government' jobs. He's got a younger sister. She writes for magazines as well.'

'Nice to see nepotism's alive and well,' Birch muttered.

The other plain clothes man nodded.

'Who found him?' Birch asked, crouching to get a better look at the body.

'A neighbour heard him screaming, called down to the security guy. He banged on the door, couldn't get an answer so let himself in and . . . bingo.'

'Where is he now?'

'Downstairs, being treated for shock.'

'What time was Corben found?'

'About nine-thirty.'

'Looks familiar,' Johnson said quietly, also studying the ravaged body.

Birch nodded.

'Forensics have already done a preliminary dust for prints in here,' the balding detective said. 'They're doing the other rooms now. Kitchen, toilet, bathroom and two bedrooms.'

'Has the body been examined?' Birch wanted to know.

'Enough for me to be able to tell you he was killed by the same person who murdered Frank Denton.'

Birch turned slightly as he recognised the voice of Howard Richardson.

The pathologist had emerged from the bathroom. He was drying his hands with his handkerchief.

'What have you been doing?' Birch asked.

'Even great men have to pee,' Richardson told him.

'Same MO,' Birch said.

'The main thing that's different is that the attack was more savage than the one on Denton,' the pathologist announced. 'The cuts to the neck are so bad, another inch or two deeper and Corben would have been decapitated. Same with the eyes. No calm removal this time. They were cut out with a serrated blade, hacked out. Probably the same one the killer used to finish him off.'

'You mean he wasn't dead when his eyes were taken?' Birch asked, frowning.

Richardson shook his head.

'Where's the other eye?' the DI wanted to know.

'We haven't found it yet,' the balding plain clothes man said. 'It could have been taken by the murderer.'

'Classic serial killer,' Birch suggested. 'Taking a trophy.' He moved forward, noticing what looked like fine dust on some parts of the body.

'Wood pulp from the torn books,' Richardson informed him.

Birch noticed that a number of hardback and paperback volumes were lying near the corpse. All had been harmed in some way but five of them had sustained particularly bad damage. Dust jackets had been ripped off and torn, bindings had been broken and split. Pages had been pulled free and scattered around like confetti, many of them over the body itself.

'Also similar to Denton is the fact that there are very few defence cuts on the hands and forearms,' the pathologist continued. 'It seems as if the killer took Corben by surprise too.'

'In a ninth-floor flat?' Birch mused. 'Who the fuck could sneak up on him in here? There are only two ways in and out. Through the front door and through those windows that open out on to the balcony. What are we supposed to do? Put out wanted notices for fucking Spiderman? Because I can't see who else could have got in and out of here without being seen. What about the front door? Was the lock picked? Any sign of forced entry?'

'None,' the balding detective said. 'The front door and the balcony windows were locked from the inside. They were still locked after the murder.'

'Just like Denton,' Detective Sergeant Johnson said.

Birch stepped away from the centre of the room and made his way to the front door of the flat, followed by Johnson.

'Corben's been butchered,' the DI said. 'Whoever killed him would have been covered in blood. Their clothes, their shoes. Everything. But look.' He gestured along the short, carpeted corridor that led to the lift. 'There isn't a mark on the floor. Not a spot of blood.'

'Perhaps the killer wore overalls to protect his clothes then dumped them before he left,' the DS offered.

'Before he left a flat that was locked behind him when he walked out?' Birch challenged.

'Could he have taken a key with him and disposed of it later?' said Johnson.

'It's possible, I suppose.' There was no conviction in the DI's voice. 'It's this business with the blood that gets me. Even if he did wear overalls he would have left some trace out here.' He turned and headed back into the flat, past the police photographer, the pathologist and the other men busy with their duties. Slipping his handkerchief from his pocket he wrapped it round the key that was in the lock of the balcony windows and twisted. The windows opened and Birch stepped out. A strong breeze ruffled his hair. He gripped the guard rail and looked down from the ninth floor of Harbour Towers into Cabot Square. Above him, another five storeys of the luxury apartment block thrust upwards into the night sky.

He glanced in the direction of the Thames, watching as a pleasure boat crammed with happy revellers chugged through the dark water.

The sound of the Docklands traffic far below seemed a million miles away.

'Nine floors up,' Birch said. 'There's no way the killer could have got in this way. And even if he was some kind of fucking human fly, those windows were locked from the inside too.' He hooked a thumb in the direction of the balcony windows. 'The only way in was past a security guard, CCTV, then up in a lift to a flat that was locked from the inside. Even if the murderer used the stairs he'd have still had to enter the building by the main door and foyer and they're covered from every angle by cameras.'

'Corben must have known his killer,' Johnson said. 'To have allowed him access to the lift. The suspect would have had to have been let into the lift by the security guard. Corben must have OK'd that. He must have known who was coming up here.'

'Then it should show up on the CCTV footage,' Birch said. 'Once we get a look at those tapes we've got the bastard.' He gripped the guard rail more tightly and gazed out once more in the direction of the river.

Progeny

The woman felt as if she'd been punched in the stomach.

All the breath was suddenly ripped from her as she stared down into the portable incubator.

Tears filled her eyes. They came suddenly and without warning.

Beside her, the man was standing motionless, his own gaze fixed on the small figure before him. He said nothing. Even though his lips moved, no sound would come forth. He searched for words to express what he was feeling but none would come.

The woman tried to swallow but her mouth and throat were as dry as sand.

The doctor spoke but what he said hardly registered. The woman felt as if she had suddenly been encased in some kind of bubble. She could see out but nothing could penetrate. Tears continued to roll down her cheeks.

She wanted to look at the doctor
(she wanted to look away from the baby)
but her gaze remained riveted on the child.

Her son.

It was as if those two words suddenly forcing themselves into her consciousness shook her from her trance-like state.

Her son.

She moved backwards on the bed, wanting to be away from the child

(was child even the right word for the form that lay in that incubator?)

as if close contact with it would somehow damage her.

One monstrous thought filled her head and refused to budge. She wondered if it would be possible to tear open the stitches that held her stomach and womb together and somehow shove the child back in.

She laughed at this absurd idea and the sound that echoed round the room chilled all those who heard it. It was the laughter of the mad.

(The damned?)

The laughter of someone who cannot accept what they are witnessing. Someone who must try to deny what they are seeing for the sake of their sanity.

The man was silent but for his laboured breathing. He actually moved forward towards the incubator, his initial reaction now turning to something resembling anger.

He wanted to know what was wrong with the child.

The doctor tried to tell him. First in medical jargon and then in words that would be more easily understood, but it was useless.

There were no words in any language to adequately describe what lay in the incubator.

The baby began to cry. Softly at first. A low, mewling sound that rose in volume and intensity until it resembled the mucoid snorting of some slaughterhouse victim.

The doctor was still speaking. Still attempting to explain what had happened.

To the woman it was as if he was trying to justify the existence of the figure that writhed in the incubator before her. Was he offering some kind of apology? Only now did she manage to tear her gaze from her son.

Her son.

She gripped her partner's arm and tried to say something to him but he shook loose, still standing over the incubator, his eyes now bloodshot as if the veins that criss-crossed the whites were about to explode.

The woman was shaking her head constantly now. As if that action would change what had transpired. Change her son.

'I'm sorry,' the doctor said.

They were the only two words she heard.

Her head was swimming. She felt as if the room was whirling around her.

She looked one last time into the incubator then blacked out.

27

'Nothing,' snapped Birch, jabbing the 'Rewind' button of the video recorder. 'Nothing that's any use to us, anyway.'

The tape whirred loudly as it rewound, the spools squealing. The sound echoed round the inside of the Incident Room. The plain clothes and uniformed police officers in there glanced at the television screen with its swiftly moving black and white images or looked around at the noticeboards and blackboards that also vied for space.

Every single one of them was festooned with photos. Interiors and exteriors of Frank Denton's house and Donald Corben's flat. Builders' diagrams. But, mostly, it was the pictures of the slaughtered men themselves that dominated the room. Dozens of them, taken from every conceivable angle. Each one designed to highlight one of their many savage injuries or the charnel house state of the rooms where they'd been butchered.

At the rear of the room there was an Action Board that showed the location of every man or woman working on the case and the aspect of it they were involved with.

'As you all know by now, Donald Corben was killed around nine-thirty p.m. last night,' Birch called, taking his finger off the 'Rewind' button. He gestured towards the TV screen, tapping the top right-hand corner with the end of his pen. There was a date and a time displayed there. 'These tapes, from the CCTV cameras covering the security gate and the foyer of Harbour Towers, show that between five-thirty and nine-thirty p.m., eight people entered the building. Five of them were residents. The other three were visitors. They've all given statements. They've all been checked out and they're all kosher. They've been eliminated from our investigation. None of those eight people who entered the building during that time killed Donald Corben.' He looked at the screen, where the black and white images still flickered.

'What about someone who came in before five-thirty?' a plain clothes man at the back of the room called.

'It's extremely unlikely the killer would have hung around in the building for three hours waiting to get to Corben, let alone longer,' Birch said dismissively. 'Anyway, all visitors have to sign in and there weren't any before five-thirty other than a couple of tradesmen in the morning. They've both been accounted for.'

'What about the stairs, guv?' another man seated near the front of the room asked. 'They're not covered by CCTV cameras. The killer might have got into the building and up to Corben's flat that way.'

'Forensics went over them with a fine-tooth comb,' Birch said. 'Nothing out of the ordinary.' He sighed. 'And that's about the only thing connected with this fucking case that isn't out of the ordinary.' He turned to one of the

112

notice-boards and tapped photos of Frank Denton and Donald Corben. 'We've got two dead men. Both killed the same way. Two crime scenes virtually identical. In both cases there was no sign of forced entry which would imply that both men knew their killer.' The DI raised a hand. 'By the way, it's Frank Denton's funeral later today. I want a couple of men there. Watch the other mourners. See if anything stands out. It's just possible the murderer might turn up. You know how some of these fuckers get an extra kick out of seeing the reactions of the deceased's family and friends. Just keep your eyes open. You two.' He pointed at two men standing by the nearest noticeboard. After a moment, he went on: 'I'm not going to go over all the details again; you've all read the pathologist's reports. You've seen the state of the bodies. You know the backgrounds of the two men and the details of the case.' He fumbled in his jacket and pulled out a packet of cigarettes, one of which he lit. 'Now, has anyone got anything worthwhile to tell me? Like how the murderer gained entry to and then managed to leave crime scenes that had locked doors and windows without showing any signs of either forced entry or exit?' The DI surveyed the occupants of the room hopefully. 'If both men knew their killer then that would explain why there was no evidence, at either crime scene, of B and E. But it doesn't tell us how the doors and windows at both places came to be locked once the murders had been committed. Who locked up behind him? He can't be working with an accomplice because if he was, how did the accomplice get out?'

'Could he have got into Denton's house and Corben's flat and just waited for them?' Detective Sergeant Johnson offered. 'There was a large attic in Denton's house. He could have hidden there. Come out when he thought the time was right.'

'It's possible, but where the hell did he hide in Corben's flat, Steve?' Birch asked. 'In a wardrobe? Besides, that still wouldn't explain how the doors and windows at both murder scenes were still locked even after the crimes were carried out.' The DI took a drag on his cigarette and blew out a stream of smoke. 'Whoever he is, he somehow comes and goes without leaving a trace. No fingerprints. No footprints. No saliva. No blood smears. Nothing. He works quickly and effectively and he vanishes.'

'Excuse me, sir,' called a young plain clothes policewoman standing near the Action Board. 'But the killer did leave traces.'

'Tell me,' Birch demanded.

'The fibres that forensics found on Corben's body were the same as those found on Denton,' said a fresh-faced man with his shirt sleeves rolled up to expose powerful forearms. 'Woollen thread.'

'And wood pulp from the ruined books, right?' Birch added.

The younger man nodded.

'Why does he destroy the books?' Birch murmured, as if the question was directed at himself rather than his colleagues.

'Maybe the killer's a pissed-off librarian,' someone near the back of the room called.

There was a chorus of laughter. Birch himself grinned.

'It's part of his trademark,' Johnson interjected. 'All serial killers have a trademark, don't they? An MO that's peculiar to them. This bastard's just adding his own little touch.'

Birch scratched one unshaven cheek.

'What about the five books that were found ripped up in Corben's flat?' he asked.

'They were the ones he was going to review for his newspaper column, sir,' the plain clothes policewoman answered.

'Any of them the same as those found at the Denton murder scene?' Birch wanted to know.

'Two of them,' the policewoman told him, glancing at her notes. '*The Fairground Phantoms* by John Paxton and *The Seeds of the Soul* by Megan Hunter.'

28

The two women hurried into the bar and made straight for the nearest booth, delighted that the place was almost empty but for some staff, one of whom was drying glasses while another was checking menus. The one with the pile of menus raised a hand to acknowledge them.

'God, I hate funerals,' Megan Hunter said, shrugging off her black jacket and running a hand through her hair. 'Especially in the rain.' She looked down at the droplets of moisture on her boots. 'It always makes the event seem so much more depressing. Even sadder than it is anyway.'

'He had a good send-off though, didn't he?' Maria Figgis offered, also removing her coat. 'I think he would have been pleased with how many people came.'

'I've never understood that, you know. What difference does it make to the poor devil who's being buried how many people turn up?'

'Ah, Megan, you don't understand, do you? You forget, we Irish like a good funeral almost as much as we do a good wedding. My dad always used to say that the only difference between an Irish funeral and an Irish wedding is that at the funeral there's one less drunk.'

Both women laughed.

'Perhaps we should have stayed longer,' Megan said.

'No. We put in an appearance to show our respects. That was enough.'

'There were more people there from publishing than I expected.'

'He was very well respected within the business. He'd been in it for over twenty-five years. I've known him for fifteen.'

Megan smiled warmly as the waiter arrived. She ordered a glass of red wine for each of them, glancing in the direction of the bar for a moment.

'His family were nice,' she observed. 'I'm sure I recognised one of his sisters from somewhere. Isn't she an actress?'

'That was his cousin. She's been in the theatre for years and a couple of films, I think. Just small parts.'

The waiter returned, set down the wine glasses, nodded politely and left.

'Cheers,' Megan said, raising her glass.

'To Frank,' Maria responded, also lifting her wine in salute.

They drank, then Megan reached into her handbag for her cigarettes. She was about to light one when she remembered that the bar had a no-smoking policy. Sighing, she pushed the cigarettes and lighter back into her handbag and concentrated on her wine.

'I didn't think that the police released the bodies of murder victims to the relatives so soon,' she mused. 'It's been less than a week since it happened.'

'I was thinking the same thing,' Maria echoed. 'There must be a good reason.' She exhaled wearily. 'First Frank and then Donald Corben.'

'I don't think too many people will miss Corben, Maria.'

Maria frowned reproachfully.

'The first two novels I wrote he absolutely slated,' Megan reminded her. 'What is it they say? Those who can do, those who can't teach and those who can do neither criticise. That was true of Donald Corben.'

'He did have a vicious turn of phrase about him, I'll admit that. But no matter what his faults he didn't deserve what happened to him. No one deserves to die like that. The newspapers said he was stabbed repeatedly. No one deserves that.'

'There are some who would disagree with you, Maria.'

'Like who? You tell me anyone who'd wish that kind of harm on a man.'

'What goes around comes around. Corben was nasty to a lot of people. Perhaps it was karma. It came back on him.'

'I can't believe you're speaking this way. Especially as we've just come from the funeral of a man who was also murdered and probably by the same maniac who killed Donald Corben.'

'How can you know that?' Megan said dismissively. 'The papers only said that both men were stabbed and their deaths may be linked.'

'They were both a part of the publishing business.'

'Corben was a critic. He wasn't in the business. All he did was make snide remarks about people who are. Especially writers.'

118

'Critics can be useful.'

'Not critics like Donald Corben.'

'Well, I doubt if we'll be invited to his funeral. Either of us.' Maria took another sip of her wine and glanced out of the window at the rain-soaked street beyond.

'I think I can live with that,' Megan said, draining what was left in her glass. She held up her hand to summon the waiter. When he arrived, she ordered two more glasses of red wine. 'I need a cigarette,' she murmured. 'I'm just going to stand outside for a minute and have a couple of drags.' As she got to her feet she reached inside her handbag and took out her mobile phone.

'Are you expecting a call?' Maria asked.

Megan didn't answer. She was already heading towards the door.

29

'We could have got the Tube then just got a cab from the station,' Detective Sergeant Stephen Johnson observed, guiding the dark blue Renault round another tortuous bend in the road.

It was lined on both sides by high hedges. Beyond them, fields stretched away to their left. To the right, trees waved gently in the breeze that had been blowing ever since they left central London.

With the sun still hidden behind forbidding banks of grey cloud, puddles of water on the road remained deep. Especially on some of the turns of the narrower roads that Johnson was forced to negotiate.

'There are some beautiful properties round here,' Birch noted, glancing at a huge white house that lay at the end of a long drive. 'You can almost smell the money.'

'How long's John Paxton lived out here?'

'Twelve years, apparently. He had a place in Mayfair before that. Sold it. Made a bloody great profit and moved out here to Amersham around the same time his first novel was turned into a film.'

Johnson nodded and was relieved to see that he was now coming to a stretch of straight road.

'I watched the film on DVD last night,' Birch continued. 'Not my cup of tea, I must admit. I don't like horror films.'

120

'Natalie loves them. She's read some of Paxton's books too. She says he's a good writer.'

'He must be doing something right. According to his agent, he's sold over forty million books worldwide. I want to know how well he knew Corben and Denton. I know he worked with Denton and, apparently, he'd had a couple of run-ins with Donald Corben. Corben had slagged his books off in reviews. They were on a TV show together about six months ago. Things got heated and Paxton threatened to put his head through a window.'

'Not very literary.' Johnson smiled.

'Copies of his latest book were found at both murder scenes. It had been ripped up and bits of it scattered over the bodies. If there's a reason for that, Paxton might even know what it is. It's probably a complete coincidence, but talking to him can't hurt. He might be interested to know that his new novel was used to decorate a couple of corpses. Perhaps he'll put it in his next book.' Birch tapped his companion on the arm and pointed at the house looming before them, protected by a tall privet hedge. 'This is the place.'

Johnson turned into the drive that curved for a hundred yards or so round a perfectly manicured lawn until it opened out before the house itself.

Both policemen clambered out of the car, shoes crunching on the gravel of the driveway.

The house had a thatched roof and leaded windows. The flower beds on either side of the front door were a riot of colour. Hanging baskets, also bursting with all manner of blooms, were fixed to the whitewashed frontage of the imposing building.

'Doesn't look like the kind of place where a horror writer would live, does it?' Johnson murmured.

'What were you expecting?' Birch smiled. 'Bodies nailed to the walls?'

Birch reached for the large metal knocker on the front door and brought it down three times.

The two policemen waited a moment then heard movement on the other side of the partition. There was the sound of a lock being released, and then the door was opened.

The man who greeted them was in his mid-forties and powerfully built, with brown hair greying at the temples. He was dressed in jeans, trainers and a red Reebok training top.

'Detective Inspector Birch,' said the man, before the policeman had the chance to speak. 'You obviously found the house without any problems. Good.'

The DI nodded and produced his identification.

'This is my colleague, Detective Sergeant Johnson.'

'I'm John Paxton,' the man said. 'Come in.'

30

'Sorry to disturb you, Mr Paxton,' Birch said as they stepped into the large hallway of the house. 'We'll try to be as quick as we can.'

'You're not disturbing me,' Paxton told them. 'I've given myself the morning off. One of the advantages of being self-employed.' He smiled again. It was an infectious, easy smile that complemented his manner. 'Anyway, I'll look at it as research. Having two detectives in my house. That doesn't happen every day.'

Birch glanced quickly round the hallway. Like the outside of the house, it was painted white, the walls decorated with several large paintings of military battle scenes. A dark wood staircase to the right led up to the first floor. Their feet beat out a tattoo on the parquet as they followed Paxton towards a door at the rear of the hall.

'Would you like a drink, either of you?' the writer asked. 'Or can't you drink on duty? Is that true or is it just a cop show cliché?'

'Tea would be nice, Mr Paxton,' Birch told him. 'Thanks.'

'Call me John, for fuck's sake. I hate formality,' Paxton said earnestly.

They followed him into a large sitting room and then into an equally spacious kitchen where he flicked on an electric kettle standing on one of the worktops, took three mugs from the wooden mug tree nearby and dropped a tea bag into each.

'Excuse me being a bit hyper,' Paxton said, smiling. 'But this is exciting in a weird kind of way. I've written about detectives before but I've never actually had any in my house.'

'You have been close to policemen before, though, Mr Paxton,' Birch reminded him.

'During the course of research for books, yeah. The police have always been very obliging when I've asked for their help on technical stuff. I was even lucky enough to have a look round the Black Museum at New Scotland Yard when I was working on one book.'

The kettle boiled and Paxton filled the mugs. He took a carton of milk from the fridge close by and indicated the sugar bowl and spoons on the worktop.

'Help yourselves,' he told the two detectives.

'And there was the time you were arrested for being drunk and disorderly,' Birch said.

'Oh, fucking hell, yeah.' Paxton nodded. 'I'd forgotten about that. Jesus, that was fifteen years ago, when I used to drink.'

'What happened?' Johnson wanted to know.

'I was in a restaurant in London having dinner with a friend,' Paxton told him, handing him a mug. 'Some bloke started giving me a load of grief, telling me my books were shit and Christ knows what else. That wasn't what bothered me, though. I mean, if you do anything for a living that's designed for public consumption then you've got to respect people's opinions if they tell you you're great or if they tell you you're

124

rubbish. But this prick started having a go at my friend too.' The writer shrugged. 'I was pissed, he was an arsehole . . . ' He allowed the sentence to trail off.

'So you hit him with a wine bottle,' Birch finished.

'He was a big bastard.' Paxton winked. 'I'd never have decked him with a punch.'

'Even though I'm smiling, I'm not condoning what you did, Mr Paxton,' Birch said.

'I wouldn't expect you to, Detective Inspector,' the writer answered, noting that Johnson was also grinning. He glanced through the window to see that the sun had finally emerged from behind a bank of cloud. 'Let's sit out on the patio and talk,' he suggested, leading them towards the back door. 'It's more comfortable. If I'm going to be interrogated, I might as well have the sun on my face while it's happening.'

'We didn't come here to interrogate you,' Birch told him, moving out on to the patio.

'I'll try and remember that,' the writer said, beckoning the two policemen to follow him.

'This garden's bigger than Hackney Marshes,' the DS said, awestruck by the sight before him.

The raised terrace looked out over a lawn protected on three sides by high, dense and perfectly kept privet. At the far end of the huge expanse of green there was a half-size football goal, complete with net and two brand new balls nestling in it.

'I have to keep fit somehow,' Paxton explained, seeing that Johnson was peering in the direction of the goal.

'You live alone,' Birch stated.

'For the last six years,' Paxton told him. 'Ever since my wife left me.' He shrugged. 'I don't blame her. I was the one who did wrong.' He nodded. 'With five different women, to be precise. I did wrong with all of them. I'm not proud of it. I know my own weaknesses. I think being a writer forces you to confront your own faults. Being stuck in a room with nothing but a computer and your own thoughts for company eight hours a day, five days a week you tend to examine the fluff in your own navel a little bit more minutely than people who do proper jobs.' He held up one hand in a gesture of supplicatory confession. 'I'm a sucker for a pretty face. Especially when it's attached to a gorgeous body.' He sipped his tea. 'There's a lot of pretty faces in and around the publishing business and when you're in my position it makes things a bit easier. I'm no Brad Pitt, I know that, but, like they say, there's no such thing as an ugly rich man.'

The writer showed them to a wooden table and chairs set next to the stone balustrade of the terrace. He invited them to sit down, then, taking a sip of his tea, looked at each man in turn.

'Well, you didn't come here to find out about my life,' he said. 'What do you want to know?'

31

'What kind of working relationship did you have with Frank Denton?' Birch asked.

'The same as I have with any editor,' Paxton said, a slight smile on his lips. 'The same as most writers do. As someone once said, we sweat blood for six months and they correct the spelling mistakes.'

'You know he was murdered?' Birch continued.

Paxton nodded. 'Only what I read in the papers,' he explained. 'That he was stabbed. Or was that the story you put out? The one you wanted released?'

Birch raised his eyebrows quizzically.

'Come on, Detective Inspector,' Paxton pressed. 'I know how this kind of thing works. You get nutters ringing in after every murder wanting to confess. So you feed a story to the media with details of a murder but you lot have made them up. So the nutters ring in and start confessing. 'Yeah, I killed him. I cut his throat then carved his dick off,' and you guys sit there knowing that the real killer is still out there. Because he's the only one who really knows what was cut off and from where.'

'Possibly,' Birch conceded.

'So was Denton stabbed or not? Or can't you tell me?'

'I didn't come here to discuss details of how

Frank Denton was murdered, I came here to find out what kind of working relationship you had with him.'

'Any editor I've ever worked with will tell you that I'm pretty easy-going. I'm not one of these arty-farty 'don't change that sentence I spent hours on it getting the texture right' types. If an editor tells me cutting something out of a book or changing a chapter will make it a better book I'll do it, nine times out of ten. Because a better book will sell better and, in the end, the only thing that matters is the money.' Paxton sipped his tea slowly. 'Denton was different. We were like chalk and cheese. Different upbringings. Different views. Everything. If I said something was black he'd say it was white. If he said today was Thursday I'd tell him it was Friday. But that didn't matter. I would still have listened to what he had to say if I thought it was constructive, if I thought it would have helped make what I'd written better.' Paxton's expression darkened a little. 'The first book I worked on for him was set on a rough council estate, like the one I was brought up on. Denton told me that the characters and situations in that book weren't realistic. That people didn't behave like that. That they wouldn't do the things I'd described them as doing.' Paxton's brow was deeply furrowed. 'What the fuck did he know? The cunt went to a boarding school and then to Oxford University. From the time he was eleven he probably spent most of his time playing the biscuit game and getting arse-fucked by prefects. His family had more money than my old man earned in the whole of his fucking life and here was this cunt telling me what was right and wrong about life on a council estate. I don't fucking think so.'

'So that was the start of your problems with him?' Birch said.

Paxton nodded. 'After that it was all downhill,' he admitted. 'Thank Christ I'd only signed a three-book deal with the publishers where he worked. As soon as it was up, I was gone.'

'And yet you still send him signed copies of your new books. Why?'

'It's pathetic, I know, but it's like a sort of literary 'up yours' every time a new one hits the top of the bestseller lists.'

'Is that how your new book came to be in the room where he was murdered?'

32

'My books get to a lot of different places, Detective Inspector,' Paxton said after a moment.

'The same novel was also found torn up and scattered around the body of Donald Corben, the critic,' Birch continued.

Paxton, who had been about to drink, paused, then slowly lowered the mug.

'Was Corben murdered too?' he asked.

Birch nodded.

'I didn't know,' the writer said quietly. 'I haven't seen a paper for a couple of days, I've been busy.' His reflective mood changed abruptly. 'He hated my books anyway. The twat probably tore it up himself.' He smiled. 'Was the copy you found at Frank Denton's place ripped up as well?'

'Yes,' Birch informed him.

'What can I say? Some people just have no respect for writers and their work.'

'You say Corben hated your books. How did you feel about him?' the DI persisted.

'He was a jumped up little prick,' Paxton said venomously.

'Any idea who might have murdered him?' Johnson interjected.

'You haven't got a notebook big enough to list the names,' Paxton said. 'You could start with every writer he's ever ripped the piss out of in his fucking reviews.'

'Would that include you, Mr Paxton?' Birch enquired.

'Critics don't mean a thing to me. Especially wankers like Donald Corben. They don't pay for their books so writers don't even get royalties from those copies.' His tone darkened. 'Most of them are failed or wannabe writers with axes to grind. They're jealous of anyone who's had anything published. Especially those of us who've been lucky enough to become successful. Critics are a waste of space. The only people who matter are the public, because they're the ones who buy the books. The ones who care about what they're reading. Not self-important bastards like Donald Corben.' He looked at Birch evenly. 'Don't expect me to shed any tears over that cunt, Detective Inspector. The only sad thing is that someone didn't top the fucker a few years earlier.'

'So, we should start interviewing writers Corben criticised as possible suspects in his murder?' Birch asked, a slight smile on his face.

'Is that what I am, then? A murder suspect? Just because you found my books at a couple of crime scenes?'

'No one said you were a suspect, Mr Paxton. It's just that there seems to have been friction between you and both of the men who've been killed. You have to admit, that fact alone might make some policemen a little bit curious. And you don't exactly seem unhappy about either death.'

Paxton shrugged. 'Is that the only reason you came to speak to me?' he enquired. 'Because my

131

books were found at both murder scenes?'

'And because of your history with the two victims. Your antagonism towards Denton and Corben.'

'Mine couldn't have been the only books found at the crime scenes. Denton was an editor, for Christ's sake. His house must have been full of books. Same with Corben.'

'As it happens, yours were among the ones that had been more comprehensively . . . destroyed. Shredded and scattered over the bodies and the rooms they were found in.'

'If I killed them, I'm hardly likely to leave such a blatant clue, am I?'

Birch shook his head.

'So, were my books the only ones destroyed?' Paxton wanted to know.

'No. There were others. We'll be speaking to the authors of those in due course.'

'Which authors? Or is that confidential?'

Birch merely smiled.

The three men talked amiably enough for another hour, then Birch looked at Johnson and nodded. He looked at Paxton and got to his feet. Johnson also rose.

'We'll let you get back to work now, Mr Paxton,' the DI said. 'Sorry for taking up so much of your time.'

The writer stood and shook hands with each of the policemen in turn.

'It was a pleasure.' He beamed. 'Like I say, I'll treat it as research. I thought you were going to be tougher on me than that.'

'And I told you, we didn't come here to

132

interrogate you,' Birch reminded him.

The writer walked them back through the house to the front door. The sun that had been blazing so brightly earlier on had now been smothered by several huge banks of dark cloud. A strong breeze had begun to whip round the house.

'Thanks again for your time,' Birch said.

'Are you working on a book at the moment?' Johnson asked.

'I'm always working on a book,' Paxton informed him. 'Either writing one, preparing one or promoting one.'

'Well, good luck with the new novel,' Birch said.

Paxton smiled. 'Thanks.'

He watched the two men as they climbed into the waiting Renault, waving as the car pulled away, then stepped back inside his house and closed the front door. He hurried into the sitting room and peered out of the window, watching as the dark blue car made its way back down the driveway and out on to the road.

Paxton waited a moment longer then reached for the phone.

He jabbed the digits hard and waited for an answer. When the receiver was picked up he recognised the voice immediately.

'Yeah, it's me,' he said brusquely. 'I've just had the police here. We need to talk.'

33

The characters are so poorly realised they're not even one-dimensional. A plot with so many holes you could drive a truck through it stumbles along like a geriatric doing the marathon, periodically interrupted by descriptions of the vilest and most obscene violence and gore imaginable. Obviously, within the limited confines of such an infantile and archaic genre as horror, one must expect this kind of thing, but a modicum of skill on the part of the writer can at least slightly enliven the kind of book only read by spotty teenagers, Trekkies and middle-aged virgins. Unfortunately, John Paxton has never possessed this skill and never will.

Birch raised his eyebrows and glanced away from the computer screen long enough to reach for the mug of tea close by. He took a sip and then scrolled down the page, scanning more of the words that appeared before him.

Sad to see John Paxton expanding his bank balance with the release of another of his fourth-rate horror books. It's just a pity he can't expand his vocabulary, his writing ability or his descriptive powers which, as ever, seem confined to sex, violence and depravity.

The DI regarded the words indifferently, moving on to the next page displayed before him.

Paxton remains a godawful writer. At one point, the heroine's eyes 'sparkle like stars'. The only thing, I must emphasise, that does sparkle in this turgid and repulsive tome from a writer anyone with more than one brain cell should rightly despise. Fortunately for Paxton, the kind of people who read his books rarely possess more than that solitary one required to enjoy his dreadful offerings.

And further on:

The literary equivalent of watching endless soap operas through a tomato ketchup gauze.

'Well, Mr Paxton, I can see why you didn't like him,' Birch murmured as he scanned snippets from reviews of other books.

He took another sip of his tea then massaged the bridge of his nose between his thumb and forefinger. He felt as if he'd been reading for hours. The disk was one of five taken from Donald Corben's flat, each containing hundreds of reviews that he'd written for his columns in the newspapers and magazines to which he had contributed. Birch had clicked on to the name of John Paxton but the sheer volume of material about the writer had surprised him. The venom contained within the reviews was unrelenting.

Why expend so much energy on someone you

obviously disliked so intensely?

The DI shook his head. What the hell had Paxton ever done to provoke Corben into tirades as long and as savage as these?

John Paxton has obviously lost the ability to distinguish where his characters (such as they are) end and he himself begins. He seems determined to live up to his reputation of violent thug in real life as well as on the pages of his badly written and hateful books.

'Getting personal too,' Birch observed quietly.

If this odious, opinionated and boorish man chooses to live like the so-called heroes portrayed in his vile books then he should favour us all by emulating those who meet the kind of appalling ends he usually reserves for them.

Birch waited a moment then slowly typed in another name and tapped his fingers gently on the desktop while he waited for it to appear. When it finally did, he nodded to himself.

Megan Hunter.

There were seven books listed there. Two novels and five non-fiction works. Birch scrolled down to the review of the first novel.

Whenever one receives the work of a newly published author it is with excitement at the prospect of finding some major new talent.

136

A burgeoning career perhaps. A new voice amidst the sea of mediocrity. Unfortunately, Megan Hunter is not that voice. This pseudo-intellectual publication marks Ms Hunter down as a name to watch but only so that all future offerings from her should be treated with caution. The caution that is spawned from such a lamentable first novel.

'Jesus,' Birch muttered to himself. He read what else Corben had written about Megan Hunter, occasionally shaking his head.

What had Paxton said about disgruntled authors wanting to kill Corben?

A bad review was hardly a motive to kill, Birch mused. If that was the case, from what he'd seen so far in Corben's files, people would have been queuing round the block to top him.

No, Birch told himself, that wasn't the answer. He ran a hand through his hair, wishing to Christ he knew what was.

Decisions

Their argument began almost as soon as the mobile incubator was wheeled out of the hospital room.

The man paced the floor frantically, shaking his head and saying that they couldn't keep the child.

The woman sat up in bed, sipped some water from a beaker and said that they had to. That it was their child. They would find a way of coping somehow.

When the doctor re-entered the room he said that there were ways they could be helped but the man, who was still pacing the floor, turned furiously on him and said they didn't want any help. That they didn't want the child. They couldn't keep it.

Not now.

Why get close to it? Why form an emotional bond with it when it was so very obviously impossible for them to raise it?

The woman disagreed.

The doctor offered his views.

The man shouted his defiance.

The doctor told them he would leave them alone to discuss the matter further. There was no need for them to make a decision as yet. There was plenty of time for them to consider their options.

The man asked the woman to consider

everything, to try to look at the matter objectively.

She reminded him that it was she who had carried the child for nine months. That she had been the one from whose belly it had been cut. Her words had no effect upon his opinion. His over-riding mood seemed to be one of anger, and she knew that while he continued in such a state of mind whatever she said to him was likely to fall upon deaf ears.

Nevertheless she told him her thoughts. Once she even cried softly as she spoke about the child but even her tears weren't enough to sway him.

They couldn't raise the child. Their son. On that point he was adamant.

He asked her to reflect on the medical implications, begged her to put those before even any moral or humanistic qualms she still harboured.

And she listened to his entreaties as calmly as she could. She even agreed with some of the points he was making, but in the deepest reaches of her mind she was aware only of a wrenching turmoil and of a pain so intense it was almost physical. She had feared the agony of the birth but what she was experiencing now was much more acute and could not be alleviated by even the strongest drugs.

After more than two hours of raging, cajoling, reasoning and shedding tears, they were no closer to an answer. At least not an answer that unified them.

They could not agree.

She wanted the child, the man did not. It was

as simple as that. They were poles apart with a gulf of fear and misunderstanding between them that seemed unbridgeable.

He left her late that night to return home, leaving her with his words ringing in her ears and her own feelings surging through her consciousness like adrenalin.

Alone, she spoke to the doctor again about her son and he repeated what he had already said. Constant medical care and attention would probably be needed, and even that would not guarantee the child's well-being.

In admirably professional and measured prose he informed her that in his opinion the child would be better off remaining where it was.

She didn't answer him.

After thirty minutes he had said as much as she wanted to listen to, but just before he left the room she asked if it would be possible for her to see her son again.

Could she be taken in a wheelchair up to where he was?

The doctor hesitated for a moment and then agreed.

The woman sat back against her pillows, wiped a tear from her cheek and waited.

34

Megan Hunter smiled as she took another glass of champagne from the tray the waiter pushed towards her. He nodded deferentially and weaved his way expertly through the hordes of people gathered in the Swirl Room of the Soho Hotel.

Like the adjoining Black and White Room and the Crimson Bar beyond it, the Swirl Room was one flight of highly polished wooden steps below the lobby of the hotel itself.

'I didn't think there'd be so many people here,' Megan said, brushing at the hem of her black knee-length skirt with her free hand. 'And I think I've spoken to, shaken hands with or kissed every single one of them.'

The swell of conversation from the three rooms forced her to lean close to Maria Figgis, who merely smiled back at her and motioned round at the table behind them that bore paperback and hardback copies of *The Seeds of the Soul* propped up to show the cover.

'It's not every day a publisher has a book nominated for a prize,' Maria offered. 'They're probably more delighted than you are. They'll be even happier when you win.'

'You sound very confident, Maria.'

'And why shouldn't I be? Your book deserves to win.' She raised her own glass in salute. 'And I'm sure your agent will be very highly thought of too. Especially when she secures you an even more lucrative deal on the back of your impending victory.'

The women smiled and clinked their glasses together in a toast before drinking.

A photographer who was making his way around the assembled throng aimed his Nikon in their direction and snapped off a couple of shots, grinning as he walked away, leaving Megan blinking at the intensity of the flash.

She reached for a canapé from one of the trays being ferried between the three rooms and bit delicately into it.

'Those are to die for,' said a voice behind her. 'But I suspect they could be fattening. So I only had one.'

Megan turned to find herself looking at the finely chiselled features of a young woman dressed in a pinstripe jacket and skirt. Her short blonde hair emphasised her flawless bone structure as effectively as her thigh-length skirt and precipitously high-heeled silver sandals showed off her slim legs. The overall effect was stunning.

'I'm sorry I had to leave you earlier, but I had to answer a call on my mobile,' Sarah Rushworth explained, flashing her cobalt blue eyes at Megan and smiling. 'Publicity never sleeps.'

'I doubt if you have to worry about putting on weight, Sarah,' Megan told her, offering her a bite of the canapé which the younger woman declined. 'And don't worry about leaving me for a couple of minutes. I'm fine.'

'I can't neglect my author,' Sarah said,

reaching out and rolling the material of Megan's white blouse between her thumb and forefinger, momentarily distracted. 'I do love silk. That's Dolce and Gabbana, isn't it?'

Even above the din of conversation the ring-tone of a mobile phone was heard and Sarah sighed and reached into her clutch bag.

'I'll have to take this call,' she said apologetically. 'I'll be back as quickly as I can.'

'Take as long as you need,' Megan told her, watching as the twenty-eight-year-old publicity director glided out of the room.

'She's certainly a beautiful girl,' Maria said. 'And, fortunately, very good at her job as well.'

'I agree with you. She just seems a little ... over-attentive at times. I know publicity people have to be ready to deal with the slightest whim but Sarah seems to have taken the art to new levels,' Megan observed.

'I wasn't aware that you had any whims.' Maria smiled. 'I'd always thought of you as whimless.'

Megan coughed and took a sip of champagne to clear her throat.

'Sarah always makes me feel inadequate,' she explained. 'Although that could be either my age or my paranoia. I'm not sure which. I don't think I've ever seen her look anything other than stunning, though.'

'I've a feeling that the way she looks tonight, she'd make Kate Moss feel slightly less than immaculate.'

Both women laughed.

'Now you know how I feel when *we're* out

together,' Maria continued.

'I'm just going to the ladies to freshen up while Sarah's busy,' Megan said. 'Otherwise if I tell her where I'm going she might come in with me, just in case there's anything I need.'

'Don't mock her enthusiasm,' Maria said, feigning reproach.

Megan walked out into the reception area, smiling to herself as she glanced at the posters of her book and her photo that had been so carefully hung in the subterranean area. There were more copies of the hardback on a table close to the entrance to one of the two screening rooms that the hotel possessed. Three members of the uniformed staff were thumbing through the book.

But it was something else that caught her eye.

Megan didn't recognise the man in the navy jacket and trousers who was walking purposefully towards her, having got to his feet when he spotted her.

She was sure this was no one from her publishers. Perhaps, she thought, he was not looking at her but beyond her to where the party was still in full swing.

Megan was only feet away from him when he reached inside his jacket, pulled out a slim leather wallet and flipped it open.

'Sorry to disturb you, Miss Hunter,' said Detective Inspector David Birch. 'I know this is an important night for you so I won't take up too much of your time, but if it's possible I'd like to ask you a couple of questions.'

35

For a moment, Megan could only nod. Then Birch smiled slightly.

'I know this sounds corny,' he said, 'but your picture . . . ' He nodded in the direction of one of the posters bearing Megan's image. 'It doesn't do you justice.'

'Neither does yours,' she told him, pointing at the small photograph that adorned his ID card. He snapped the thin leather wallet shut and slipped it back into his pocket.

'Thanks. I wish I could agree. Anyway, now we've got the mutual appreciation society stuff out of the way is there somewhere quieter we can talk?' the policeman asked. 'It sounds a bit frantic down here.'

'There's a library and a drawing room upstairs for guests' use,' she informed him. 'We can talk up there.'

Birch stepped back and motioned for her to lead.

'Can I ask what this is about?' Megan said.

'It's nothing for you to worry about. Just call it tying up a loose end.'

There was a chorus of loud laughter from the Swirl Room.

'I'll tell you when you can actually hear what I'm saying,' Birch added. 'By the way, I'm sorry to disturb the party.'

Megan nodded and began heading across the

reception towards the stairs that would take them up to the ground floor of the hotel. Birch walked slightly behind her.

'Megan.'

She turned as she heard her name.

Sarah Rushworth was hurrying towards them, her high heels clicking on the wooden floor.

'What's going on?' the younger woman wanted to know, looking first at Megan with an expression of concern.

'It's nothing to worry about,' Megan told her.

'Who are you, if you don't mind me asking?' Sarah demanded, turning her gaze on to Birch. 'I don't know you. Have you got an invitation?'

He showed his ID once again.

'That's my invitation,' he said flatly. 'I won't keep Miss Hunter from her party any longer than I have to.'

'I should come with you, Megan,' Sarah insisted.

'Just go and tell Maria I'm upstairs in the library, please. I'll be back soon.' She glanced at Birch. 'Won't I?'

He nodded.

Sarah hesitated a moment longer then turned and headed back towards the party.

Birch, with Megan leading the way, headed up the stairs, the raucous din from the party subsiding the higher they climbed. When they reached the ground floor, Megan motioned to a door on her right. She pushed it open and led the way into a large room, decorated in muted colours, replete with sofas and armchairs and dominated on three sides by huge bookcases.

'Do you mind if I have a drink?' she asked him. 'It might calm my nerves a bit. This is the first time I've been interrogated by the police.'

Birch smiled.

'Help yourself,' he told her. 'But I'd hardly call this an interrogation.'

'Would you like a drink?' she asked him.

'I'll have a mineral water, please,' the DI said, watching as Megan removed a Bacardi miniature, a bottle of Coke and some Perrier from a small, glass-fronted fridge that nestled in a cupboard beneath one of the bookcases. She placed the drinks and glasses on the table next to the nearest sofa, then seated herself at one end while Birch took up a position at the other.

'Now am I allowed to ask what this is about?' she began, filling her glass. 'Why are you here? It must be important.'

'You're aware that Frank Denton and the critic Donald Corben were murdered recently?' he said, sipping his own drink.

'I was at Frank's funeral. I read about Donald Corben.'

'Well, copies of your new book were found at both murder scenes. I know that probably doesn't sound unusual, what with Denton having been your editor, and it looks as if Corben was getting ready to review your latest book for one of the columns he wrote. The strange thing is that on both occasions, your book had been ripped up and scattered around the room. Portions of it were found on the corpses of both men.'

'Oh, God,' Megan breathed.

'I just wondered how well you knew either of the men personally. If you had any idea why your book in particular should have been one of the ones torn up and used to help . . . decorate the murder scenes. It's probably a complete coincidence but it's my job to make sure that's all it is.' He sipped his drink. 'Can you tell me something about your book, please? It might have some relevance. Maybe only to the killer, but . . . ' He allowed the sentence to fade away.

Megan sucked in a deep breath, held it for a moment, then exhaled.

'It's about a thirteenth-century Italian writer and philosopher called Giacomo Cassano,' she began. 'He was a contemporary of Dante. Who himself was famous for the *Divine Comedy* — Dante's *Inferno*, as most people know it.'

'I've heard of Dante.' Birch smiled. 'I saw *Seven*.'

Megan laughed warmly. 'I'm sorry, I didn't mean to insult your intelligence by suggesting you didn't know who Dante was,' she said.

'I'm just more of a film fan than a reader. The main kind of reading I do these days is confessions, coroner's reports or eye witness statements. Sometimes interesting but the plots leave a bit to be desired.'

Again Megan laughed and Birch found it was an infectious sound. From where he was sitting he could also smell the scent of her perfume.

Remember what you're here for, dickhead. So, she's a gorgeous woman. Big fucking deal. Show some professionalism.

'About your book,' he continued. 'You were

talking about this writer, Cassano.'

'He believed that all creative people had been given a gift by God. Whether they were painters, sculptors, writers or musicians. It didn't matter. Their abilities were given to them at birth, but God would exact some kind of payment for having given those gifts. You know people say that creative types suffer for their art, well, Cassano took that theory to its extreme. He believed that for everything good that had been given by God, something bad would happen to balance it.'

'How bad?'

'Well, if you look at some of the greatest creative people in history then Cassano's theory seems correct. For instance, Beethoven, one of the most amazing composers ever, went deaf and couldn't hear his own music. Christopher Marlowe was murdered. The philosopher Nietzsche went mad. Caravaggio, the painter, was murdered. There are so many more examples. They all had incredible gifts but they all paid a terrible price.'

'Do you believe Cassano's theory? You're creative. What price are you going to have to pay?'

They looked at each other fixedly for a moment, then the silence was broken by Birch.

'So Cassano maintained that creative people were the ones at risk of some kind of celestial payback.'

'I've never heard it put that way.' Megan smiled. 'But yes.'

'Denton wasn't creative. He only added his

opinions to work that had already been done by others. Corben wasn't creative either. All he did was criticise what had been created by someone else.' The DI sipped his drink and tapped distractedly on the back of the sofa. 'What happened to Cassano in real life?'

'Well, the Church at the time condemned him as a heretic for his teachings and his beliefs. Despite the fact that he said these gifts of creativity were God-given. The Church thought he was being blasphemous to suggest that the same God would then punish the very people he'd given those gifts to.' She sighed. 'He was tried before a papal court in Florence in 1287. They decided not to execute him but they wanted his writings and teachings to stop. So they cut off his hands so he couldn't write, and tore out his tongue so he couldn't preach. Then they blinded him.'

'How?'

'His eyes were gouged out.'

'Jesus.'

'I know, it's terrible. Even until the time of his death he always maintained his love of God, and yet — '

'No, I don't mean that.' Birch cut across her. 'You said his eyes were gouged out?'

She nodded.

'Do you know how Denton and Corben were killed?' Birch persisted.

'Only what I read. They were stabbed.'

'Yes, they were, but other things were done to them too.' He aimed an index finger at her. 'The same kind of things that you've told me was done to the man you've just written about. Your book was found torn up at the murder scenes. I'm wondering if the killer read your book.

'It's been serialised in *The Times* for the last four weeks. Anyone could have read it.'

36

'I'm exploring avenues,' Birch told her, wiping some condensation from his glass. 'Or clutching at straws, depending on your choice of terms.' He drank. 'The thing is, at the moment, the only thing linking Denton and Corben, apart from the way they were killed, is the fact that they both had torn-up portions of your book scattered on and around their bodies. Can you think of anyone at your publishers who didn't like Denton?'

'Someone who hated him enough to murder him? No, I can't.'

'What about Corben? Do you know anyone who hated him enough to kill him?'

'Lots of people hated Donald Corben.'

'Including you?'

'Hate's a strong word.'

'I saw some of his reviews for your books. I wouldn't blame you for disliking him.'

'If everyone who'd ever had a bad review decided to kill a critic there'd be none of them left.'

'Would that be a bad thing?'

Megan grinned and shook her head.

'So, how well did you know the two dead men?' Birch persisted. 'On a personal level.'

'I'd met Corben a couple of times briefly but Frank and I had known each other for six or seven years.'

'On a purely professional basis?'

Megan eyed him warily for a moment, then took a sip of her drink. She nodded.

A little hesitant?

Birch smiled reassuringly at her.

'Do authors and editors usually get friendly?' he enquired. 'I'm assuming that if you work with someone closely over a period of time then some kind of bond builds up between you.'

'It depends on the author and the editor. I'm sure some do have wonderful relationships that extend beyond the workplace. Mine and Frank's wasn't one of those. It was always strictly business.'

'Sorry if it seems like I'm prying, but it goes with the job.'

'You said that my book was *one* of those found torn up and scattered around the murder scenes. What about the others, or is that confidential too?'

'Copies of John Paxton's latest book were also found destroyed at both crime scenes. He's already been questioned.'

Megan shifted her position on the sofa and reached for her glass, apparently not noticing that it was empty.

'Do you know Paxton?' the detective continued.

'Everyone in the publishing business knows John Paxton's name.'

'I didn't ask if you knew his name, I asked if you knew him.'

'We've met a few times.'

'What did you think of him?'

'I thought you came here to ask what I knew about Frank Denton and Donald Corben. Not John Paxton.'

There was a defensive note in her voice that Birch wasn't slow to detect.

'It's probably nothing,' he told her. 'But the fact is that, like you, he — or his book at any rate — is one of the links between the two murders. Inasmuch as both your book and his were found with the dead men.'

'You said that the killer might have read what I wrote about Cassano and copied what was done to him. Imitated the punishment Cassano received. You should read Paxton's books. There are far more ingenious and inventive ways of killing people described in those.'

'So I hear. Do you read his books?'

'Occasionally. I like them.'

'A horror fan, are you? I wouldn't have thought they'd have been on your chosen reading list.'

'Just because I write non-fiction books about historical figures doesn't mean I only read academic works.'

'Paxton had had run-ins with both Denton and Corben. Do you think he was capable of killing them?'

'You should ask him that.'

'I'm asking you.'

'I've met him a few times and I've read some of his books, but that doesn't mean I know how his mind works. Just because he writes about murder and death doesn't make him a suspect, does it? After all, he's not the only horror writer

154

in the world. Just the most successful.'

Birch nodded and got to his feet.

'I've taken up enough of your time,' he said cheerfully. 'I'd better let you get back to your party. And, by the way, congratulations on the award for your book.'

'I haven't won yet.'

'Congratulations anyway,' he insisted, waving away her words. His tone darkened slightly. 'Listen, if you hear anything that you think might be useful to me then give me a call, please.' He handed her a dog-eared card that he took from his wallet.

'What kind of thing?' Megan smiled. 'A confession?'

'Anything.' He extended a hand and she shook it warmly.

'This party is going to be over in an hour or so,' she told him. 'Only four or five of the people who work for my publishers are staying at the hotel tonight and most of them will probably spend their time in the bar. If you'd like to hang around we can talk again later. There might have been some things you forgot to ask me.'

'That's very kind of you, Miss Hunter, but I doubt if that young lady downstairs who was guarding you will let me near you twice in one evening.'

'Don't worry about Sarah. She just gets a bit over-enthusiastic. Publicity directors have a habit of doing that.'

'I'll take your word for it. In the meantime, I should be getting back to work.'

'At this time of night?'

'Murder investigations don't have set hours, unfortunately.'

'What time will you go home tonight?'

'It's not really important. It isn't as if I've got anything to rush back for.'

'No wife?'

'Not any more. The second one was a casualty of the job. Unfortunately I paid her less attention than some of the cases I was working on.'

'Did the same thing happen with the first one?'

'She died.'

'I'm sorry.'

Birch nodded. 'You're trying to tell me that there's no one waiting at home for you?' he said, trying to inject some levity into his tone. 'I find that hard to believe.'

'Giacomo Cassano may well have been right when he said that we all have to sacrifice something in exchange for success. I've sacrificed more relationships than I care to remember.' She looked down at his card, then pushed it into her handbag. 'If you change your mind about that drink you know where I am.'

'Are you staying at the hotel tonight? You live in London.'

'Author's perk. It's my publisher's way of treating me. A night in an executive room.' She smiled. 'They're treating me again in a couple of days' time when I have more interviews scheduled.'

Birch held her gaze a moment longer before preparing to turn towards the door that would lead him out of the library and into the hotel reception. 'If I don't come back tonight, then perhaps another time?'

'I'd like that.'

He made to leave.

'Detective Inspector Birch,' she said suddenly.

The policeman turned to face her.

'I know this sounds terribly presumptuous,' Megan continued. 'But if you want to take a copy of my book with you, there are plenty of them around. You never know, you might even read it.'

'I think I will,' he said. 'Thank you.'

'Let me know what you think.'

Birch nodded and headed for the door, closing it gently behind him.

Megan watched him go, a smile still playing on her lips. She saw him pause by a pile of books on a table close to the hotel entrance. He picked one up, glanced at the front, then left.

Only when she'd seen him walk out of the main doors did her smile drop away as quickly as a stone from an outstretched hand.

37

There was a welcomingly cool breeze blowing in off the Thames as Birch clambered out of the Renault.

He loosened his tie a little more and undid another button at the neck of his shirt, enjoying the feel of the air against his hot flesh.

The detective looked up at the tall, monolithic structure that was Harbour Towers. It jutted up into the night sky like an accusatory finger. He locked his eyes on the ninth floor. On the balcony of Donald Corben's flat.

No way up there other than from the inside. Not unless you had grappling hooks and crampons.

Birch smiled to himself and headed for the large metal gate that led into the immaculately kept grassy courtyard beyond. He showed his ID to the security guard and told the man where he was going.

There was a loud electronic buzz and the gate swung back on its hinges. The closed circuit cameras on either side of the entrance whirred as they recorded his passing.

Birch walked through, looking briefly in the direction of the river to his left then concentrating on his route up to his chosen destination.

There was a CCTV camera above the main entrance. Even now it would be recording his passage through into the foyer of the building.

Another camera above the concierge's desk moved slightly, a red light blinking on it.

Again Birch showed his ID, then he continued on towards the lift at the end of the corridor.

There was another camera mounted there.

Five cameras in the space of a hundred and fifty yards.

The policeman hit the 'Nine' button and waited for the lift to arrive.

Five cameras and yet not one had picked up anyone or anything out of the ordinary the night Donald Corben had been butchered.

The lift arrived and Birch stepped in and rode it to the ninth floor, where he got out and walked slowly towards the door of the flat he sought.

There were still blue strips across the entrance.

POLICE DO NOT CROSS.

The words were printed in large white letters on the strips. The door of the flat was firmly locked.

As it would have been the night Corben was murdered.

'So, how did you get in, you bastard?' Birch murmured, regarding the partition. 'Did he know you? Did you knock and he just let you in?' The DI slid a credit card from his wallet and eased it into the crack between the door and the frame, manoeuvring the thin strip up and down until he heard a click. He smiled to himself and stepped inside the flat, closing the door behind him.

'Right,' he said quietly to himself. 'You're in.' He walked past the bedrooms and the kitchen on his left into the sitting area. Forensics had only completed their work on the flat that day so the room smelled of chemicals and it was still littered with some of the debris of the fateful night when Corben had been killed. The blood that had stained walls, floor and even ceiling bright red not so long ago had now dried black. The cleaners would be in tomorrow, Birch thought. Ready to scrub and sponge away all traces of the horror that had been perpetrated in this place.

He crossed to the balcony doors and unlocked them.

'You certainly didn't come in this way, did you?' he muttered, closing them again. He turned and looked round the room. 'So, you killed him. Butchered him and then you left. But without leaving a fingerprint anywhere.' The DI walked back towards the door of the flat and stepped outside. 'But who locked the door behind you afterwards?' He took a step back into the flat. 'Unless you took a key and locked it yourself after you'd finished.' He opened the flat door again and looked out into the corridor. 'Is that what you did, you bastard?'

★ ★ ★

Birch wasn't sure how long he sat in his car outside Frank Denton's house in Putney.

With the driver's side window rolled down, he gazed intently at the empty dwelling, surveying the front door and windows. The same thoughts tumbled through his mind as those he'd entertained at Donald Corben's flat, only here, if anything, his confusion was even greater.

No forced entry,' he muttered, taking a drag on his cigarette. 'Nothing taken and doors and windows locked after you left. Only here it wasn't so simple, was it? You could have taken a key and locked the door behind you after you left but there were bolts on the inside of the door too. How come they were still on?'

The DI took a final drag then hauled himself out of the Renault, stepped on his discarded cigarette end and headed towards the house.

There were lights on in most of the other houses in Merrivale Road. He wondered how many of their occupants were watching him as he walked from window to door then across to the other front window.

Any point in looking inside?

The place was due to be cleared by relatives the following day. One last look couldn't hurt.

Just in case you missed something first time round.

Birch walked back to the car and leaned against it, staring fixedly at what had been Frank Denton's house.

What am I missing?

Was there another way in and out that hadn't been discovered yet?

How about the chimney? Perhaps you're looking for a psychopathic Santa Claus.

In spite of himself, Birch smiled at his own musings.

This one's a clever bastard.

He walked round to the driver's side and slid

back behind the wheel, gazing at the house for a moment longer. Then his attention was caught by something on the passenger seat other than the two notebooks, a late edition of the *Standard*, a half-empty bottle of Lucozade and a thin manila file. He reached for the copy of *The Seeds of the Soul* he'd placed there upon leaving the Soho hotel.

Birch opened it at the contents page and scanned the chapter headings:

1. *Thirteenth-century Italy*
2. *The Florentine Heretic*
3. *In Praise of God*

The detective sucked in a deep breath. He flipped to the section marked *List of Illustrations*. There were several reproductions of woodcuts of Giacomo Cassano.

The first showed him at his writing desk, quill in hand. The second was simply of his face. He'd been a clean-shaven, long-haired individual.

Another showed him kneeling on the Ponte Vecchio, surrounded by people, his tongue and eyes torn out, his hands severed.

There was one of Dante. Another of Guido Cavalcanti. Some scenes from Dante's *Inferno*.

He turned back to the contents page, his eye drawn to another chapter heading.

Into Hell.

Birch reached for another cigarette and lit it. Then, by the light inside the Renault, he began to read.

*   *   *

The DI had no idea how long he'd been immersed in the book when the ringing of his mobile dragged him out of his studies.

He dropped the book back on to the passenger seat and flipped open the phone, sitting motionless behind the wheel as the voice at the other end of the line spoke to him.

Birch waited until the other voice had finished, then he dropped the phone beside Megan Hunter's book and started the Renault's engine.

The sound cut loudly through the relative quiet of Merrivale Road. The detective stepped hard on the accelerator, his face set in hard lines. He glanced down at the dashboard clock and wondered how quickly he could make it to his destination. Even the cool air rushing through the open driver's window couldn't dry the perspiration that had beaded on his forehead.

He felt his heart thudding hard against his ribs.

38

'Who found her?'

Birch paused momentarily outside the door of room 413 of the Soho Hotel and looked questioningly at Detective Sergeant Stephen Johnson.

'Half the hotel heard her screaming,' Johnson informed him. 'Reception had seven or eight calls reporting it. One of the receptionists came up to see what the problem was. She let herself in with a pass key and found her.'

'Anyone see anything?'

'No.'

The DI looked at the door of the room, running one hand up and down the frame and the edge of the partition itself.

'No forced entry again?' he murmured.

Johnson shook his head.

'Door was locked when the receptionist arrived,' he informed his superior.

'Mind you, that's no surprise this time. Hotel room doors lock automatically when you close them, don't they?'

'True. The windows in the room were locked on the inside as well, though. So, it looks as if he entered and left by this door.'

'Anything stolen?'

'Not as far as we can tell. She had some expensive clothes and shoes in her overnight bag but they weren't touched. There's still cash and credit cards in the room. Her handbag hasn't even been opened by the look of it. Robbery wasn't the motive, just like it wasn't with the other two.'

'No blood out here,' Birch noted. 'Just like outside Corben's flat.'

'Maybe the killer wore overalls again.'

Birch nodded wearily. 'What about the other guests?' he asked.

'We cleared the floors. The guests are downstairs in the bars and dining room. Some of them aren't too happy, but — '

'Fuck them,' snapped Birch, cutting across his companion. 'Let them wait. So nobody saw anyone leave this room, get in the lift or leave the hotel immediately afterwards?'

'All the guests on this floor have been interviewed, so have any staff who were working in or around the reception, foyer or bars on the ground floor. None of them saw anyone leave. We've still got the other guests to take statements from, though. Perhaps one of them might have seen something.'

'There've got to be stairs leading down from all floors. He could have used those to get out.'

'They come out in the reception area. Also, there's a service lift that room service and housekeeping staff use but that comes out right next to the kitchen. No one in the kitchen saw anything around the time of death.'

'Which was?'

'About midnight. That's when her screaming was heard.'

'Those stairs,' Birch said thoughtfully. 'Maybe

the killer didn't use them to go down and out through the reception. He might have used them to go up.' The DI jabbed an index finger skyward. 'If he could have made it to the roof he could have got away over the top of the buildings next door to the hotel.'

'It's possible,' Johnson mused. 'But you would have thought someone would have seen.'

'Maybe someone who hasn't been interviewed yet. Keep it in mind, Steve.' He sucked in a deep breath and nodded towards the door of room 413. 'Right, let's have a look.'

A flight of three stairs led up to the bedroom and bathroom area. From the bottom of the steps, Birch could see thick smears of blood on the white door of the bathroom straight ahead of him. There was more of the crimson fluid on the wall.

He reached the top and turned to look into the bedroom.

There were four other men engaged in various tasks, including a photographer who nodded sagely at Birch and continued snapping away. The other three were working in different parts of the room. One was carefully dropping something reddish pink into a clear evidence bag.

It only took one glance for Birch to realise that it was an index finger.

There was blood everywhere.

The carpet was soaked in it. Spurts had jetted on to all four walls. The white duvet that adorned the bed itself looked as if it had been dyed crimson.

Howard Richardson was leaning over the object in the centre of the carnage.

The pathologist turned away from his work for a moment to nod a greeting to Birch, who skirted the worst of the bloodstains on the carpet round the bed in order to get closer to the thing that lay upon it like some hideously battered oversized doll.

'Watch yourself,' Richardson said quietly, standing back momentarily and motioning to the canopy above the bed.

There was blood dripping from it.

'Arterial spray,' Richardson explained as Birch narrowly avoided one of the crimson droplets. 'From the neck wounds.'

Birch leaned closer to the torn, bloodied rag that had once been a human being.

'He took both eyes again,' the DI stated.

'No sign of them in here or the bathroom,' the pathologist told him.

Birch sighed and looked down at what remained of the naked body of Sarah Rush-worth.

39

'Everything so far points to it being the same perpetrator who killed Frank Denton and Donald Corben,' the pathologist said.

'Same murder weapon?' Birch enquired, studying the savagely mutilated body.

Richardson nodded. 'A curved, serrated blade. And the cuts are left to right, same as before.'

'It looks as if he nearly took her fucking head off,' the DI breathed, inspecting the deep lacerations round the dead woman's neck.

'One more cut to the base of her skull and he would have done.'

'She was killed in here, obviously?' Birch said thoughtfully. 'On the bed. So how did the blood get on the bathroom door?'

'As you saw, there's blood all the way from the bathroom to the bed,' Richardson said. 'I would assume she tried to run. He dragged her back to the bed to finish the job.'

'Wait a minute,' the DI said, raising a hand. 'No forced entry, right? So, she opens the bedroom door to let him in. She would have seen him through the spyhole first so it was someone she knew and recognised. Maybe even someone she was expecting.'

'She didn't order anything from room service,' Johnson offered. 'Every call's logged. Nothing for this room.'

'Right, so the killer wasn't dressed as a fucking

waiter. That much we know,' Birch continued. 'She looks through the spyhole, sees who's on the other side and lets him in. He attacks her there.' Birch jabbed an index finger towards the top of the three steps. 'She starts screaming. He throws her on the bed, continues stabbing her. Guests hear the screams and call down to reception. The murderer leaves. The receptionist arrives and finds the body. Job done.' The DI rubbed his cheek, his attention still riveted by the woman's corpse.

'It's the first woman he's killed,' Johnson murmured.

'Any traces of semen?' Birch wanted to know.

'We haven't done vaginal and anal swabs yet but it doesn't look like it,' Richardson said. 'If you want my professional opinion, rape wasn't his motive. Any sexual thrill he might have got came from the killing itself. In fact, there are several stab wounds around the vagina. One of them severed a portion of her labia.'

Birch glanced at the blood-clogged area the pathologist had indicated and saw a sliver of red-stained slippery tissue about two inches long lying between Sarah Rushworth's parted legs.

'She wouldn't have opened the door naked, would she?' the detective mused.

'Not unless it was someone she was expecting,' Johnson interjected.

'Her dressing gown's on the floor,' Richardson said. 'She was stabbed at least three times while she was wearing it. She wasn't naked when she let the killer in.'

'How long did the murder take?' the DI wanted to know.

'From beginning to end it couldn't have been more than seven or eight minutes.'

'He worked fast. Like he did on Denton and Corben.'

'He had to,' suggested Johnson. 'There was more chance of him being seen in a place like this.'

'The bastard's getting more confident, isn't he?' Birch said. 'Maybe over-confident.' The knot of muscles at the side of his jaw throbbed angrily. He pointed to some small fragments of matter on one punctured breast. 'Is that what I think it is?'

'Wood pulp,' Richardson told him. 'We removed more of it from her abdomen and face.'

'Where's the book?' Birch said flatly.

Richardson walked round to the other side of the bed, bent and retrieved an all too familiar hardback book.

The copy of *The Seeds of the Soul* was bent back in the middle, the spine cracked, the binding torn. Several pages had been pulled from the book, ripped up into small pieces and scattered over the bed.

'Couldn't forget his trademark, could he?' the DI murmured, watching as Richardson laid the blood-spattered tome on the bedside table.

'The wood pulp didn't come from that book,' Richardson continued. 'It came from this one.' He slid one of the bedside cabinet drawers open a little further and, using one gloved hand, took out another volume.

The second book had been even more comprehensively destroyed, but, despite the damage done to it, Birch recognised it immediately.

'*The Fairground Phantoms*,' he said.

'Sarah Rushworth took it from downstairs in the library,' Detective Sergeant Johnson informed his superior. 'Guests can borrow the books in there for the duration of their stay.'

'How come Paxton's book's in there?'

'All of his books are. Apparently, he stays here whenever he's got business in London. All the staff know him. Sometimes he even gets a free room, just so the hotel can advertise he's a valued customer. He sent them an advance copy as a gift. He thanks them in the acknowledgements of all his novels.'

'Jesus Christ,' Birch murmured. 'So we've got everything we had at the previous two murder scenes.'

Richardson cleared his throat. 'We've got something we haven't had before,' he announced.

'What?' Birch demanded.

'Fingerprints,' the pathologist told him.

'Why the fucking hell didn't you tell me that when I walked in?' the DI snapped. 'So, the bastard *has* got over-confident. Can you identify him from the prints?'

'If he's been arrested before. But it's not quite as easy as that.'

Birch looked puzzled.

'What I'm going to tell you will sound insane,'

171

Richardson said evenly.

'Everything about this case is insane, Howard. Just tell me, will you?'

'I think that Sarah Rushworth was killed by more than one man.'

40

For long moments, Birch's expression didn't change; then, gradually, a twisted grin appeared on his face. He held up both hands and turned away from the body and from the pathologist.

There was a large armchair in one corner of the room and he seated himself in it.

'So more than one person got into this locked room tonight without being seen,' he said. 'Cut a woman to pieces, scattered bits of ripped-up book over her then sneaked out without anyone catching sight of them? Is that what you're telling me?'

'I told you it'd sound insane,' Richardson repeated.

'You never suspected more than one killer where Denton and Corben were concerned.'

'There were no prints at either of those crime scenes. At least none that we found. I'm going to check Corben's body again when I get back to the morgue.'

'And what about Denton? What are you going to do about him?'

'I'll need an exhumation order. The initial examination showed no signs of fingerprints beyond the fragments round Denton's eyes. There may be none when I re-examine the bodies. But I need to be sure. This wasn't negligence on my part, David.'

'Then what the fuck was it?' rasped the DI

angrily. 'I wouldn't have released Denton's body so quickly if I'd thought there was still work to be done on it. How much more have you and your team missed that we don't know about?' He ran a hand through his hair. 'What are you playing at, Howard?'

'I'm not playing, David,' Richardson said, through clenched teeth. 'And nothing else was missed. I made a mistake. I apologise for that. Everyone makes mistakes now and then.'

'Well, none of us can afford to,' the DI retorted. 'Not on this case.' He let out a long breath, trying to compose himself. 'Where the hell did you find the prints on Sarah Rushworth?'

'There was a partial print under her tongue. I think the killer may well have been trying to remove it. Rip it out. Like her eyes. The other was on one of her fingernails.'

'He tried to rip out her tongue?' Birch repeated, his eyes straying to the battered copy of *The Seeds of the Soul* lying beside the bed.

What had Megan Hunter said about Giacomo Cassano? 'They tore out his tongue so he couldn't preach. Then they blinded him.'

'So, the print under her tongue and the one on her fingernail came from different people?' the detective continued, getting to his feet.

'When we're fingerprinting we can occasionally identify abnormalities of the fingers,' Richardson said. 'The print underneath Sarah Rushworth's tongue came from someone with abnormally short fingers — the technical term is brachydactyly. The one on her fingernail came from a person with webbed fingers — syndactyly. I'd say the index and middle fingers.'

'One of the killers has his index and middle finger joined?'

Richardson nodded. 'And not just by the skin. Judging from the size of the print, the fingers are fused together by the bones. That was the only reason we spotted it. Same with the one under her tongue. Short fingers or not, he got enough purchase on it to tear some of it away from her lower palate. If it hadn't been protruding the way it was, chances are we wouldn't have seen it.'

'So are we looking for two killers, both with malformed hands?' Johnson wanted to know.

'I didn't say that,' the pathologist countered. 'I just told you what I found. At least one of them has some kind of deformity to one, possibly both hands.'

'Will you still be able to lift a print from under Corben's tongue if there's one there?'

'I don't see why not.'

'And from Denton?'

'If there's a print there I'll find it. But first I need his body.'

'I'll arrange the exhumation order,' Birch confirmed. He turned to Johnson. 'Let's go to work on the guests. It's weird enough that nobody saw one killer. I don't believe anybody could have missed two.'

Instinct

They were keeping the child.

The doctor had heard the words, and for a moment he had thought again about trying to explain the difficulties that would arise. But such was the determination in the woman's expression and tone that he had decided to keep his thoughts to himself.

The man had barely spoken and the doctor had sensed something akin to suppressed rage within him. A fury at what he saw as the senselessness of pursuing this particular course of action.

But the woman was not to be dissuaded. She would be allowed home in a day or two. She'd already been in the private room for over a week and, during that time, she'd spent longer each day with her son. Either she had visited him or he had been brought to her in his mobile incubator.

As her physical strength had returned so, it seemed, had her implacability. As her body repaired itself, her mind kept apace, stiffening her resolve and steeling her determination until the doctor was convinced that no one on earth could have talked her out of the decision to keep her son. Despite what she knew and what she had been told.

The man
(the father)

176

was a different proposition.

Time and again, from the moment the child had been born, he had expressed his reluctance to accept him. He seemed able to see beyond the biological ties. To fully grasp the situation he and the woman would face once they had taken their son out of the hospital.

And, again, the doctor had explained that the first year or so of the boy's life would involve a series of visits to the hospital. That the child would require courses of treatment, probably even operations, if anything like a reasonable quality of life were to be maintained.

While the woman accepted this with grim determination, the man seemed reluctant to even discuss it.

The doctor had thought, on more than one occasion, of trying to stop the woman taking her son away from the medical care he so desperately needed, but there was no lawful way for him to achieve that. All he had ever been able to do was impart his knowledge and his misgivings should the boy leave the sterile and specialised environment that was all he had known since his birth.

The arguments between the man and the woman had lessened in intensity over the past few days, but only because it now seemed futile to argue with the woman. Her mind was made up and the man knew from experience that her will was strong. If she believed in something, then nothing would divert her from that goal.

In this case, her goal was to take her son out of

the hospital, to care for him. To be a mother to him.

The man had no corresponding desire to be a father to the boy. He had very little interest in even seeing the child again, let alone in helping to raise it.

He said he was being realistic, that the woman was being stubborn and short-sighted, but she ignored his entreaties. Turned a deaf ear to his rages and refused to accept his dismissal of their son.

If that was how he felt, she had told him, then so be it. She would not abandon the child. And if it meant the end of their relationship then she was prepared to accept that. She would raise the child alone.

When she'd said that, the man had regarded her with a look in his eyes that was a short step from hatred.

He'd left the hospital earlier than usual that evening, wanting to be away from her. Needing to escape the cloying, antiseptic surroundings of the medical building that he'd come to know and, lately, to despise, since the birth of

(he couldn't bring himself to say the words) his son.

But he knew he would return the following day. He accepted that he would be on hand to help the woman when she left the hospital.

What he wouldn't do, and he was as firm in his resolution as she, was ever accept the child he had fathered as his own.

Never.

41

There was a wonderful peacefulness about the library of the Soho Hotel. Birch glanced at his watch.

3.56 a.m.

Not really surprising at this time of the morning, is it?

The DI sat back in one of the armchairs and raised his glass in salute.

'I know we shouldn't be doing this,' he said, smiling. 'But who gives a shit? Cheers.' He took a long swallow of the Jack Daniel's, feeling the liquid burn its way to his stomach.

In the seat next to him, Detective Sergeant Johnson nodded and sipped at his own vodka and Coke.

'So, this is how the other half live,' muttered Birch, looking around. 'Over two hundred quid a night for a room. Do you reckon the department would swallow that on expenses?'

Johnson grinned. 'I doubt it.'

A long silence descended, eventually broken by Birch.

'Seventy-three guests and twenty-one members of staff,' he continued. 'And not one of them saw fuck all.'

'They haven't all been interviewed yet, guv. One of them might have got something worthwhile to say.'

'That's true. Who did you speak to from

Megan Hunter's publishers?'

'The sales director and an editorial big nob. Neither of them saw or heard anything.'

'Nor did the MD or the head of foreign rights.'

'What about Megan Hunter herself?'

'Nothing. But I'm going to talk to her again. Find out more about this book she's written. See if I can figure out why the killer would want to keep leaving it at every murder scene.'

'Someone trying to frame her?'

'Her or John Paxton? His books are always found at the scenes too. If someone wanted to frame either of them there must be easier ways.' With one index finger he wiped a droplet of moisture from the outside of his glass.

'If Howard can find prints on the bodies of Denton and Corben then we might be in,' Johnson said hopefully.

'I'm not holding my breath.' Birch downed more of the liquor. 'What's the motive?' he said finally, his voice low.

'What's *their* motive. What if forensics are right about there being two killers?'

'Then not only are we up shit creek, we've lost our paddle, the boat's sinking and the water's full of sharks.' He raised his glass once again in salute, his eyes straying to the bookshelf opposite. To one particular part of that shelf.

The spines of fourteen books showed the name of John Paxton.

'Who's got it in for Paxton and Megan Hunter?' Birch mused. 'Why was Sarah Rushworth the one murdered tonight? There were other people here from Megan Hunter's publishers. Why her?'

'We're not going to know that until we know the motive, are we?'

Birch looked at his companion.

'Go home, Steve,' he said. 'Get some sleep. Spend a few hours with your wife. There's nothing more we can do until morning anyway.'

'It is morning,' Johnson reminded him, glancing at his watch.

'You know what I mean.'

'What about you?'

'There's something I need to check on before I go.'

'And you don't want me to know what it is?'

'Go,' Birch repeated. 'Before I change my mind.'

He watched as his companion finished his drink then got to his feet, fishing in his jacket pocket for his car keys.

'Thanks, guv,' Johnson said.

Birch smiled.

The DS left and Birch was enveloped by the welcome solitude once again. He finished his drink then got to his feet and crossed to the bookshelf where John Paxton's books were displayed. The detective ran his finger across the spines of the assembled hardback volumes, creating a sound like dripping water.

The gap was where *The Fairground Phantoms* had been.

He turned and headed out into the foyer.

★　★　★

As he drove, Detective Sergeant Stephen Johnson kept his car window open, allowing a cooling breeze into the vehicle. The sounds and smells of early morning London drifted in too. He glanced down at the dashboard clock. Another twenty minutes and he'd be home.

He was about to switch on the radio when his mobile rang. The detective signalled, swung the Astra into the side of the road and reached for the phone.

He recognised the number that was flashing on the screen.

'Yes, guv,' he said.

'What I said I had to check on,' Birch said. 'I've done it.'

'And now can you tell me what it is?'

'You know you told me that John Paxton was a frequent visitor to the Soho Hotel? I got a receptionist to run through their computer records of guests. Paxton stayed here twice in the last three weeks. The first time was when Frank Denton was killed. The second was the same night Donald Corben was murdered.'

'Jesus,' murmured the DS.

'That's not the only thing. I spoke to the doorman and the concierge who were on duty on those two nights. They both remember seeing Paxton leave the hotel each evening, but neither of them remembers seeing him come back in.'

'But, guv, they must see dozens of people in any one evening. They could have forgotten.'

'All the staff here know Paxton, you told me that yourself. The two guys I spoke to tonight both said he always stopped and chatted to

182

them, signed fucking books for them.'

'Then they could have just missed him when he came back in on those nights.'

'It's possible, but it's a hell of a coincidence, isn't it? The doorman and the concierge both happen to be otherwise engaged when Paxton comes back to the hotel. How convenient.'

'Could he have come in another entrance?'

'There is no other entrance. To get back to his room he'd have to enter the hotel through the main doors and he'd have to pass the concierge's desk. Now, if you discount that both guys happened to be looking the other way when he got back each night, that means that when our first two victims were killed, Paxton was not in the Soho Hotel. And, as far as we know, he didn't return there on either night. So where the fuck was he?'

42

The slow dripping of a tap into a metal sink was the only sound within the morgue.

Howard Richardson barely noticed it as he scribbled down the salient points of his report. Every now and then the pathologist would glance over his shoulder in the direction of the two sheet-covered corpses behind him as if seeking inspiration from the motionless bodies. For the most part he was content to peer over the top of his half-moon glasses, stopping once to chew on the end of his expensive pen.

When the double doors that formed the entrance to the morgue opened, Richardson turned to see who had entered. Was it another body for him to work on? Some poor unfortunate who'd met an untimely end? Perhaps one to temporarily join the other four already stored in the refrigerated lockers that formed almost the whole of one wall of the main room.

The pathologist smiled when he saw that it was Birch and Johnson.

'Before you ask,' he said. 'My report isn't finished.'

'I couldn't give a toss about the paperwork, Howard,' Birch told him. 'Just tell me what you found.'

The pathologist crossed to the slab nearest his

desk and pulled back the sheet covering the body beneath.

The two detectives looked down at the mutilated corpse of Sarah Rushworth.

'What a waste,' muttered Johnson.

'Every murder's a waste,' Birch said, also fixing his attention on the young woman's body.

'I gave you most of the details on this one at the actual scene,' the pathologist said. 'Examination hasn't revealed much more than you already know. All I will say is that the attacks seem to be getting more savage. For instance, the cuts on Sarah Rushworth are deeper than those on Denton and Corben. Also, the fact that he seemed to have removed Denton's eye with his fingers and with no evidence of frenzy and yet Corben's eyes and Sarah Rushworth's were hacked out. That would seem to indicate a growing loss of control with each successive murder. That could be why he left prints last night but not in the previous two attacks. As you suggested, he might be getting careless.'

'Was there sexual interference with the girl?' Birch enquired. 'You weren't sure of that last night.'

'No. Vaginal and anal swabs showed no traces of semen, saliva or any other secretion. She wasn't raped before, during or after death.'

'Well, let's be thankful for small mercies, shall we?' said Birch sardonically. 'What about Corben? Did you find any prints on him?'

'No,' Richardson said, almost apologetically.

He stepped across to the next slab and removed the sheet from the body that lay there.

All three men gazed down at the corpse of Donald Corben.

'You checked his tongue?' Birch pressed.

'I checked everywhere, David. There were no prints.'

'What about the possibility of two killers? Anything to support that in Corben's case?' Johnson asked.

'Not as far as I could ascertain.'

'The physical evidence at the scene — fibres, footprints and stuff like that — didn't point to more than one murderer,' Birch reminded them.

'It didn't at Sarah Rushworth's either,' Richardson offered. 'Or at Frank Denton's house. It was only the different types of fingerprints on the woman's body that made me suspect there could be more than one murderer.'

The three men stood in silence for a moment, their attention still held by the bodies before them.

'Perhaps only one acted in the first two killings but he had an accomplice last night,' Birch murmured.

'It's possible,' the pathologist admitted. 'By the way, did you have any luck getting that exhumation order for Denton?'

'The Home Office granted a licence,' Birch told his colleague. 'No problems. The gravedigger and the undertaker are being notified. The gravedigger has to identify the grave before it can be dug up and the undertaker has to ID the coffin itself before it's opened. But we're on for tomorrow night. All exhumations have to take place under cover of darkness, as you probably know. So it'll be about midnight when we bring him up.

'As Denton was buried in Wandsworth cemetery, I'll arrange for re-examination to take place in the mortuary of the Springfield Hospital,' Richardson said. 'It's the closest and best equipped.'

Birch nodded. 'Yeah, I know it.'

'David, I'm sorry this has had to happen,' the pathologist confessed. 'As I said to you last night, there was no negligence on my part during the initial examination of Denton's body. There was nothing to indicate there might be fingerprints in the mouth. But I apologise — it was an oversight.'

'I know that,' Birch said. 'I think we were all on short fuses last night. Mine just burns a bit quicker than most.' He smiled. 'Listen, Howard, if I thought you were going to find something worthwhile tomorrow night when you re-examine Denton, I'd dig the poor fucker up myself.'

'What do you want to do about Paxton?' Detective Sergeant Johnson asked.

'We'll question him again,' Birch announced. 'Him and Megan Hunter. After all, not only was her book found at last night's murder scene, she was actually in the hotel when Sarah Rushworth was murdered.'

'When do you want to question them?'

'According to his agent, Paxton's due in London tomorrow for some kind of promotional work. We'll have a word then. His agent told him we want to interview him again.'

'What about Megan Hunter?'

'I'll speak to her tonight.' Birch looked again at the two dead bodies lying before him, thoughts racing uncontrollably through his mind.

43

As she listened to the voice at the other end of the phone, Megan Hunter glanced across at the small carriage clock on her desk. She realised she'd already been on the line for close to twenty minutes. The voice at the other end had fluctuated between calm and furious but Megan had listened impassively when she had to and returned the verbal barrage with equal ferocity when she'd felt it had been necessary.

'All right,' she said, trying to stem the tide from the other end of the line. 'Calm down. It's not a problem. I know how to handle myself.' She tapped one well-manicured nail on a pile of paper on the desk beside her keyboard.

The caller said they were more than aware of that.

'What's that supposed to mean?' she asked.

The word trust was mentioned.

'When it comes to a matter of trust I don't think you're quite so well qualified to lecture, are you? And no, I'm not being sarcastic. I've told you, I know what to do. Stop treating me like a child.'

When, the caller wanted to know, could they meet up again?

'You, of all people, should know how difficult that's going to be in the next couple of weeks,' Megan said wearily. 'I think it's best if we just stay clear of each other for the time being.' She shifted position on her chair, drawing one slender leg up beneath her.

There was silence at the other end and, for a moment, Megan thought the caller had hung up.

'Are you listening to me?' she persisted. 'I said I can handle it and I will.'

Another pause, then the caller's tone softened slightly. The question took Megan by surprise.

'I haven't even thought about my book winning the prize,' she confessed. 'Maria asked me that when I spoke to her this morning but, frankly, that's the last thing on my mind at the moment. But thanks for asking, anyway.' She felt her own temper cooling a little. 'This is a difficult time for both of us. I realise that and I want to see you again but I think it's dangerous at the moment.'

The caller insisted that there had to be a way.

'Then you tell me how,' she demanded. 'You've got far more to lose than I have if the truth is discovered. You understand what I mean? Soon this won't mean anything to me. Nothing will.' She brushed some dust from one leg of her jeans, pulling at a thread on the turn-up.

The caller said they could meet at a hotel.

'That's impossible,' Megan said flatly.

Perhaps, the caller suggested, the meeting could take place at her flat.

'No. Not yet. It's too soon,' she said. 'Don't push it.' Her tone hardened. 'You know why.' She sucked in a deep breath. 'I don't care about that.' There was something approaching anger in her words now. 'Listen, don't ring me here again. If you have to contact me then call me on my mobile but not unless it's important. An emergency.'

She glanced at the carriage clock once more, then down at her bare feet.

'Listen,' she told the caller. 'I'm going to have to go. I'm expecting another call in five minutes.'

The voice asked if the other call was important.

'It is to me,' Megan growled. 'I'll ring you tomorrow if I get the chance. I promise. You're not the only one that's busy, you know.' She drew in a weary breath. 'Yes, I'll call if I can. OK.' She held the phone tightly for a moment. There was a hiss of static on the line, the only sound between Megan and the caller. It was she who finally broke the silence. 'I'm not sorry for what's happened,' she said, her voice cracking slightly. 'Don't expect me to be.'

She hung up.

As she lifted her hand away from the receiver, she noticed that it was shaking slightly.

Nurture

The woman insisted that she could be left alone with the child. With her child.

The nurse did not agree. She stood like a sentinel at the bottom of the bed while the woman hovered over the portable incubator, looking down at her son. She wanted to lift him out and hold him. Eventually she asked the nurse if that would be all right.

The nurse hesitated for a moment, then nodded.

With infinite care, the woman reached for the tiny form inside the incubator.

The child made a gurgling sound. A liquid mewling that made it sound as if it was making the noise through a throat clogged with mucus. There was clear fluid dribbling thickly from its wide nostrils but the woman seemed unconcerned. She lifted the boy to her chest and held him there, feeling his hands pulling at her left breast.

She looked at the nurse and asked if he could be fed.

The nurse informed her that he already had been earlier that morning. He was currently having difficulty retaining fluid

(it was one of the symptoms the doctor had warned her about),

as was obvious by the stench coming from his nappy.

192

But the woman seemed untroubled by the smell and unimpressed by the nurse's words.

The boy again clawed at her breast and she pulled down her nightdress, exposing the milk-swollen mammary.

The nurse took a step towards her, urging her not to breast-feed the child. In the woman, clutching her son, the words provoked a feeling of defiance and she moved the child's head nearer to her left nipple.

The baby bucked more powerfully in her arms now, smelling her milk. Wanting to suckle.

It began to salivate. The mucus mingled with the thick, gelatinous fluid already seeping from its nose and the woman felt the sticky wetness against her breast. She could feel the boy's warm and eager breath rasping over her prominent nipple. And, all the time, she held the nurse's challenging gaze as she lifted the child closer to her.

Again the nurse asked her not to feed the boy, told her that his digestive problems would only be exacerbated by ingesting his mother's milk, but the woman seemed oblivious of the words. She looked down at her son, untroubled by the stench that seemed to be growing more intense by the second. Unworried by the sight of the thick mucus dribbling down his face from his flaring nostrils. Caring nothing for the liquid rasping that came from deep in his throat.

She pressed him to her left nipple and felt his warm, fluid-filled mouth close over the throbbing teat.

The small mouth slid over the nipple at first

and the boy used his hands to reach for her breast, trying to attach himself to the appendage, seeking the milk he craved.

The nurse was shaking her head, advancing on the woman now, telling her to stop what she was doing for her own sake but also for the sake of her son.

Her son.

The woman looked down at the tiny form in her arms and she pushed his head forward to meet her nipple. There was a moment of discomfort as he fastened his lips round the teat and then she felt the suction as he started to feed.

The nurse shook her head and backed away slightly.

The woman held the child tightly to her, her eyes closed almost in ecstasy, as if it were a lover paying attention to her nipple rather than her own offspring.

Milk dribbled down the boy's chin, mingling with the other fluids already smeared there.

He made a sound deep in his throat. A noise that seemed beyond the vocal range of a child so young. A low, rumbling gargle of satisfaction.

There was a vile hissing sound that the woman knew was more noxious voiding into the nappy. The smell that arose became almost intolerable but she kept the baby at her breast. Some of the puerile faecal matter was beginning to seep out of one side of the nappy.

The nurse was now imploring her to put the baby back in the incubator and, finally, the woman relented and pulled the child gently away from herself.

Milk was running from her nipple, some of it dripping on to the child.

Her child.

The boy flapped his arms in her direction, wanting to continue feeding. The nurse was already preparing to wheel the incubator away but the woman stopped her, looking down at her son, his face smeared with milk, sputum and mucus.

She smiled at him.

44

As Birch rode the lift to the twenty-eighth floor of the Hilton Hotel on Park Lane he inspected his reflection in the mirrored wall. He straightened his tie, brushed away some imaginary flecks of dust from the sleeve of his charcoal grey suit and ran a hand through his hair again. Then he bared his teeth at the image staring back at him.

You'll do.

When the lift bumped to a halt he stepped out and turned to his left towards the cocktail bar called Windows. A uniformed member of staff nodded curtly towards him as he wandered into the bar, the sound of an acoustic guitar drifting on the warm air.

He drew one or two glances from a group of noisy guests seated in the large leather armchairs close to the bar's entrance but the person he sought was waiting further inside, looking out of the huge picture windows that offered a magnificent panoramic view of London.

As the detective moved closer, the figure turned towards him and smiled.

Megan Hunter was wearing a red halter-neck dress, the hem of which stopped just above her knee. She had a light-weight black jacket draped round her shoulders and the high-heeled sandals she wore accentuated the very pleasing shape of her legs and showed off a perfect pedicure. Her blonde hair was slightly tousled.

Birch could think of any number of clichés to describe her appearance but the one that seemed most apt was breathtaking.

He nodded and smiled as he sat down opposite her.

'You didn't mind meeting here, did you?' she asked, sipping her cocktail.

'Not at all,' he assured her. 'It's very nice. Thanks for asking me.'

'I wasn't sure if this was even . . . what's the word, acceptable.'

'What? Going out for dinner with someone? I don't think I'm going to find myself pounding a beat tomorrow because of that.'

'Even if I am a suspect?'

'No one said you were a suspect, Miss Hunter — '

'Please, Detective Inspector,' she cut across him. 'If we're going to sit in one of the most famous restaurants in London and eat dinner then I'd appreciate it if you called me by my first name.'

'Sorry. Force of habit.'

'And, if it's not breaking any rules, I'd like to call you by yours. It's David, isn't it?'

'Or Dave, if you feel more comfortable with that. I'm not overly struck on Davey boy, but if you must . . . '

Megan laughed. 'I think I can manage with David,' she told him, grinning.

'Thanks, Megan,' he replied, motioning to the waiter. 'Mineral water, please.' The man scuttled off to get his order.

'Am I going to be the only one drinking tonight?' she said, sipping her cocktail.

'Technically I'm still on duty. But don't let me cramp your style. If you want to get pissed then be my guest.' They both smiled. 'I'll just apologise in advance if my mobile rings but with the investigation being so far along . . . ' He allowed the words to tail off.

'It's OK. I understand.'

The waiter returned and set down Birch's mineral water, poured some, and then retreated.

'I was glad when you agreed to come tonight,' she told him. 'If we're going to talk I just thought it'd be nice to do it in more pleasant surroundings.'

'You mean instead of me dragging you down to New Scotland Yard?'

She laughed again. Birch was aware once more of how infectious that sound was and he couldn't help but smile himself.

'Let's take our drinks through to the dining room,' she said, raising her glass and reaching for the bill. 'I'll get these. After all, it was my choice of venue. I asked you to come here.'

Birch shook his head. 'I know this might sound old-fashioned but I'll pay,' he insisted, peering down at the bill.

'Thank you very much.' Megan smiled.

'Fucking hell,' Birch whispered, reaching for his wallet, then, to Megan: 'Excuse me. Nine quid for a cocktail and a mineral water. Maybe I *should* have taken you down to the Yard. It'd have been cheaper.'

45

As the sun sank lower behind the skyline of London, it spilled its colour across the heavens like blood on blotting paper.

'The city looks beautiful from up here,' Megan observed, wiping one corner of her mouth with her napkin and gazing out over the vast metropolis. 'It looks cleaner.'

'It doesn't always look that clean from where I see it,' Birch told her.

'No, I suppose not. You must have seen some horrible things over the years.'

'Not stuff you'd want to hear about over dinner.' He pushed a forkful of food into his mouth.

'Why did you become a policeman?'

'I can't even remember now.' He shrugged. 'I'm not going to give you some bullshit about wanting to rid the world of evil people.' He grinned. 'But I'm sure my reasons were pure enough at the time. Over the years they've changed. I've changed. My second wife used to tell me that all that mattered to me was the case I was working on. That I was nothing without it.'

'Do you think she was right?'

'Maybe it is all I've got, but I can live with that. Some people call it an obsession.'

'What do you call it?'

'Being focused. I won't let anything get in the way of my work.'

'Not even two marriages?'

'I didn't decide to end the first one.' There was an edge to his tone that Megan wasn't slow to pick up. 'I wasn't expecting my wife to die of cancer.'

'I'm sorry,' she said quietly.

'What about you?' Birch enquired, reaching for his drink. 'Do you ever get sick of writing?'

'No. It's a very privileged position to be in. I earn enough money to continue doing a job I love and it doesn't really feel like a job anyway.'

'What did you do before you became a writer?'

'I temped. I worked in bars and restaurants as a waitress so that I could earn enough money to go back to college and get a teaching qualification. Then I taught at a couple of secondary schools, but I was writing all the time. Trying to make the breakthrough. I think I was more surprised than anyone when it finally happened and my first book was published.'

'It must be a great feeling, walking into a bookshop and seeing your book on the shelf.'

'Like catching a murderer is to you, I would imagine.' She held his gaze. 'Probably what it'll feel like when you get the person who killed Frank Denton, Donald Corben and Sarah Rushworth. After all, that's what we came here to talk about, isn't it?' She took a sip of her red wine. 'How close are you? Or is that classified?'

'Confidential, you mean. You've seen too many American cop films.' He smiled. 'I know you didn't kill Sarah Rushworth, if that's any consolation. I'd be willing to bet a rather large amount of money you didn't murder Frank

Denton or Donald Corben either. What I would like to know is why torn-up copies of your latest book keep turning up at the murder scenes.'

'If I could tell you that, David, I would. I just hope the press don't get hold of it. I don't think the public knowing that copies of *The Seeds of the Soul* have been found scattered around three crime scenes would be beneficial to my sales.'

'I bet John Paxton wouldn't worry if the papers knew that his latest book's also been found close to every victim. No such thing as bad publicity, is there?'

'Well, I'm not John Paxton.' She glanced out of the window and drained what was left in her glass.

'Did Paxton know Sarah Rushworth?'

'Of course he did,' Megan said matter-of-factly. She looked directly at Birch. 'They had an affair.'

46

Birch sat forward in his chair.

'How do you know?' he asked.

'The managing director of the first publishers I ever worked for once told me that in the book business it's difficult to turn over in bed without someone else in publishing knowing about it. He was right.'

'How long ago did this affair take place?'

'About eight or nine years. Sarah had just joined Paxton's publishers. Straight out of college. She was only nineteen. He was a big name, even then. Rich, influential and powerful. He made a habit of bedding impressionable young secretaries and publicity girls. She wasn't the first to fall for his charms and she won't be the last.'

'Have you got any idea how long it went on for?'

'About six months as far as I know, that's all. Paxton gets bored easily.' She looked unwaveringly at the DI. 'You think he's got something to do with these killings, don't you?'

'His latest book was found shredded and spread over each victim. He didn't get on with Frank Denton. He hated Donald Corben and now you tell me he had an affair with Sarah Rushworth. Also, as far as we can tell, his whereabouts, at least on the nights of the first two killings, are sketchy. He seems to be linked at every turn. And yet . . . '

'What?'

'My gut feeling? My hunch? Copper's instinct?' He shook his head. 'I don't think Paxton killed any of them.'

'So what's your hunch?'

'I wish I had one. All I've got are three corpses, a couple of barely useable fingerprints and more loose ends than a fucking string factory.'

'So what do you do next?'

'For what it's worth, we interview Paxton again tomorrow. The body of Frank Denton is being exhumed and re-examined tomorrow night in the hope that we can find something we missed first time round. Other than that, all we can do is sit around with our thumbs up our arses waiting for the next murder.'

'My God, David. Are you that convinced there'll be one?'

'I'll be very surprised if there isn't. This bastard's getting bolder. He's enjoying his fucking work. If Sarah Rushworth was the last victim I'll be amazed.'

'So why did you want to speak to me again if you don't suspect me of the killings?'

'I want to know more about Giacomo Cassano.'

'How's that going to help you catch this murderer?'

'I don't know yet. But you told me Cassano was blinded and had his tongue ripped out. All three victims have had their eyes gouged out and' — he leaned forward conspiratorially

— 'this is confidential, but the murderer tried to tear out Sarah Rushworth's tongue.'

Megan felt the colour drain from her cheeks.

'Oh, God,' she murmured.

'If the killer is using your book as some kind of inspiration for the murders then he's either read it or he already had previous knowledge of Cassano's life and death. Especially the way he was tortured. Where could he have got that kind of information? What other books have been written about Cassano?'

'None that I know of. Mine's the first. I haven't even seen his name mentioned in English-language encyclopaedias or bibliographies. All my research was done in Italy and, even there, information was difficult to come by at first. There was a small portrait of him in the Palazzo Colonna gallery in Rome. But I would never have found it if not for one of the curators of the Uffizi gallery in Florence.'

'I've heard of that,' Birch told her. 'I saw *Hannibal*.'

Megan smiled. 'He helped me find information about Cassano,' she explained. 'Pointed me in the right direction. And, before you ask, that curator died eight years ago.'

Birch nodded. 'If there was so little information about Cassano to begin with, how did you find out about him in the first place?' he asked.

'I was researching a book on Dante. This would be ten or eleven years ago now. While I was going through some of his correspondence, Cassano's name began to crop up more and more. They'd written to each other. Compared ideas. It became clear that he'd been a major influence on Dante. A mentor, but something more than that. The more I learned about Dante, the more I understood what Cassano had done for him.'

'Meaning?'

'It's always been agreed by scholars that the equivalent of the first draft of the *Divine Comedy* was written by Dante around 1308. I found evidence in his correspondence with Cassano that a first draft had been written as early as 1299.'

'How come you found this evidence if everyone else before you had missed it?' Birch wanted to know.

'Most of the letters from Cassano to Dante had previously been censored or destroyed by the Church. Some of Cassano's followers rescued some of them and hid them. I was just lucky to find them. There's no great mystery about it, David. How many times do you see books or articles published these days claiming to reveal previously unknown information about famous people? Someone wrote an article not long ago stating that Churchill had sent hit squads into Germany to try to assassinate Hitler in 1943. No one else had ever found that kind of archive material before despite the reams of stuff that have been published on Churchill over the years. It's the same principle.'

Birch nodded. 'What was the difference between the first draft of the *Divine Comedy* and the one that was eventually published?' he wanted to know. 'Did Cassano write the one everybody knows? Just like someone else supposedly wrote all of Shakespeare's plays?'

'No, but after Cassano read the first draft he wrote to Dante urging him to rethink his vision of Hell as described in the *Divine Comedy*. He said that the description was inaccurate. He told Dante that he could help him depict Hell as it truly was.'

'How?'

'He promised to show Dante Hell itself.'

47

'And how did he propose to do that?' Birch enquired.

'I told you about Cassano's philosophy when it came to artistic people.'

'You mean the business of having to pay some kind of price for possessing a God-given talent. Yeah, you mentioned it.'

'Well, there was more to his beliefs than that. The Church wanted him silenced for the other things he was saying and writing too. He believed that anything created by the power of thought, of creativity, could be transferred from the mind into the actual work. That those who created could enter the worlds they themselves had given birth to.'

Birch raised one index finger to silence her.

'Hang on,' he said, smiling. 'You've lost me. Say that again in English, will you?'

Megan sucked in a deep breath. 'Cassano believed that, for instance, if someone painted a landscape they could enter that landscape any time they wanted to.'

Birch shook his head. 'Let me get this straight,' he said. 'Cassano believed that painters could become a part of their own work? That's just a self-portrait. Haven't hundreds of painters over the years done that?'

'No, you don't understand, David. That's not what I mean. Think of a painting like . . . ' She tried to visualise a suitable subject. 'I don't know . . . *The Haywain* by Constable.'

'Is that the one where the kid's lying down drinking from the pond?'

'No. I think that's called *The Cornfield*, but if that's the one you know then we'll use that as an example.'

'My mum had a Woolworth's copy of it over the fire-place when I was a kid,' he explained, smiling. 'That's the only reason I know it.'

'Right, now picture that scene,' she told him. 'Cassano believed that because Constable gave it life, he could become a part of it if he wanted to. That he could enter that painting, move around in the fields he'd sketched. Walk down that pathway that leads between the trees. Even wade in the pond that the boy you mentioned is drinking from.'

Birch could see genuine excitement in Megan's eyes as she warmed to her subject.

'Go on,' he urged.

'Do you know the painting *When did you last see your Father??*' she asked.

He nodded.

'The same with that,' she continued. 'Cassano would have believed that the artist, Yeames, because he painted it, would have been able to enter that room where the boy is being interrogated. Would have been able to sit on one of the chairs and watch and listen to the questioning.'

'How did that theory apply to other creative people? How did Cassano believe it worked with writers?' Birch wanted to know.

'He thought that if someone wrote a description of a character or a place they would be able to see that person or to visit that place. Because they'd created them. Cassano believed that art was merely a physical manifestation of the creative thought processes. That a thought could become tangible. For instance, if I was to write a scene describing a cake shop then I could enter that shop, look at the things on sale. Touch them. Smell them and even taste them. I could describe a bedroom, the cotton sheets, the scented candles all round it, and I could lie on that bed and feel those sheets against my skin. Smell the aroma of those candles.' She paused for a moment. 'And if I wanted you there with me then I would write you into that scene and you'd be in bed next to me.'

They looked at each other for what seemed like an eternity, neither of them speaking.

The silence was finally broken by Birch.

'So, if someone was dying of a disease,' he began, 'then they could write themselves into their book as cured, and they would be?'

'No. Not if the disease was real to begin with. Someone with cancer couldn't describe themselves as being cured because the tumour wasn't a product of their imagination. Cassano maintained that only things created by the mind could be controlled and manipulated by their creator. An illness like cancer isn't controlled by the mind, it attacks the body without the host being able to stop it.'

'Then how could real people enter their own creations? You said you could enter a bedroom you'd written about, but how? You already exist. You're real, it would only be the setting that was imaginary. That contradicts what Cassano believed.'

'No it doesn't, David. The creator can control their own actions within that imaginary scene, can interact inside it because it wouldn't exist but for their creativity.'

'You're starting to lose me again,' he confessed.

'I'm trying to keep it as simple as I can,' she told him.

'Thanks,' he snorted. 'I appreciate you taking my ignorance into account.'

'That wasn't what I meant,' she snapped, a note of rebuke in her voice. 'It's a very difficult concept to explain. To anyone. Especially someone as cynical as you.'

'It does sound crazy.'

'You asked me to explain Cassano's teachings and I've just done so.'

'What about you?' Birch murmured. 'Do you believe it?'

'I believe that Giacomo Cassano believed it. That was part of his philosophy. The seeds of the soul were what Cassano called those thoughts that became tangible.'

'So, according to Cassano, painters could enter their paintings, writers could become a part of their books, right?'

Megan nodded and sipped her wine.

'How does this tie in with Cassano's relationship with Dante?' the detective wanted to know.

'After Cassano told Dante that his depiction of Hell was inaccurate in the first draft of the *Divine Comedy*, Dante visited him. Cassano wrote Dante into Hell. He described it, on paper, then he added the character of Dante. Dante could then wander freely through Hell. When he returned, his visualisation of it had changed completely. The depiction that appears in the copies of the *Divine Comedy* after that are of the Hell that Dante saw at first hand.'

'If Cassano put Dante into Hell then how did he get out again?'

'Cassano wrote him out. As simple as that. The character of Dante was featured in a passage that described him leaving Hell. Cassano wrote that, upon his return to this world, Dante had the appearance of a man who had looked the most repulsive and depraved evils imaginable squarely in the eye. He also said that Dante's right hand was cut across the palm. An injury inflicted by one of the demons of Hell. He also wrote that Dante was carrying a stone he'd picked up from the path on the way to the lowest level of Hell.'

'So, not only did Cassano say that writers and painters could enter their own works, he also believed they could bring things out again?'

Megan nodded.

Birch looked to his right. Night had fallen over London and the detective could see thousands of lights shining below him from the windows of buildings, the glow of street-lamps and the headlights of vehicles. He looked at his own reflection in the glass for a moment then turned back to face Megan once more.

'Tell me more,' he said.

★ ★ ★

They arrived on huge pallets, in boxes and in crates.

Hundreds of thousands of them. Delivered by lorry, by van, by post and by car.

Bookshops all round the country, the length and breadth of Britain, received their copies of *The Fairground Phantoms*.

Many of the shops had been displaying posters of the book's cover and of its author for weeks before. A large number had employed extra staff to cope with the expected rush for copies. Some were opening early.

Shelves that had previously held twenty titles were cleared to make way for the new tome. Tables at the fronts of stores were piled high with the book. Shops unable to obtain enough copies of the printed version had ordered extra of the audio edition, read by John Paxton himself.

Most of the large bookselling chains through-out the country had given over their windows to Paxton displays, many also featuring his previous works and the DVDs of those that had been filmed.

During the next week, a number of shops would host signing sessions. Paxton would turn up and meet his adoring readers. Put his signature in their books. Laugh and joke with them as was his way. He would arrive in the evenings at some, speak amusingly about his books, and then enjoy the plaudits of those who took the time to come and hang on his words.

Everything was in place for the launch of *The Fairground Phantoms*.

In many of those same bookshops, now crammed so full of John Paxton's newest offering, Megan Hunter's biography of Giacomo Cassano was placed carefully in the new titles section.

Come the morning, it too would be sold. In vastly smaller amounts and to completely different readers, but it was there.

That was all that mattered.

48

They were the last ones to leave the dining room of Windows. The restaurant staff stood around unobtrusively until Birch and Megan finally got to their feet and prepared to go. Birch paid for the meal with a credit card, refusing Megan's offer to settle the bill. He helped her on with her jacket and they left.

As they rode the lift towards the ground floor they stood on opposite sides of the car and Birch couldn't resist looking her up and down.

She smiled when she saw his gaze upon her.

'I hope I've been of some help to you tonight, David,' she said quietly. 'I've really enjoyed myself.'

'Good.' He nodded. 'I appreciate your time.'

Ask her if she wants to do it again, dummy. Do it now before the fucking lift reaches the ground floor.

The lift bumped to a halt at the tenth floor and three men in their early thirties stepped in. All of them looked at Megan. One of them smiled, nudged his nearest companion in the ribs and raised his eyebrows.

Birch looked at the men with distaste.

Pricks.

He took a step across to Megan.

The lift reached the ground floor, and as the doors slid open the three men hurried out, laughing loudly. The first of them looked back

214

again at Megan and smiled crookedly, then licked his lips.

The trio disappeared out through the main entrance of the hotel.

'Fucking dickheads,' Birch grunted. Then his mood lightened as he felt Megan slip one arm through his as they walked to the door.

'Can I drive you home?' he asked. 'It's the least I can do after dragging you out tonight.'

'Thank you, David.'

Her heels clicked on the floor and one of the receptionists glanced in her direction, as did two guests seated on one of the sofas in the centre of the foyer. Birch wasn't surprised at their stares.

The automatic doors opened to allow them passage on to the forecourt and the uniformed doorman nodded politely. He prepared to beckon one of the waiting taxis across but Birch shook his head.

'We're all right, thanks, mate,' he said, leading Megan over to where he was parked.

He opened the passenger door of the Renault and she slid gracefully in. Birch walked round to the driver's side, got behind the wheel and started the engine.

'Right,' he murmured. 'Let's get you home.'

Megan looked at him, the smile still on her lips.

'So, am I off the wanted list now?' she enquired. 'I mean, I'd like to be able to tell my agent that my publicity appearances for my book won't be limited to Holloway.'

'Are you doing stuff in London for the next couple of days?'

'Then Manchester, Birmingham, Edinburgh and Dublin. You've got my number if you need to get in touch. If there's anything else you want to know.'

Birch nodded. 'I'm still trying to figure out some of the things you told me tonight,' he admitted.

'About the seeds of the soul? Cassano?'

'Mostly.'

'I know you don't believe it, David. It's difficult for anyone to understand, let alone a cynic like you.'

He looked at her and smiled. 'I'm going to take that as a compliment,' he informed her.

'Being called a cynic?'

'I've been called a lot worse in my time.'

They drove in silence for a while then the policeman spoke again.

'Just let me get this straight in my head,' he began. 'What do you think Cassano showed Dante? When he . . . sent him to Hell. Do you believe it? That a man could have that kind of power? You can understand me being sceptical, Megan.'

'All I know is what I found out during the course of my research, David. Read my book.'

'I tried.' He sighed. 'Painters who can come and go in their own pictures. Authors who can write themselves into their own books.' Birch shook his head. 'How did that theory work for musicians, then? Did Mozart turn into a bloody violin before he wrote a symphony?'

'You asked me what Cassano believed. I told you.'

'Whatever Cassano thought, preached or wrote during the thirteenth century doesn't get me any closer to the bastard who killed Denton, Corben and Sarah Rushworth, does it?'

He guided the car along Holland Park Avenue, his gaze fixed ahead, his mind so full of thoughts it felt as if it was going to explode.

'You can drop me on the corner,' Megan said, touching his arm and gesturing just ahead to the turning into Norland Square.

'I'll see you to your door,' he told her. 'Just in case.'

'If I'm not a suspect any more, does that mean I'm likely to become a victim?'

'I wish I knew, Megan. Until we find out what this bastard's motive is I can't tell you for sure one way or the other.'

He brought the Renault to a stop in a space close to her front door.

'I know this is the worst kind of cliché,' she began, 'but would you like a coffee? At least that way you'll be sure that I get inside my flat safely too.'

'Good point,' he said. 'Go on then. You twisted my arm.'

Megan smiled as he switched off the engine.

They walked together to the front door of the building and Megan let them in, ushering the detective into the hallway.

Even if they'd been aware of the presence hidden by the darkness on the far side of Norland Square, neither of them would have seen the one who watched them.

217

49

'Come in,' Megan said, stepping inside the flat.

Birch nodded and accepted her invitation. He followed her into the sitting room, standing awkwardly at the threshold as she moved quickly around switching on the lamps. She shrugged off her jacket and laid it across the back of the sofa.

The room was welcoming, the subdued lighting adding to the relaxed feeling generated by the colours the flat was decorated in.

'Would you like some music?' Megan asked, pausing before the CD player.

'As long as it isn't rap.' Birch grinned.

Megan selected a disc, pushed it into the machine and lowered the volume so that it was little more than a background presence.

'Tea, coffee or something stronger?' she asked.

'Just tea, please,' he said, still standing on the threshold of the room.

'David, come and sit down.'

Birch walked tentatively towards an armchair and perched on the edge of it. He watched her as she opened the balcony windows, the curtains billowing slightly as a breeze stirred them.

'It's a beautiful place,' he said, looking round the room.

'Thank you. It's got a beautiful mortgage to go with it.'

'You work in here,' he observed, nodding

towards the computer on the desk in one corner of the room.

'Sitting room and office,' she confirmed. 'I've got a laptop in the bedroom too.'

'In case you get inspired during the night?'

She smiled at him and headed towards the sitting room door, pausing to turn and look back at him as she reached it.

'If you want to change the music, there are more CDs over there.' She pointed towards the player. 'Have a look. There might be something you prefer. I like to think I've got pretty broad taste when it comes to music.'

She disappeared towards the kitchen, the brilliant red of her dress looking luminous in the warm light.

Birch got to his feet and wandered towards the CD player, running appraising eyes over the large collection of discs displayed on shelves above and around the machine. There was everything from classical to jazz, the Rolling Stones to Lucie Silvas, Keane to Iron Maiden. He allowed the disc she'd inserted to continue playing and moved slowly across the room to the overstocked bookcases.

Again the choice of volumes was eclectic to say the least. Fiction that spanned everything from James Joyce to the latest trash bestsellers. Poetry. Non-fiction. There were even a number of books on photography. He took one down and glanced at it.

How To Take Great Pictures boasted the title. 'It's a hobby.'

Birch looked up when he heard her voice. She

nodded in the direction of the book he was holding.

'I'm never going to be Annie Leibovitz but I enjoy it,' she told him.

'You took some of the pictures in your book, didn't you? I checked out the credits on them.'

'So you did look at it?'

'I looked at the pictures,' he told her, grinning.

'Sugar in your tea or honey?' she wanted to know.

'Sugar please.'

She smiled and disappeared once again.

Birch put the book back in its place on the shelf and continued scanning the other volumes there.

He studied the spines of several tomes all side by side on a shelf and realised they looked familiar. The name John Paxton stood out in large letters on each of them. Birch took one down and flipped it open at the title page. It was signed.

For Megan, hope it scares you, all the best, John.

He took down another further along the shelf.

That too was signed.

For Megan, best blood-spattered wishes.

Yeah, very funny.

Birch replaced it and removed another.

For Megan, from the man whose writing is marginally better than his back rubs.

Birch raised his eyebrows.

Love John.

Love John. It was a bit of a step forward from 'All the best', wasn't it?

He pushed the book back into position on the shelf and was about to take down the copy of *The Fairground Phantoms* when a letter lying close to Megan's computer caught his eye. It was with a number of other pieces of correspondence but it was the heading at the top of the paper that caused the detective to glance more inquisitively at it.

The Redman Private Clinic.

It bore the previous day's date. Birch glanced in the direction of the door then back at the letter, using a biro to lift the letter above it and allow himself better access to the words printed on the headed paper.

The clinic, as far as he could see from his hasty inspection of the embossed letters at the top of the page, was in Hertfordshire.

He saw words like medication, treatment, examination and prognosis. There was an appointment date on it.

Just in time he heard Megan approaching the sitting room and he took two long strides away from the desk, transferring his attention back to the rows of books before him. A moment later, Megan entered carrying a small tray with two mugs, a sugar bowl, a milk jug and a miniature teapot on it. She set the tray down on the table in the middle of the room and began filling the mugs with tea.

'Very civilised,' Birch said approvingly. 'It'd have been a tea bag in each mug and water straight from the kettle at my house.'

She pushed his mug towards him and watched as he perched on the edge of the chair opposite and spooned in sugar.

Megan made herself comfortable on the floor close to him, undid the straps on her shoes, pulled them off and drew her legs up beneath her.

'I've been thinking about what you told me,' Birch began. 'About Cassano. About his ideas and his philosophy. The whole thing about artists being able to become a part of their work.'

'And you still think it's crazy?' she said, sipping her tea.

'The truth?' he challenged. 'Yes I do.'

Megan held his gaze for a moment, her expression giving no clue as to her thoughts.

'What would convince you that Cassano was right, David?' she said, finally.

'A lot more than your explanation, Megan. Fascinating as it was.'

'All right. If you won't believe what I told you, let me show you.'

Exile

They hadn't argued. The closest the man had come to losing his temper had been one or two piercing looks. For the rest of the time he'd sat virtually motionless on a chair in the private room of the hospital while the woman spoke.

She had talked until it seemed that she was drained of words. And every one of those words had been impassioned and ripped from deep within her soul.

More than once tears had rolled down her cheeks as she'd spoken. Spoken of their son.

The man had looked away when she'd mentioned the child, as if the act of averting his gaze would somehow negate the boy's existence. But no matter how many times he looked away, she had continued with her tirade and he had heard the words despite his desire to block them out.

She had asked him to come with her to see the boy but he had refused. He had, he told her, no desire to see the child.

Their child, she reminded him.

However, despite the fact that the boy was as much his as the woman's, he stubbornly clung to the misguided and ridiculous hope that ignoring the child would somehow distance him from it.

He had told her that he wanted no part of its upbringing and she had accepted that. It had surprised him at first, but as she spoke and time ticked inexorably by he heard the determination in her voice and he saw it in her face. He knew now that nothing he could say or do would make her forsake the child.

Their child.

He shook his head as the words filled his mind. He would not, he could not, accept the boy, despite the fact that he had fathered him.

The woman's argument for keeping the child was more than persuasive, though. It was implacable. Nothing on earth was going to make her abandon her offspring and the man knew that now. So he listened helplessly as she spoke. At first he had wanted to walk out of the room, perhaps even walk out of her life, but he knew that he could not. So he sat in that sterile room, sometimes gazing out of the window, and allowed her words to wash over him.

But enough of them penetrated his muddled thinking for him to realise that she would accept his leaving as long as she had the child. If this was maternal instinct then even he had been surprised by its power and ferocity.

However, amid her pleas, entreaties and demands, the woman had spoken words that had been difficult for her. Words that had carved themselves deeply on his consciousness. She had said she understood the problems they would face raising their boy. She had repeated what the doctor had warned them of. And he knew that somewhere within her was the common sense that overrode even her strong emotion.

They would take the child from the hospital when the time was right. They would return it

224

when it needed medical care. She repeated that she would not abandon it.

Never.

As long as she lived, she would always look upon the child as their son. No matter what. When he had said that he could not feel the same way, she had looked at him not with dismay or sadness but with something approaching rage, but still they had not argued.

She had told him what she wanted to do and, with great reluctance, and not a little fear, he had agreed.

And now the time was close.

50

Birch peered at Megan over the rim of his mug for a moment before he lowered it, a slight smile on his lips.

'And what are you going to do to show me?' he asked. 'Send me to Hell like Cassano supposedly did to Dante?'

Megan's face was impassive. There was no trace of a smile there.

'I'm trying to help you understand,' she said, a little reproachfully. 'I told you what Cassano believed. Now I'm offering to show you but you think it's some kind of joke.'

'I didn't say that, Megan.'

'Then what are you saying?'

'Listen, you said yourself that Cassano, naturally, believed in his own philosophy. But you didn't say whether you thought it could actually be done.'

'I told you Dante supposedly returned from Hell carrying a stone he'd picked up there and with a gash on his hand sustained when a demon cut him.'

'*Supposedly* returned. *Supposedly*.'

They looked at each other in silence for a moment then Birch spoke again. 'Think about it logically. A painter who can enter something he's committed to canvas? A writer who's able to become a part of what he's written? It's a fascinating idea, but — '

'Ridiculous,' she cut across him irritably. 'That's what you were going to say, isn't it?'

'Megan, you said it yourself. It was a belief. Nothing more.'

'And I'm telling you that sometimes logic isn't the only answer, David.'

'Well, in my world it is. And in this case it is. Logic's the only thing that's going to help me find the killer of Denton, Corben and Sarah Rushworth.'

'You were the one who wanted to know about Cassano, David. All I did was to answer your questions. I was trying to help. I needed your attention, not your unqualified belief.'

'I'm a copper,' he snapped. 'Part of my job is pursuing leads. Don't sound so surprised because I'm trying to chase one down. Cassano's teachings, your book and what you've told me could be a crucial part of this case. I need to understand, Megan. On my terms.'

Silence descended once again. Megan drained what was left in her mug then poured herself more tea from the small pot. She offered some to Birch but he shook his head.

'I'd better go,' he said, exhaling deeply. He got to his feet. 'Leave you in peace.'

Megan too stood up. Without her high heels she was several inches shorter than Birch and the DI thought how vulnerable she looked. He saw a sadness in her eyes that he'd not noticed before.

'I had a lovely evening, David,' she told him. 'Thank you.'

'Perhaps we can do it again sometime,' he said.

'When I'm not a murder suspect?' She smiled.

He nodded.

She walked him to the front door of the flat.

'Thanks for the tea,' he said, aware that the words sounded awkward. His heart was thumping a little faster than usual. 'I'll be in touch.' He turned to go but paused. 'Lock the door behind me,' he told her. 'And keep it locked. The same with your windows.'

She nodded.

'David,' she called as he walked towards the stairs that would take him down to the front door. 'Think about what I told you. Sometimes belief is all you need.'

'I think I'll stick with logic,' he said, forcing a smile.

She watched him for a moment longer then closed the door behind him and double-locked it. She padded quickly back into the sitting room and then out on to her balcony. Beneath her, she could see him preparing to open the driver's door of the Renault.

'Ring me,' she called down to him.

He raised a hand and smiled up at her.

'Go back in,' he urged.

She watched him slide behind the wheel. He started the engine and guided the vehicle out into the road. She watched it disappear into the traffic and then she retreated back inside the flat, closing the balcony windows behind her.

She locked them both.

51

The television was on but the sound was barely audible. Every now and then Birch would glance at the screen, the flickering images the only light in his sitting room apart from the dull glow of the lamp perched on top of the set.

He sucked in a deep breath and reached for his cigarettes, lighting one and drawing heavily on it. There were already several dog-ends in the ashtray on the edge of the table before him. Next to it was a bottle of Jack Daniel's and a glass.

The DI poured another measure and rolled the crystal between his palms, his attention momentarily caught by some movement on the television screen. He gazed blankly at the Italian football that was showing, watching a white-shirted player rattle a shot against the crossbar of the opposition. The ball bounced back into play and was cleared.

Birch glanced back at the table before him.

It was covered in photos. Black and white. Colour. All sizes. They showed the bodies of Frank Denton, Donald Corben and Sarah Rushworth.

The detective picked up the closest one and gazed raptly at it.

It was of the left profile of Corben's face and showed, in stark close-up, the empty eye socket, the lacerations round it and the other wounds on the face. One nostril had been split wide by a blow from the same blade that had been used to remove the eyes.

Birch put the photo back and selected one of Sarah Rushworth. In it her lower abdomen and the top of her thighs were shown, once again, gouged deeply by the serrated knife that had taken her life. The next picture was a close-up of her butchered labia, the remains of her outer lips torn and shredded by several monstrously powerful cuts.

The DI took a sip of his drink, gritting his teeth as he felt the liquor burn its way to his stomach.

He put down the photo and turned his attention to the first of the manila files that also occupied a prominent place on the table.

Autopsy reports, crime scene interviews, witness statements. The words appeared to blur into one, and the more he read them, the less sense they seemed to make.

With an exhalation of frustration, he dropped the file back on to the table and sat back on the sofa.

He assumed the match on TV had reached the half-time stage because there were now advertisements appearing on the screen every couple of minutes. Birch stared disinterestedly at them. He didn't have a problem with constipation. He didn't want a loan with very low repayment interest. His need for a stair-lift, he hoped, would be a long way off and he definitely wasn't worried about finding the right kind of pantie-liner. The ads finished. Birch sipped more of his drink.

He leaned forward again, reaching for the first of the two books on the table.

The detective hefted the copy of *The Seeds of the Soul* before him, flicking through it rapidly, pausing at the photographs in the middle. He turned to the inside flap of the dust jacket and looked at Megan Hunter's photo.

You were right. It doesn't do her justice.

He smiled to himself and thought about her sitting opposite him that evening in the restaurant. It had been a long time since he'd taken a woman out for dinner.

It may well be even longer before you do it again unless you get a break in this fucking case.

He traced the outline of her face with one index finger then gently closed the book and set it back down on the table.

The next one he picked up with a little more urgency.

He opened *The Fairground Phantoms* and began to read.

⋆ ⋆ ⋆

When she heard the buzzer sound on the flat's intercom, Megan frowned. She glanced at her watch. It had been a good half-hour since Birch had left. Unless, she mused, he'd forgotten something and had returned to claim it. And yet, looking round her sitting room, she could see nothing lying around that belonged to the detective.

The buzzer sounded again.

Also, she thought, if Birch had returned, he

231

would have called first, wouldn't he? Not just turned up like this. Not in view of his warnings to her about protecting herself.

Her heart began beating a little faster as she heard the buzzer sound a third time.

Whoever was out there seemed intent on gaining entry.

For a moment she considered venturing out on to the balcony but realised it would be a futile exercise. The main entrance to the flats was hidden by the porchway and only a dull nightlight illuminated it.

She moved to the intercom, licking her lips nervously.

The buzzer sounded again.

Megan reached out and jabbed the button that allowed her to communicate with the caller.

'Hello,' she said falteringly.

'Let me in, Megan.'

She recognised the voice immediately.

'What do you want?' she asked.

'Just open the fucking door, will you?'

She hesitated a moment longer before hitting another button on the control pad by the door.

'It's open,' she said. 'Come up.'

She unlocked the front door of the flat and stood at the threshold waiting. She heard heavy footfalls on the stairs as her visitor ascended, quickly reaching the landing. Megan stepped back and ushered him in.

John Paxton smiled at her.

52

Dressed in just a short vest top and a pair of black panties, Megan felt strangely vulnerable before Paxton, who made no attempt to disguise his slow, appraising glance up and down her body.

She followed him into the sitting room, reaching for the housecoat she'd draped over the back of the sofa. She pulled it on.

'A sudden attack of modesty?' Paxton said. 'Don't bother on my account. It's nothing I haven't seen before.' He slumped unceremoniously into the nearest armchair and looked at her.

'What do you want, John?'

'Where did you go with that copper tonight?'

Megan looked puzzled.

'Oh, come on, Megan,' he said. 'I was sitting watching you when you got back. Where did you go?'

'He wanted to ask me some questions.'

'You don't wear that red Dior dress of yours for a grilling in some fucking interview room at New Scotland Yard.'

'We went out for dinner. We went to Windows. Not that it's any of your business.'

'Very romantic.'

'It wasn't meant to be romantic. He wanted to ask me some questions. I suggested he did it over dinner.'

'And he hasn't stayed the night? Fucking hell, Meg, you must be losing your touch. I'd have thought you'd have been fucking his brains out by now.'

'Get out,' she rasped, pointing to the door. 'I knew you could sink low, John, but I didn't expect you to start spying on me.'

'So, did you fuck him?'

'None of your business,' she snarled.

'No, you didn't,' Paxton said, shaking his head. 'He wasn't here long enough. You don't like to rush, do you, Meg? You like it slow. Nice relaxed build-up. That's what gets you going isn't it? Then, once you're there, you're a fucking tiger, aren't you?'

'Say what you came here to say or go now,' she said venomously.

'What did he want to know?' Paxton enquired.

'He asked what I knew about Frank Denton, Donald Corben and Sarah Rushworth.'

'He asked me that as well. He wants to interview me again tomorrow.'

'I know, he told me. He also told me that they're going to exhume Denton's body tomorrow night to re-examine for anything they might have missed.'

Paxton nodded slowly and contemplatively. 'What else did he ask?'

'He wanted to know about my book. About Cassano and his theories.'

'Why the fuck did he want to know about that?' Paxton demanded, a bemused look colouring his features.

'He thought there might be a link between my

book and the killings.'

'And does he still think that?'

'No.'

'What did you tell him about Cassano?'

'I tried to explain his theories. What he believed. I'm not sure I made myself clear, though.'

'And what did you tell him about the murders of Denton, Corben and Sarah?'

'I told him I didn't know how copies of my book and yours came to be torn up and scattered over the bodies.' She shot Paxton a withering look. 'What did you tell him when he interviewed you?'

'The same thing, obviously.' Paxton stroked his chin thoughtfully, the anger in his tone lessening slightly. 'Did he ask about me?'

'He asked if I knew you.'

'But you didn't tell him about us?'

'There is no us, John. Not any more. I've told you that a dozen times. It had to end. You know that.'

'Does he know I was here the nights Denton and Corben were killed?'

Megan shook her head.

'I told you, he doesn't know that anything ever went on between us,' she told him. 'No one knows.' She spoke the words slowly and deliberately. 'No one will ever know.'

'He could find out. There's a lot of history between us, Megan. Twelve years is a long time.'

'We haven't been together for twelve years, John,' she sighed. 'You were too busy with your career, your wife and all the other women.' She sucked in a deep breath. 'We saw a lot of each other at the beginning, but after the first year what was it? The odd night here and there? A lunch? A dinner? The odd chance meeting at some book launch? Whatever we had has been dead for a long time.'

'You didn't say that last time I was here.'

There was a long silence, finally broken by Paxton.

'I wanted to be there for you if you needed me,' he said quietly. 'At least tell me you know that.'

She nodded. 'I think you'd better go, John,' she murmured. 'If the police are watching my flat or your house then they'll know you've been here . . . ' She allowed the sentence to die away.

Paxton got to his feet. 'I wanted to be around when you needed me,' he reminded her. 'Don't blame me for that.'

'Goodbye,' she said, without looking at him.

He paused, preparing to say something else, but the words wouldn't come.

'Megan,' he said as he reached the door of the flat.

'Just go,' she told him, with an air of finality.

53

Birch sucked in a deep, rasping breath and closed his eyes momentarily as Megan Hunter closed her hand a little more tightly around his erection.

She was straddling his groin, on her knees so that her own moist sex was close to his swollen testicles. She smiled down at him and continued to move her hand gently up and down his shaft.

The pillows had been scattered from the bed during their frantic movements and the sheet too had been discarded and lay on the floor.

Megan moved forward slightly, still holding his penis, and manoeuvred herself so that she could rub the tip of his erection against her own sensitive clitoris.

She continued to do this for a moment or two, her eyes closed and her breathing guttural. Then she lifted herself up a fraction and guided his erection into the warm wetness of her cleft.

Birch looked at her, gripping her thighs, allowing his hands to slide up her slim torso until he reached her breasts. He gently kneaded them in his hands, thumbing the erect nipples until Megan groaned even more loudly.

Unable to control herself any longer she finally lowered herself slowly on to his erection, her breathing becoming quicker as he slid deeper inside her. Birch also gasped, sliding his fingertips away from her breasts to the smooth skin of her back. He traced patterns down her spine until he reached the small of her back. She quivered as he gently massaged the area just above her buttocks, finally cupping her bottom in both hands as she began to rock slowly back and forth upon him.

As she pressed down on to him she leaned forward and they kissed fiercely. She gripped his shoulders, her well-manicured nails digging into his flesh. Her hair brushed against his face and he drank in yet another of her scents. The aroma of her perfume and her skin, the heavier, muskier smell of her sex and perspiration all mingled together in his nostrils. It was an intoxicating mixture and Birch had to pull away momentarily to gasp his pleasure. A long strand of clear saliva stretched from her bottom lip to his, momentarily joining them like some kind of clear umbilicus.

And all the time, the sensations grew more intense until both of them were gasping loudly. Moving against each other with an urgency that signalled both were close to reaching their peak.

She dug her nails more deeply into his flesh. So hard that he winced, but the combination of pleasure and pain was exquisite and he did nothing to stop her. He wanted to wallow in this feeling.

'Sometimes belief is all you need,' she whispered.

She kissed him again and he felt her movements becoming more rapid. She gasped something under her breath and he felt her muscles begin to tighten around his penis.

Birch held her buttocks, aiding her in her movements, his hands occasionally sliding on to her thighs or up her taut back muscles.

She whispered his name then kissed him again.

'Look at me,' he said breathlessly.

She lifted her head and met his gaze, now very close to her climax. She closed her eyes again but he put one hand to her face with incredible gentleness and stroked her cheek.

'Look at me when you come,' he urged. 'Don't close your eyes.'

She pressed even more firmly against him and moved with ever more frantic movements on his stiffness until she began to shake uncontrollably.

'Megan, look at me,' he gasped again and she held his gaze, their eyes seemingly magnetised. He held her face with both hands now and her eyes were wide as the orgasm swept through her. She moaned her pleasure and it felt as if they were looking into each other's souls.

'Sometimes belief is all you need,' she whimpered, then again she said his name, but more loudly this time. And she drove her nails deeply into his shoulder, raking the other hand across his chest, grazing him there too before she finally sat back, shaking as the final spasms of climax shook through her.

Then, barely pausing, she lifted herself up and her long fingers encircled his slippery shaft again, working away smoothly and gently on the hard, glistening flesh.

She took one index finger and pressed it to his lips, allowing him to taste her, then she shuffled on to her knees and raised her buttocks into the air, her back arched, inviting him to enter her from behind.

Birch clambered up on to his knees and pressed the head of his penis against her wet labia, holding it there for a second before pushing forward, making her gasp again. He gripped her hips, knowing that the pleasure that had been building for so long would shortly be released. And she pushed herself back to meet every one of his urgent thrusts until it was his turn to shudder.

She turned her head and looked over her shoulder at him as he drew close to his own climax, perspiration now running down his face and torso.

Megan arched her back, still watching him. Then she gasped as she felt the first outpouring of his orgasm inside her. He thrust into her and she pushed back willingly against him, seeing his face contorted with pleasure.

And she smiled.

★ ★ ★

The glass fell with a thud to the floor beside the sofa.

Birch sat forward, momentarily disorientated. He was gasping loudly, his mouth and throat dry.

'Shit,' he murmured, putting a hand to his head, wondering why the room wouldn't stop spinning.

'Megan,' he said quietly, looking round as if expecting to see her in the sitting room with him.

He blinked hard, trying to clear his mind as well as his vision. He looked at his watch.

'Fuck,' he grunted.

Go to bed.

And still the room seemed to be turning. He looked at the bottle of Jack Daniel's.

You've drunk too much. Get to bed now.

He licked his lips and tasted something familiar. Something . . .

Birch touched one index finger to his mouth and brought it away slowly. There was a pale stain on the tip. He licked it.

Lipstick.

Sometimes belief is all you need.

As he tried to rise, he felt pain in one shoulder and he rubbed it with his free hand. It was sore.

He got to his feet, stepping on the copy of *The Fairground Phantoms* that lay on the carpet, and stumbled out of the sitting room and through into the downstairs bathroom. He turned his back to the small mirror above the sink there and eased his shirt from his shoulder to inspect the painful area.

There were four deep scratches in the flesh of his back just above the shoulder blade. As if someone had dug their fingernails hard into the flesh.

54

John Paxton watched the sun glinting on the Thames as he gazed distractedly out of the window, a glass of orange juice in his hand.

Only when he heard voices outside in the hotel corridor did he turn away from the superb view.

Detective Inspector David Birch and Detective Sergeant Stephen Johnson entered the Savoy suite, Johnson looking around admiringly at the sumptuous surroundings.

Paxton shook hands with the two policemen and motioned to the coffee table and chairs in the centre of the room.

'Have a seat,' he said. 'Can I get you a drink? A cup of tea or coffee?'

'No thanks.' Birch smiled. 'We won't keep you any longer than we have to. Your agent told us how busy you are.'

'He gets very protective,' Paxton grinned. 'He's just safeguarding his fifteen per cent.'

'You've got a lot of interviews to do, then?' Johnson asked.

'I started at eight this morning on the phone to a radio station,' the writer told them. 'Journalists from the *Telegraph* and the *Mirror* have already been here. You just missed the guy from *FHM*. The next one is from either the *Standard* or *Time Out*, I forget which. They all ask the same fucking questions anyway. You get a script in your head after a while. It just throws

242

you when one of them asks you something you actually have to think about. Something intelligent.' He smiled again and downed what was left of the orange juice. 'But that doesn't happen very often.' He regarded the two detectives impassively. 'I'm guessing the questions you're going to ask me are going to be different from the kind I've answered so far. What can I do for you this time?'

'Sarah Rushworth,' Birch began. 'You knew her. In fact you knew her very well.'

'We worked together. She did the publicity on a couple of my books.'

'And you're aware that she was murdered and that a copy of your latest book was found torn up and scattered round the scene?' Birch continued.

'I knew she was dead.' Paxton hesitated a moment, unable to hold Birch's gaze. 'I didn't know about my book being found with her.'

'Did you see her the night she was murdered or at any time during that day?' the DI persisted.

Paxton shook his head.

'Did you phone her?' Birch continued.

Again the writer shook his head.

'So when your affair with her finished, you didn't contact her any more after that?'

Paxton smiled but it never touched his eyes.

'It was an amicable split, Detective Inspector,' he said. 'Just like all the others. They all knew what they were doing. They all played by the rules. None of the women I've had relationships with have been in them to try and end up as the next Mrs Paxton. It was fun for me and it was

243

fun for them. Simple as that. They got to spend nights in top-class hotels. Ate at the finest restaurants. Some of them even got things bought for them. And me. I got what I wanted too. It was a reciprocal thing.'

'You said that the affairs were the reason your wife left you,' Birch reminded him. 'Was there any one relationship in particular that she mentioned?'

'You mean what was the final straw that broke the camel's back, right?' Paxton shook his head. 'It was a combination of all of them. Cheating on my wife wasn't a mistake, Detective Inspector. Getting caught was the fucking mistake.'

'So you didn't see or have any contact with Sarah Rushworth the day she was murdered?' Birch repeated.

Again Paxton shook his head.

'If I had I'd tell you,' he confessed. 'If someone's trying to frame me for these killings by leaving torn-up copies of my book lying around then I'd like to know who the fuck it is.'

'Can you think of anyone who might want revenge against you?' Birch said. 'Who'd want to frame you?'

'I've upset a few people over the years with my work, my attitude and the way I've lived my life, but I can't think of anyone who'd be so pissed off they'd try to get me banged up for three fucking murders.'

'What about Megan Hunter?'

Birch saw the flash of uncertainty register on Paxton's features.

'What about her?' the writer asked.

The DI shrugged. 'She said she knew you.'

'A lot of people know me.'

'Her book's been found at the scene of every murder the same as yours has. I'm not implying anything, I'm just telling you what I know. Was she one of the women you had an affair with? One of the ones who played by the rules? You said that all the splits with other women had been amicable. It might not have been that way with Megan Hunter.'

'I've never had an affair with Megan Hunter,' Paxton lied. 'What makes you think I have?'

'I didn't accuse you of having an affair with her. I'm a detective, Mr Paxton. It's part of my job to consider everything, including the possibility that you and Megan Hunter might have had an affair and that it could have caused her enough pain for her to want to get even with you. Like I said, I have to look at every angle, especially when I've already got three corpses on my hands and might end up with more.' Birch got to his feet and extended his right hand. 'Thanks for your time,' he said. 'We won't keep you any longer.'

The writer hesitated a moment, then shook the offered hand.

'I'll tell you what I told Miss Hunter,' Birch said as he and his companion reached the door of the suite. 'Watch yourself. The three victims so far have all been connected in some way to the book business. If you're not a killer you might be a target.'

★ ★ ★

'What do you think?' Birch looked at his companion as they climbed into the waiting Astra.

'If you mean do I think Paxton's our killer then I'd have to say no,' the DS confessed.

'I agree with you, and I'm pretty sure no one's trying to frame him either. Which doesn't help us much, does it?' Birch winced as he pulled on his seat belt. The strap felt tight against the raw flesh of his shoulder. He thought about mentioning the dream to his companion but then thought better of it.

'Where to, guv?' said Johnson, starting the engine of the Astra. He guided it carefully out of the forecourt of the Savoy, avoiding a silver Mercedes that was pulling in to disgorge some passengers.

'Hertfordshire,' Birch said flatly, gazing out of the side window.

'What the hell's in Hertfordshire that's so important?' the DS wanted to know.

'The Redman Private Clinic,' Birch told him.

55

'Next junction,' Birch noted, taking a final drag on his cigarette and dropping the end out of the Astra's open passenger window.

He jabbed a finger in the direction he wanted Johnson to take and again adjusted his seat belt, once more aware of the discomfort where the strap was rubbing against his shoulder. Thanks to the volume of traffic, the journey from central London had taken close to two hours.

During that time the two detectives had talked endlessly about the case, but, despite repeatedly going over the facts as they knew them, neither was closer to an answer of any sort.

'Let's just hope to Christ that forensics can find something when Denton's body's exhumed tonight,' the DI complained.

They left the motorway where Birch indicated and, within fifteen minutes, the car was travelling along much narrower roads flanked first by expensive-looking properties with perfectly manicured hedges or stone walls, and then by fields and trees.

The stink of exhaust fumes was replaced by the fresher air of the Hertfordshire countryside.

'Tell me again why we're here, guv,' Johnson said, following the directions given to him by his superior.

'When I was in Megan Hunter's flat last night I saw a letter with headed notepaper from the

247

Redman Private Clinic,' the DI told him. 'I want to know what she's coming here for.'

'If you don't mind me asking, what's that got to do with our investigation? If she's coming to a private clinic for some kind of treatment, I don't see how that affects this case.'

'Megan Hunter's books have been found at every murder scene,' Birch reminded him.

'But you said yourself you didn't think she was involved in the murders. I don't get it. There must be other leads we could be following.'

'Like what?' Birch snapped, rounding on his companion. 'We've exhausted every fucking lead we've got so far. Three people are dead and we're still no closer than we were at the beginning to finding out who killed them. If we were back at the Yard we'd just be going over statements and reports we've already looked at a hundred times before.' He ran a hand through his hair. 'I want to know why Megan Hunter has been visiting this clinic. I'm leading this investigation and I think it's important.'

'So it's personal, not business.'

'Have I ever pulled rank on you, Steve?'

'Not that I can remember.'

'Well then, mark this down in your diary as the first time. Now just drive the fucking car.'

They rode for a way in silence, the DI gazing out of the side window again, lost in his own thoughts. More than once he rubbed gently at his sore shoulder. Only when he saw a large blue sign up ahead did he seem to stir from his musings.

'Next left,' he said, indicating the sign.

Johnson nodded and swung the car into the driveway of the Redman Private Clinic, following the gravel thorough-fare up towards the expanse of tarmac outside the main entrance.

The clinic was a red-brick two-storey building set in a large expanse of grounds, surrounded by well-kept flower beds and neatly clipped privet hedges. Topiary animals stood sentinel along both sides of the driveway and before the short pathway that led up to the main entrance. There was a large pond and small ornamental fountain in the middle of a Japanese garden. As the two policemen climbed out of the car, the sound of running water was a pleasantly soothing accompaniment to the buzzing of bees attracted to the colourful array of plants and flowers.

'And they say money can't buy everything,' Johnson mused, looking round at the picturesque setting and building. 'It can buy decent medical treatment in the best surroundings by the look of it.'

Birch ignored him and walked briskly up the path towards the main entrance.

The automatic doors whirred open to allow the two detectives access to the air-conditioned reception area.

A man in his fifties in pyjamas and a dressing gown was seated in reception reading a paper. There was a tray of tea on the table before him. He glanced up at the two newcomers then returned to his paper.

The receptionist, a woman in her thirties with

her hair pulled back tightly, was on the phone as the two detectives approached her desk. She smiled at them and nodded, holding up a hand as if to keep them at bay until her phone conversation was over.

'Yes, that's fine, Mrs Daniel,' she said, her hand still poised in the air. 'Next Monday at nine-thirty with Dr Jardine. Yes. Goodbye.' She put down the receiver and turned her best and most practised smile on the policemen. 'Can I help you?' she asked cheerfully.

'I'm Detective Inspector Birch,' the older man said. 'This is Detective Sergeant Johnson.' Both men showed their ID. Birch saw the smile fade rapidly. 'You've got a patient on your books, Megan Hunter,' Birch announced. 'I'd like to speak to the doctor who's treating her.'

'That's not possible, I'm afraid,' she told him apologetically.

'It's important,' the DI persisted. 'Could you contact the doctor in question, please?'

The receptionist looked from one man to the other, her smile now gone completely.

'I think Miss Hunter's doctor is in surgery at the moment,' she said, glancing down at something on her desk.

'We can wait,' Birch told her. He turned and headed towards one of the chairs on the other side of reception. Johnson smiled at the woman then joined his superior. Both men settled themselves. The DI reached for a pamphlet about the dangers of high blood pressure. Johnson contented himself with gazing out of the large picture window towards the Japanese garden beyond.

'How long do we wait?' he asked.

Birch glanced at his watch. 'As long as it takes,' he said.

56

Neither of the policemen actually saw the receptionist making her way out from behind her desk and across to them. Birch was gazing distractedly out of the window at the clinic's grounds. Johnson was looking at a copy of *Good Housekeeping* that he'd retrieved from one of the other tables.

The receptionist coughed theatrically as she drew nearer to them and Birch turned to face her.

'Dr Crombie's free now if you still want to see him,' the woman said slowly.

'Thank you.' Birch nodded.

'If you go through those double doors,' she motioned to the partitions away to the right, 'his office is on the right-hand side.'

The two policemen headed off in the direction she'd indicated, each of them checking the name plates on the dark wooden doors as they made their way down the corridor the receptionist had pointed out. Birch spotted the name they sought, nodded towards the door, then knocked.

A voice from inside told them to enter.

Dr Jason Crombie, a balding man in his late forties, rose as they walked in, smiled welcomingly and shook hands with both men.

'Please sit down,' he said cheerily. 'How can I help you?'

'It's about one of your patients,' Birch began. 'Megan Hunter.'

Crombie's smile faded slightly.

'Yes, the receptionist mentioned it,' he said.

'How long have you been treating her?'

'I'm sure you don't need me to tell you that all dealings and conversations between a doctor and his patient are protected by a confidentiality agreement. Not to mention the Hippocratic Oath.'

'I'm fully aware of that, doctor,' Birch said. 'Perhaps I should make you aware that all medical records can be seized if necessary.'

'With the correct paperwork and procedure?' Crombie smiled.

'Yes.'

'I'm assuming you have that paperwork with you.'

'I don't want to see Megan Hunter's medical records,' Birch assured him. 'I just want to know what condition you're treating her for.'

'Patient confidentiality covers written and spoken exchange of information. I'm not required, under law, to tell you anything I don't want to about my patients.' He sat forward in his seat and steepled his fingers before him. 'You must realise, I have no desire to be difficult or to obstruct your investigation, but I have Miss Hunter's well-being at heart. Please understand that.'

'I do understand, doctor,' Birch told him. 'And I'm not asking you to compromise your position or Miss Hunter's in any way. I just want to ask you one or two questions about her condition.'

'How did you know she was receiving treatment here?' Crombie enquired.

'That's not important. All I need to know from you is what she's receiving it for.'

'If I don't tell you, I'm assuming that the necessary action will be taken to seize the medical records you require. Is that correct?'

Birch nodded. 'You'll save all of us a lot of time and trouble if you just answer my questions, doctor,' he said. 'You'll probably also save Miss Hunter a good deal of inconvenience.'

'Considering her circumstances, I'd do anything I can to prevent that,' said Crombie, his voice fading a little. He exhaled deeply.

'Whatever you tell us won't go beyond the three of us,' Birch assured him.

'I must confess to being something of a fan of hers.' The doctor shrugged. 'I've always found her to be a very intelligent and gifted woman and I've thoroughly enjoyed her books.' Again he sighed. 'This is a wonderfully rewarding career most of the time. Seeing patients making full recoveries is very fulfilling, but one accepts that for every triumph there will be a disappointment. A patient will slip away despite all our efforts. I've been in practice for more than twenty years but it still doesn't make those moments easier to bear.'

Birch listened intently, his gaze never leaving the doctor.

'Every life is precious, Detective Inspector,'

Crombie continued. 'But one feels the loss of some more acutely than others. The young particularly. Children. Teenagers. You must feel a similar kind of loss in your own job, especially when you see people dying who are supposed to be beginning their lives.'

Birch nodded.

'I apologise for my monologue.' The doctor smiled. 'I should get to the point. Answer your question. You wanted to know what I was treating Megan Hunter for.'

The DI adjusted his position on the chair and nodded almost imperceptibly.

'She has cancer,' Crombie said wearily. 'An inoperable brain tumour. One of the most aggressive I've ever seen. She's dying.'

57

Birch felt as if he'd been punched in the stomach. He swallowed hard, his brow furrowing more deeply as he continued to look at Crombie.

The doctor merely shrugged helplessly.

'We've given her drugs, of course,' he continued. 'They have minimal effect on the tumour's growth, though.'

'What about radiation therapy?' Birch wanted to know. 'Chemo?'

'She refused all treatment except the drugs. It's almost as if she's accepted it. I think my admiration for her has grown as the time has come closer.'

'How long has she got?'

'Three months, possibly six if she's lucky.'

'But I've seen her. She doesn't look as if she's dying.'

'There's been a little weight loss but other than that very little outward change. It won't manifest itself until the last month or so.'

'How long have you been treating her?'

'Seven months, this time. She came to me complaining of some loss of feeling in the toes of her right foot. Only intermittently. There were few other symptoms. She comes to us every year for a medical anyway. We did a full body scan. That was how we found the tumour. A biopsy showed it to be malignant.'

'Who knows she's ill?'

'You and your colleague now. My staff. Other than that, I don't know who she's chosen to tell.'

'Jesus Christ,' Birch sighed.

'As I said, I would appreciate it if you didn't make Miss Hunter aware that you know of her condition,' the doctor said.

Birch nodded. 'Why did she refuse the radiation treatment?' he enquired.

'She knew that it would only delay the inevitable anyway. That and the chemotherapy could have slowed the growth of the tumour somewhat but not cured it. Miss Hunter was made aware of the side effects.' He smiled affectionately. 'She said that she liked her hair the way it was. That she didn't want to end her life with a head like a boiled egg. Those were her exact words. As I said, my admiration for the way she's accepted her condition is boundless. Most patients with terminal illnesses usually go through three very distinct phases.'

'Denial, anger, and then acceptance,' Birch interjected. 'I know. My first wife died of cancer. I know how it affected her.'

'I'm very sorry,' Crombie said.

Birch attempted a smile. 'Yeah, so am I.'

'Miss Hunter certainly hasn't displayed either of the first two phases at any stage since she was first diagnosed. Certainly not in the presence of myself or any of my staff, anyway.' He lowered his voice reverentially. 'What she does in private, of course, is another matter.'

Birch got to his feet and extended his right hand in Crombie's direction.

The doctor shook it warmly.

'Thank you for your help, doctor,' the DI said. 'We'll get out of your way now.'

'I wish the information I'd given you could have been different.'

Johnson also shook the doctor's hand then the two policemen turned and headed for the door of the office.

As he reached it, Birch hesitated, looking back at the medical man.

'I'm sorry, doctor. You said you'd been treating her for seven months 'this time',' he said. 'Has Megan Hunter received treatment here at the clinic before?'

'Yes,' Crombie told him.

'For the same condition?'

'Oh, good gracious, no.' The doctor smiled wistfully. 'It was for something altogether more pleasant, I'm happy to say. She had her baby here.'

58

It was a moment or two before Birch found the breath to speak. He merely looked accusingly at Crombie as if the information the doctor had just imparted should have been given as soon as the men met.

'How long ago was this?' he breathed, finally, stepping back inside the office with Johnson, who closed the door behind them.

'Well, I'm a little hazy on details,' Crombie confessed, 'as it's not my department, but I'd say it must be ten years now.'

'The doctor who delivered the child. Does he still work here?'

'No. He left, shortly afterwards as a matter of fact.'

'Have you got any idea where he is now?'

'He died, poor chap. Took his own life to be precise. Terrible business. I think he blamed himself for what happened to the child.'

'What do you mean?'

'It died. It couldn't have been more than a year old. It comes back to what I was saying about seeing tragedy in what's an otherwise rewarding career. Doubly sad when you consider that Miss Hunter is now so ill. First she had to suffer the death of her baby and now this. It makes you wonder why some people seem destined to suffer more in their lives than others.'

'Why did the doctor who delivered the child

blame himself for its death?' Birch persisted.

'As I said, I don't know the details.'

'Would there still be records of the birth in your maternity unit?'

'I would think so.'

'I need to see them.'

'Detective Inspector, this really is becoming something of an invasion of Miss Hunter's privacy now.' He held up both hands and shook his head. 'No, I'm sorry. This time I have to refuse and if you feel that I'm obstructing the law in some way then I'm prepared to take the consequences. If you want to examine the gynaecological records you'll have to come back with the necessary paperwork.'

Birch nodded. 'Fair enough,' he said. He stood motionless for a moment longer, his eyes never leaving Crombie's.

The whole scene looked like the frozen frame of a feature film. Then Birch turned and the film was running again.

The two policemen left the office, Crombie walking out with them as if to ensure that they actually left the building.

As the trio reached the reception area the woman seated behind the desk there glanced up worriedly.

'It's all right, Louise,' Crombie said. 'These gentlemen are leaving now.'

She nodded and reached for the phone that had just begun ringing.

'Thanks again for your help, doctor,' Birch said. 'We may well be back to have a look at those birth records.'

'Feel free, Detective Inspector. If you have the necessary paperwork with you when you arrive there should be no problem. However, if you do decide to pry further into this unfortunate case then perhaps you'd be decent enough to inform Miss Hunter.'

'But not inform her that you spoke to me about her illness?' Birch said ironically.

'That was information given in good faith,' the doctor snapped. 'I was trying to help. To spare Miss Hunter any further suffering.'

'I appreciate that. If you want to make sure that I don't have to come back and examine those birth records perhaps you can just do one more thing for me.'

'What is it?'

'Can you remember who the father of Megan Hunter's baby was?'

'Very clearly. He isn't the sort of man you forget easily once you've met him. He's a writer too. Very successful. His name's John Paxton.'

59

'Why the fuck didn't you tell me?'

Birch paced the floor of the hotel room agitatedly, occasionally glancing at Megan Hunter who was seated on one of the chairs close to the largest window. Her laptop, propped on the desk in one corner of the room, was switched on, the screen glowing dully. Megan was gazing out at the traffic in the street below.

'We've already been over this, David. We had dinner so that you could ask me some questions about Frank Denton, Donald Corben and — '

'I know what the questions were about,' Birch interrupted angrily.

'I answered your questions,' Megan continued, her voice low. 'I didn't think I was there to confess my secrets to you.'

Birch shot her an angry glance, dug his hands in his jacket pocket and reached for his cigarettes.

'This is a non-smoking room,' she reminded him.

'What the fuck does that matter?' he rasped. 'Nothing's going to matter to you in six months, is it?'

Megan lowered her head slightly and nodded. When she looked at him again there was a slight smile on her lips.

'No, you're right,' she said sardonically. 'What's a little secondary smoke to someone

262

dying of cancer? A bit like shutting the stable door after the horse has bolted.'

'Megan, I'm sorry,' he said, clamping his jaw together as if wishing he could have kept the words behind his teeth. 'I'm so sorry. I didn't mean that.' He took a step towards her.

'Don't worry about it, David,' she told him, getting to her feet. 'People say things all the time that they don't mean.'

She crossed to the mini-bar and extracted a miniature of Bacardi and some Diet-Coke which she poured into one of the glasses nearby. She turned and looked at him, her eyes moist. 'Join me?'

He nodded.

'Don't tell me, mineral water?' She grinned, reaching for a bottle of Perrier.

He took it from her, his fingers brushing against hers in the process.

'I'm sorry for what I said,' he repeated, watching as she returned to her seat by the window. 'I just can't believe that you said nothing about your illness. Let alone that — '

'That it was terminal?' she cut in. 'It's hardly the kind of thing you bring up over dinner, is it, David?' She took a sip of her drink, her tone hardening slightly. 'Besides, if you hadn't been snooping round my flat you'd still be none the wiser, would you?'

'I wasn't snooping. I told you that. I saw the letter from the clinic. I was curious.'

'You were just doing your job.' She raised her eyebrows.

'I saw enough letters like that before my first wife died.'

'So you thought that visiting the clinic might give you some clue as to whether or not I was the murder suspect you were looking for. You wanted to see if I was being treated for some kind of mental problem? Some kind of schizophrenic or sociopathic condition? Was that it? Or were you just concerned about my health?'

'I suppose so. Maybe.' He drew in a deep breath. 'Fuck it. I'm not sure what the hell I was looking for.'

'Well, now you've found something. Well done.' She raised her glass in mocking salute.

'Who else knows about your illness?' he wanted to know. 'Your agent? Your publishers? Did Frank Denton or Sarah Rushworth know?'

Megan laughed, but there was no humour in the sound.

'Do you think I killed them because they knew I was dying, David?' she sneered. 'No one knows. Not even my parents. What's the point in telling anyone? Nobody can do anything to help me. Why burden them with that kind of knowledge?'

'But the doctor said a biopsy was done. That operation and your recovery would have taken at least a week. Your agent would have wondered where you were.'

'I told her I was going on holiday. It was all very simple.'

There was a heavy silence, broken by the detective.

'Does John Paxton know?' he said flatly.

264

Birch saw the look of surprise and uncertainty flicker momentarily across Megan's features.

'Why would I tell John Paxton something like that?' she challenged.

'He was the father of your child, Megan. He has a right to know, doesn't he?'

She glared at him. 'You really have been busy, haven't you, David?' she rasped. 'No wonder you're so good at your job. What else did you find out about me?'

'You told me the first time we met that you couldn't turn over in bed without someone in publishing knowing about it,' he reminded her. 'How the hell did you and Paxton manage to keep your relationship secret? Never mind the fact that you had his child?'

'When you're as wealthy as John Paxton you can keep anything secret.'

'So how long did your relationship with him last?'

'What business is it of yours?'

'Because you lied to me, Megan. If you lied about that, what else have you lied about?'

'Does this mean I'm a suspect again?'

He raised both hands as if in surrender. 'Jesus,' he breathed. 'I just want to understand.'

'Understand what?' she snapped. 'My illness? My relationship with Paxton? My child?' A single tear rolled down her cheek. 'You're a detective, David. If you want to find out about those things then I'm sure you will. With or without my help.' She drained what was left in her glass. 'Now, if that's all, I'd appreciate it if you left. I've been working hard today. I've got a lot of interviews tomorrow. I'd like to get an early night.' She brought the empty glass down hard on the table and returned to gazing out of the window.

Birch hesitated for a moment, then turned and headed for the door.

With his back to her, his fist already closed round the door handle, he spoke softly.

'I'm sorry,' he told her.

'Don't be,' she answered.

Still gazing out of the window she heard the door close behind him as he left.

60

As he drove through the night-time traffic, Birch felt as if he was drunk. Intoxicated by the amount of information he'd imbibed that day.

Get a fucking grip.

He hit his brakes hard, almost running into the back of a taxi that was stopping to pick up a fare.

Concentrate.

His mind was spinning. The details of Megan's illness. How the hell had she managed to keep it secret from so many people for so long? And the child she had given birth to. Paxton had been complicit in that deception, but why?

And, as if that wasn't enough, there had been the dream. A dream he was reminded of every time he felt the soreness in his shoulder. He hadn't even had time to mention that to her. With the catalogue of revelations he'd already faced, it had seemed almost insignificant.

Almost.

It was a dream. Nothing more.

But dreams didn't leave scars, did they?

Then what was it? You're supposed to deal in facts. Cold, hard facts.

In the dream she had scratched him and now he bore the deep lacerations on his shoulder that could only have been caused by fingernails.

'Sometimes belief is all you need.'

Birch heard Megan's voice inside his head and

it distracted him enough to alert him to the red light he was approaching. He eased down on the brake and sat waiting, his window open, his eyes fixed firmly ahead.

Belief in what? What she'd told him about her own book? About the beliefs of some little known thirteenth-century Italian philosopher?

The DI glanced up at the lights that were still on red.

'Come on, come on,' he murmured, agitated.

He glanced at his watch and saw that it was approaching 11.10 p.m. If the traffic was light enough he should make it to his destination by midnight, he reasoned.

The lights changed to green and Birch accelerated away a little too quickly, his tyres spinning momentarily.

The breeze blowing through the window dried the sweat on his forehead. The night was warm. Sticky and uncomfortable.

Megan Hunter is dying.

He shook his head.

That's got nothing to do with your investigation. And the fact that she had a child by John Paxton ten years earlier? A child that died close to its first birthday. Has that?

He drove on.

It's personal stuff. It's not going to help you find whoever murdered Denton, Corben and Sarah Rushworth, is it?

A vision of Megan's face forced its way into his mind.

She'd be dead in three to six months, the doctor had told him.

What a waste of a life. Just like your own first wife. Is that why the feelings are so strong? Bringing back memories, isn't it? She's almost the same age as your first wife, too, isn't she?

He shook his head as if to clear it. With one hand he fumbled for the switch that would turn on the car stereo. Perhaps some music would distract him from this constant swirl of thought.

A child. Fathered by John Paxton. Why had she lied?

He turned the volume higher.

That's got nothing to do with this case. Forget it.

Birch shifted in his seat, wincing when he felt pain from his badly scratched shoulder again.

The dream. Pleasure and pain in one. So vivid.

'Fuck it,' he rasped, glaring ahead, coaxing more speed from the car.

He looked again at his watch.

Other things to consider now. Focus. Get your fucking head straight.

Another fifteen minutes and he'd be at his destination.

61

Birch brought his car to a halt beside one of the emergency vehicles already parked outside the main entrance to Wandsworth cemetery.

Next to them he saw a Ford and a large, gleaming BMW, both of which had men seated behind their steering wheels. There was also a flatbed truck parked close to the gates and Birch could see half a dozen shovels on it as he swung himself out of the Renault and reached for his cigarettes.

Howard Richardson, clad in his familiar green overalls, waved cheerfully from the open back doors of one of the waiting ambulances. Birch acknowledged the pathologist's greeting then screwed a Rothman's between his lips.

'Everything's ready, guv.'

Birch recognised Detective Sergeant Johnson's voice and nodded as he cupped a hand round his cigarette to light it.

'The gravedigger and the undertaker are here,' Johnson continued, nodding towards the drivers of the Ford and the BMW respectively. 'Lights have been set up round Denton's grave so we can see what we're doing.'

'Let's get this over with then,' the DI said, setting off for the main gates of the cemetery, which had already been opened to allow the passage of any vehicles. As it was, only the truck moved slowly forward, trundling up the wide tarmacked central driveway.

Birch, Johnson and Richardson, flanked by two of his assistants, all followed. They were accompanied by several torch-carrying uniformed officers who walked on either side of the gravedigger and the undertaker. The bizarre little cortège made its way through the cemetery, Johnson glancing off to his right in the direction of Wandsworth Prison.

'I wonder how many we've put in there over the years?' he mused, nodding towards the monolithic structure.

'Not enough,' Birch answered, his eyes fixed straight ahead. He glanced at Richardson. 'Once they dig Denton up and you get him back to the morgue, how long before you can complete the re-examination, Howard?'

'I'll be dusting for prints primarily in the places I didn't check before,' the pathologist told him. 'So it shouldn't be more than two or three hours before I've got some news for you.'

Birch nodded, aware of the loud puttering sound of a small portable generator just ahead.

He saw the truck slow down then come to a halt. Two men clambered out of the cab, lifted shovels from the back of the vehicle and headed off in the direction one of the uniformed officers was indicating with the powerful light of his torch. A halo of light from round the grave also marked the site. The gravedigger and the undertaker followed, the latter almost tripping over one of the cables that ran from the generator.

'It's going to take them a while,' Birch

271

murmured, looking in the direction of the workmen who were just disappearing over a slight rise. He sucked on his cigarette.

'That's the trouble with cemeteries in the dead of night,' Johnson quipped. 'Nowhere to get a drink while you're hanging around waiting for a body to be exhumed.'

Birch managed a smile. He was about to say something when one of the uniformed men came running towards him.

'Sir,' he said breathlessly. 'Could you come with me, please?' The man was already turning, heading back the way he'd come.

Birch, Johnson and Richardson set off at speed with him.

As they reached the top of the small rise, Birch could see the problem.

The four arc lights that had been set up at each corner of the grave illuminated the area perfectly with a cold white luminescence.

Birch and his companions advanced upon the scene, slowing their pace as they reached the graveside.

The flowers that had decorated Frank Denton's final resting place were scattered in all directions. Bouquets still wrapped in cellophane had been hurled everywhere to expose the dark earth beneath, which was itself uneven and disturbed. The gravestone had been pushed over. It lay at an angle to the head of the grave, cracked and spattered with water from the overturned vase that had been knocked from the marble plinth which had supported it.

'How the hell did this happen?' Birch wanted

to know, his eyes taking in the scene of devastation. 'When did you get here, Steve?'

'Over an hour ago,' Johnson told him, his eyes never leaving the desecrated grave. 'I watched the lights being set up and put in place. We've had men on site since ten-thirty tonight.'

The DI surveyed the destruction calmly, the knot of muscles at the side of his jaw throbbing.

'I don't see how anyone could have got to the grave,' Johnson murmured.

'Well somebody did, didn't they?' demanded Birch. 'Let's get Denton's body out of there. We'll worry about how this happened later.' He turned to the two men with shovels and pointed at the disturbed plot. 'Bring him up, fellas.'

'There'll be footprints,' Richardson remarked, looking at the grave. 'The ground isn't that hard.' He dropped to one knee a yard away from the detectives.

'There could be physical on the earth of the grave itself,' Birch offered.

'My priority is examining Denton's body,' Richardson said.

The two men with shovels were already hard at work, grateful that the dirt they were turning had been recently dug.

'Why desecrate his grave?' Birch mused. 'Is the killer taking the piss?'

'There's no way the murderer could have found out Denton was going to be exhumed tonight,' Johnson said.

'Then it's a hell of a fucking coincidence, isn't it? If it is the murderer, he picks the one night he knows we're going to be here to do this.' Birch shook his head, his gaze fixed on the two men who were digging. He was still watching them when he heard a dull thud.

It was the sound of metal on wood.

Both of the diggers stepped back.

'Now what?' Birch said through clenched teeth. He moved closer to the edge of Frank Denton's resting place and looked down.

The lid of the coffin was clearly visible, barely two feet below the surface.

The box lay slightly askew. Birch could see several deep scratches on the lid and sides of the coffin.

'Give me that,' he said, taking the shovel from one of the workmen, who seemed only too happy to surrender the tool.

The DI stepped down into the shallow grave, pushed the shovel under the top of the casket and lifted.

The lid came away easily and Birch peered inside.

The body of Frank Denton was gone.

62

For long moments, Birch and his companions were transfixed by the sight of the empty coffin. Then the DI drove the shovel angrily into the freshly turned earth.

'Somebody talk to me,' he rasped, turning to look at Johnson.

The DS could only shrug as he stepped down into the shallow hole alongside his superior.

Birch knelt close to the battered lid of the coffin and inspected the marks that had been gouged into the wood.

Richardson joined the two detectives, running one index finger over a particularly deep gash in the casket close to where one of the screws had been.

'Claw hammer,' he murmured. 'You can see the two marks made by the hooks.' He indicated similar flaws on the side of the box. 'It looks as if one was used to prise the lid open. Either that or a crowbar.'

'What's that?' Birch enquired, glancing down at something metallic gleaming in the dirt by his feet.

Richardson stooped to pick it up.

'One of the coffin screws,' he announced, holding it up like a trophy between thumb and forefinger. He dropped it quickly into a small, clear plastic evidence bag that he'd taken from his pocket.

'Why take the body?' Johnson wanted to know. 'Unless there were prints on it the killer was afraid we'd find.'

Birch waved the idea away.

'The killer couldn't know what we did or didn't find on the body first time round,' he said dismissively. 'He'd have no reason to suspect we were going to exhume Denton and re-examine him and, even if he did, he couldn't have known when that was going to happen.' Birch sucked in a deep breath. 'And yet he got in here tonight, dug up the coffin, took Denton's body, then put the fucking box back again.' The DI surveyed the grave once more, his anger and frustration building by the second. 'It would have taken him a good hour to dig down to Denton's coffin on his own. Probably the same amount of time to put it back and re-cover it and yet we've had men here for an hour and a half or longer and not one of them saw anyone come or go. Let alone someone carrying a body they'd just disinterred.' He licked his lips, struggling, but failing, to keep his temper. 'What the fuck is going on here?'

Richardson was leaning over the silk-lined coffin, running his fingers over the material. He paused and licked the end of one index finger then pressed the digit into one corner of the casket and raised it before him.

There were several small white particles sticking to it. He tapped Birch's shoulder with his free hand and pushed the finger towards the detective so that he could get a clear view.

'Wood pulp,' Birch stated flatly.

'There's more of it on the underside of the coffin lid,' Richardson noted. 'And in the box itself.'

'And here,' Johnson added, indicating more of the confetti-like substance at the edge of the grave. He stepped up and began looking down at the dark earth around the hole, seeking more of the flimsy matter.

'We'll dust the coffin for prints,' Richardson said. 'And the headstone.'

Birch said nothing. He merely stood motionless, gazing at the scene before him.

A slight breeze blew across the cemetery. It sent some of the wood pulp fluttering into the air. Birch watched the fragments disappear into the night sky like snow carried on a winter wind. Disappearing.

'I want the entire cemetery sealed until forensics have been over it,' he said. 'We're going to nail this bastard.'

63

There was a horrible familiarity about the feeling that filled Birch as he sat in the small, dimly lit room. A re-emergence of feelings he'd done his best to suppress for so many years. He lit another cigarette, ignoring the No Smoking sign on the wall, gazing into space. Lost in his own thoughts. The room at the Springfield Hospital where he and Johnson now sat had transported him backwards in time. To the night when his first wife had died.

He could still recall, all too vividly, the details of that night. As her illness had taken a more firm and unbreakable grip, he'd spent as much time as possible at her bedside. Even when she'd slipped into a coma he'd sat next to her, holding her hand and speaking quietly to her. Telling her about the case he was on.

Couldn't even forget about work when your wife was dying, could you?

The nursing staff had told him that he could do nothing for her and that he'd be better off at home. They'd call him if there were any developments. But Birch had ignored their suggestions. He didn't want to be away from her, even though she was deep in the coma and slipping further away from him every day. He was going to lose her eventually but he had wanted to ensure that he spent every spare second at her side.

He'd tried to prepare himself for what he knew was the inevitable, but when that time had come the news had still hit him with the force of a sledgehammer. He felt as if his soul had been made of glass and the news of her death had shattered that fragile and ethereal part of him. Perhaps for ever.

He remembered sitting in a room like the one in which he now sat, a part of him still refusing to believe that she was dead. Even when he had said goodbye, planting soft kisses on her forehead, nose and lips, he had wondered

(prayed?)

if, for one glorious second, she was going to open her eyes and look up at him. Tell him everything was going to be all right. As he'd left her room the tears had come.

That was why a nurse had guided him to a room like this one and held his hand while he sobbed like a child. It was pain unlike anything he'd ever felt in his life before or since. He was sure that no physical agony could ever match the suffering he'd undergone that night.

He remembered a doctor and a priest coming into the room at some stage. The priest had asked him some questions about faith and Birch could remember telling him that it was difficult to believe in God when he saw the kinds of things he saw from day to day in his job. Even more difficult now the woman he had loved more than anything else in the world was dead. Birch could still remember what he had said to the priest that night.

'They say God moves in mysterious ways,

don't they? Well, I'll tell you what, he's got me fucking stumped this time.'

The DI managed a slight smile at the recollection and Johnson, nursing a plastic cup of strong coffee from the vending machine, saw it.

'Something funny, guv?' he asked.

Birch shook his head, dragged away from his musings by his companion's question.

'No, Steve,' he answered. 'Nothing. Nothing at all.' He dropped his cigarette end into his own cup and got to his feet, pacing the small room slowly. 'How much longer is Richardson going to be?' he wondered aloud. 'We've been here three hours already.'

'I still don't get it,' the younger man said. 'Why desecrate Denton's grave? Why take his body?'

'You don't get it? Join the fucking club.'

The door of the room opened and both men looked round expectantly.

Howard Richardson entered and crossed to the table in the centre of the room. He had removed his green overalls and now looked immaculate in a dark grey suit, his half-moon glasses perched on the end of his nose. He was carrying a thin plastic file with him which he laid on the table.

'The reports are in there,' he announced, tapping the file. 'Everything we've got so far.'

'I'll read them later. Just give me the short version,' Birch asked.

'The coffin was dug up by the same person or persons who murdered Sarah Rushworth,' the pathologist announced. 'There are prints all over the box itself. Identical to the ones found at the last murder scene. They indicate the presence of more than one man, one with syndactylic fingers, the other with brachydactylic.'

'What else?' Birch demanded.

'The coffin lid was removed with a claw hammer as I originally thought. The marks on the lid were caused by the shovel that dug it up.'

'Two men?' Birch mused. 'Both of them coming and going unseen.'

'That's what it looks like,' Richardson answered. 'But the curious thing is that preliminary examination of the ground around the grave showed only one set of footprints.'

Birch frowned. 'So two guys dug up Denton's body and stole it, but only one left tracks?'

'It's ridiculous, I know.'

'That's one word for it,' the DI retorted. 'What about the wood pulp? The same as the stuff found at the three murder scenes like you said?'

'No. That's the curious thing. The paper book printers use is usually cheap stuff. The wood pulp we found in and around the coffin was of a different texture. It was finer, not coarse like the paper they actually print books on. More like typing or computer printer paper. The reason I made that mistake back at the cemetery is because the paper had been so badly pulverised.'

Birch scratched his cheek, the bristles grating against his fingertips.

'We found the wood fibre inside the coffin, as you know.' Richardson paused for a moment before looking at each detective in turn. 'We also found this.' He reached into his jacket and pulled out a folded evidence bag, which he placed on the table next to the plastic file. 'It was in a tear in the lining of the casket.'

The two detectives moved closer to the table and both saw that what was inside the bag was clearly the top half of a page from a book.

Birch picked up the bag and read, through the clear plastic, the words printed at the top of the page.

The Fairground Phantoms.

64

'I want Paxton brought in,' Birch said flatly.

'Arrested?' Johnson asked. 'What for? We've already interviewed him twice and you said yourself you were sure he hadn't got anything to do with the killings.'

'We interviewed him at his home and in his hotel suite,' Birch reminded his companion. 'He was more relaxed then. He was on his own territory. Let's see how he responds inside an interview room.'

'None of the prints found on the coffin or the head-stone belonged to Paxton,' Richardson interjected.

'Maybe not, but what the fuck was this doing inside the box?' Birch held up the portion of page from Paxton's book.

'Paxton couldn't have dug up that coffin and removed the body,' the pathologist protested. 'Not in the time established. It isn't possible. Even if he did, why put a page from his own book there? He'd know it would lead you straight to him.'

'Well, once we get him back to the Yard we'll find out what game he's playing,' Birch snapped.

'When do you want to pick him up, guv?' Johnson asked.

'Now,' Birch said, already turning towards the door.

The two cars moved swiftly along the virtually deserted streets, encountering little traffic at such an early hour of the morning.

Birch led the way, often driving faster than necessary and occasionally having to slow the Renault slightly to allow Johnson to keep up with him.

The DS had asked whether Birch wanted support but the older man had said no. He couldn't foresee any problems with Paxton, and even if there was some protest from the writer Birch had no doubt that he and Johnson could handle it themselves.

Birch turned his car into the forecourt of the Savoy. He parked and clambered out, watched by a porter who, moments later, saw a second car arrive and come to a halt behind the Renault.

The detectives made their way through the main door of the hotel, past the porter who merely looked on silently as the two men strode onwards through a deserted reception towards the lift that would take them up to Paxton's room.

'What's the charge?' Johnson asked as the lift rose.

'Conspiracy to commit murder,' Birch told his companion. 'Unless we stick with plain old grave-robbing.' He raised his eyebrows.

'Guv, you don't really think — '

'Ask me what I think after we've interviewed him again,' Birch cut in.

The lift bumped to a halt and the detectives

strode out, heading for the suite they knew Paxton occupied.

The DI knocked firmly on the white-painted door and waited.

'Perhaps he's entertaining.' Johnson smiled. 'Some publicity girl probably. Either that or he's out and about somewhere.'

Birch ignored the comment and knocked again. Harder and more forcefully.

Still no answer.

There was a click from behind them and the door of the room next door opened a fraction. A man peered out sheepishly, saw the two detectives and retreated back into his own room.

Birch banged again on the door of Paxton's suite.

'Come on,' the DI muttered. 'How fucking long does it take to get out of bed?'

He hammered four times with his fist.

When he still heard no sounds of movement from inside, Birch stepped away from the door, his eyes focusing on a white house phone on the wall a few yards away. He picked up the receiver and jabbed the button marked 'Reception'.

'Hello,' he said. 'Yes, it's Mr Paxton in room 816. I can't find my key. Can you send someone up to let me in, please?'

The receptionist said that someone would be there immediately.

Birch replaced the handset and returned to the door, where he leaned against the frame.

A moment later a bell sounded and the lift doors slid open to reveal the same porter who'd seen the detectives arrive.

285

'Open it, please,' Birch instructed, flashing his ID and indicating the door behind him.

The porter hesitated a moment, then took a plastic pass key from his pocket and slid it into the lock. The green light flashed and Birch pushed past him into the room.

The stench hit him immediately.

'Get him out,' the DI said to Johnson, who thanked the porter and gently urged him back out into the corridor.

Birch slapped on light switches and the suite was illuminated by half a dozen lamps.

Johnson stood beside him and the two detectives gazed as though hypnotised at what lay before them, the smell now clogging their nostrils like noxious gas.

The younger man blew out his cheeks.

'My God,' he said flatly.

'I don't think God had anything to do with this,' Birch murmured quietly.

65

John Paxton was spreadeagled on the bed. The duvet, sheets and blankets looked as if they'd been carefully and systematically immersed in blood. Barely an inch remained uncovered by the crimson liquid, which was congealing in places. Huge arterial spurts had sprayed two of the walls. More of the sticky red fluid had soaked into the carpet round the bed. There were splashes on the ceiling, the furniture and a painting that hung above the bed.

'Same MO,' Johnson said, walking further into the room behind his superior.

'Looks like it,' Birch confirmed, gazing at the ruined body of the writer.

Paxton's torso had been split open from sternum to groin, his intestines torn free of the cavity. A length of bloated, bloodied entrail hung down as far as the gore-sodden carpet. Birch couldn't help but think that the body looked like an animal carcass hung in a slaughterhouse. The place certainly smelled and looked like an abattoir.

Where Paxton's genitals should have been there was nothing more than a gaping red hole, dried blood forming a crust round the ragged edges.

His head, severed just below the chin, was propped jauntily on one of the pillows.

Both eyes were missing.

'Looks like the killer took his time,' Birch said. 'Did the job he wanted to do on the other three.'

'Someone must have heard,' Johnson offered. 'Paxton must have screamed . . . ' The sentence trailed off.

Birch walked over to the windows and gently eased back the net curtains.

'Windows are locked from the inside,' he said. 'Same as the door.'

'Just like the other three,' Johnson mused. 'Reckon Paxton knew his killer as well?'

'It looks that way,' Birch conceded.

He turned back to look at the butchered corpse and saw the by now all too familiar specks of matter he had come to dread.

There was wood pulp on the body and on the floor beside the bed.

'Have a look in the bathroom,' he instructed. 'See if there's anything . . . unusual. It looks as if he might have had company.' He pointed to two empty glasses on one of the bedside tables. There was some dark liquid left at the bottom of the taller one. Birch crossed to the table, ducked down and sniffed.

Bacardi in there with the Coke.

Next to it was a whisky tumbler that also still contained some fluid. Birch sniffed the contents of that as well.

Had Paxton been drugged? Was that why no one heard anything while he was being carved up? Poor fucker was already flat out when the killer went to work?

He could hear Johnson's footsteps echoing on

the marble floor as he inspected the contents of the bathroom.

Birch moved slowly round the bed, his gaze never leaving Paxton's corpse as he scanned every single horrific wound and laceration. There were several very deep cuts to the chest and shoulders, one of which had gouged away so much flesh it had exposed a collar bone.

Apparently oblivious of the cloying odour of blood and excrement, the DI moved nearer to the bed, inspecting the severed head more closely.

There were a few scratches round the blood-filled sockets where the eyes should have been, but other than that the skin of the face looked remarkably unblemished. The lips were parted slightly, and Birch could see that more blood had welled over and dribbled down the chin.

The DI fished in his inside pocket for a pen and tried to open the mouth, fearing that rigor mortis may have set the jaws as solidly as tetanus. He was delighted to find that his worries were unfounded. The mouth opened easily. Several large clots of congealed blood fell away, further staining the already ruined sheet and pillowcase beneath. Birch peered into the mouth. It was like gazing into an open wound.

The tongue was gone.

'Nothing unusual in the bathroom,' Johnson announced, re-entering the bedroom. 'Nothing to suggest anyone else has been here tonight.'

'We'll see what forensics say,' Birch answered, his gaze still fixed on the severed head. He used his pen as a pointer, indicating the areas round Paxton's eyes and mouth. 'I reckon he was dead before his eyes and tongue were taken. It looks as if the killer cut off his head first and then took them. There doesn't seem to have been much struggling from Paxton. If there had been there'd be more cuts and scratches around the eyes and mouth.'

Johnson moved closer to the corpse and looked down at the hands.

Apart from a deep gash across the palm of the left and another between the index and middle finger of the right, there was little damage.

'Hardly any defence cuts,' the DS observed. 'That's weird.'

'Perhaps one of the first stab wounds killed him,' Birch remarked. 'That one, probably.' He pointed at a large wound just below the sternum. 'If he died quickly that'd explain why there was no screaming. Once Paxton was dead, the killer would have been able to take his time.'

'How long do you reckon he's been dead?'

Birch shrugged. 'Five or six hours, tops. That'd put the time of death between ten and eleven.'

Birch again found his attention drawn to the tall glass on the bedside table next to the whisky tumbler.

Prints on there with a bit of luck. Prints all over the place probably.

He stepped back.

'Get on the blower, Steve,' he said, still running appraising eyes over the appalling scene before him. 'Get some support over here.

Interview as many guests as you can to start with. Somebody might have seen or heard something. Call in the forensics team and anything else you need. You know the drill. Same routine as usual. You can handle it until I get back.' He was already turning towards the door.

'Where are you going, guv? If you don't mind me asking.'

'I'll speak to you later,' Birch said. He smiled. 'You wanted a bit more responsibility, didn't you? Now you've got it.'

Johnson was about to say something else, but realised that his superior was already gone.

He stood silently in the room, glanced down once more at the butchered remains of John Paxton, then reached for his phone and stabbed in a number.

66

'I didn't expect to see you again.'

Megan Hunter rubbed a hand through her tousled hair and pulled her robe more tightly around her. 'Especially not at this time in the morning. I told you earlier that I've got interviews to do tomorrow and that I wanted to get a good night's sleep — '

'This is important,' Birch cut in. 'I wouldn't have disturbed you if it wasn't.'

Megan sighed. Birch thought how pale she looked. The dark rings beneath her eyes made it look as if someone had smudged charcoal on the flesh there. Without make-up she looked wan and pallid.

Was it just tiredness or her illness?

'I need to talk to you,' he said quietly. 'It'd be easier to do that inside your room rather than out here in the corridor.'

Megan stepped aside almost reluctantly and ushered him into the hotel room.

Birch stood with his hands behind his back, watching as she flicked on a couple of the lamps then clambered on to the bed, drawing her slender legs up beneath her.

'OK, are you going to tell me what's so important?' she asked, motioning for him to sit.

'I wanted you to hear this from me,' he told her, perching on the end of the bed.

Megan shrugged.

'John Paxton was murdered in his hotel room tonight,' the detective said. 'By the same person who killed Denton, Corben and Sarah Rushworth.'

She looked blankly at him for a moment.

'Nothing to say?' he asked quietly. 'You don't look very shocked at the news. Especially considering you and Paxton were lovers. You had his child.'

'Ten years ago.'

'Do you ever think about it? About what might have been between you and Paxton?'

'Did you come here to tell me he was dead or to psycho-analyse me?'

'I was curious.'

'Goes with the job, I suppose.'

'You had an affair with Paxton ten years ago.'

'So did a lot of other women,' she countered. 'Ask his wife. If anyone had reason to kill him it was her.'

'You got pregnant by him and had his child. What you had between you must have been more than just a fling. Were you in love with him?'

'What's that got to do with his death?'

'That's what I'm trying to work out.'

'Just because you come here and tell me that John Paxton's been murdered and I don't burst into tears you think there's something strange. When I got pregnant, it wasn't planned. Accidents happen.' She pulled a couple of pillows behind her and lay back on them.

'How did Paxton react when he found out you were pregnant?'

'He didn't want me to have the baby. He said it would be ruining my career before it even started. I'd already had my first novel published.' She smiled bitterly. 'Of course, he also didn't want his wife to find out what had happened. He offered to pay for an abortion but I insisted on having the baby.'

'Are you Catholic?'

'No, I'm not, but Catholics don't have the monopoly on conscience when it comes to abortion. I considered having it adopted or even keeping it.' She lowered her gaze a little, her voice softening. 'But there were problems. The child was born with Cushing's syndrome. It's a problem that affects the pituitary gland. It causes the baby's body to develop at twice the rate it should. It can also cause deformity because the body can't cope with such accelerated growth.'

'Is that why the baby died?'

Megan nodded. 'I was prepared to look after him,' she said. 'Paxton wanted no part of it, apart from offering to give me some money every month. Even the doctors advised against it, but it didn't matter in the end.' She looked at him. 'He was just over a year old when he died. But you already know that.'

'So you got pregnant around the time you were researching your book on Dante. The time you first found out about Giacomo Cassano and his theories.'

'What's that got to do with anything?'

'Was Paxton with you in Italy?'

'The baby was conceived there.'

'Did he know about Cassano's teachings? This

idea of creative people being able to enter and leave something that had originated in their mind?'

'Yes, he did.'

'And he believed it?'

'What's this got to do with his death, David?'

'We found a piece of his latest book inside Frank Denton's coffin when we exhumed it tonight. The coffin, by the way, was empty. Denton's body had been stolen. Could Paxton have been responsible? There was wood pulp in the casket too, just like there was at every murder scene. Could Paxton have written a passage or a chapter of a book and described the body of Denton being stolen?'

'Are you trying to tell me you suddenly believe what I told you about Cassano's teachings?'

Birch slowly shrugged off his jacket, then he tugged off his tie and began unfastening his shirt buttons.

'What are you doing?' Megan demanded.

He opened his shirt slightly, pulling the material away from his shoulder to expose the still-red scratches there.

'Do you know how those got there?' he asked.

Megan shook her head.

'I dreamed about you the other night,' he told her. 'You and I. We were having sex. You scratched me. Here.' He patted the red marks on his shoulder. 'In the dream, I kissed your back. You've got a mole on your left shoulder blade and another on the small of your back, to the left of your spine. How could I know that unless I'd seen them? Unless I'd seen you naked?'

Megan got to her feet and began slowly undoing the belt that held her robe together. She pulled it free and shrugged the material off, allowing it to drop at her feet. Birch watched unblinking as she stood naked before him, his gaze taking in the sensuous contours of her body. She turned slowly and he looked at her back.

Especially at the mole on her left shoulder blade. It was slightly larger than the one on the small of her back.

'Sometimes, belief is all you need,' she said quietly.

67

Birch shook his head slowly. He felt as if someone had wrapped his body in freezing bandages.

'I don't expect you to believe it, David,' she told him, bending to retrieve her robe and pull it back on. 'I know it's alien to your way of thinking. That it contradicts all rationality. But what more proof do you want?'

'How does it work?' Birch said quietly, watching as she fastened the robe once more. 'What do you do?'

'I can't explain it to you.' She shrugged. 'I'm not even sure myself. All I know is that Cassano was right. That his theories were correct. Something imagined within the mind of a writer, or anyone else creative, extends beyond the word on the page or the paint on the canvas. The world an artist invents can become real to the one who created it. They can interact with it. Become a part of it. Enter and leave it.'

Birch felt his heart thudding harder against his ribs.

'And Paxton knew this too?' he said. 'Believed it? Knew how to use this power?'

Megan chuckled. 'I'm not sure power is the right word,' she said and there was a hint of derision in her voice.

'Whatever the fuck it is,' Birch snarled.

'Yes, he knew.'

'Did he kill Denton, Corben and Sarah Rushworth?'

'He didn't have to.'

'Don't talk to me in riddles, Megan,' Birch hissed. 'He killed them all, didn't he? And he stole Denton's body too. Using this . . . thing, this power that Cassano talked about.'

'The seeds of the soul,' she reminded him gently.

'I don't believe it,' Birch said flatly.

'You don't want to believe it. You're frightened to believe it. Frightened of the power of the mind. Of your own mind.'

He shook his head.

'Do you believe that you and I made love the other night?' she asked. 'You said yourself that there was no other way you could have known about the moles on my back. No other explanation for how you came to have those scratches. You must have believed, David, or you wouldn't be here now.'

'Did it happen?'

'What do you think?'

'Just give me a straight answer,' he rasped, getting angrily to his feet.

'Do you believe it happened, David?' she persisted.

He glared at her, as if seeking the answer to her question in her eyes.

'Yes,' he said, finally, his voice little more than a whisper.

When she smiled at him, Birch again wondered if what he saw in that expression was something like scorn. Or triumph?

'I wanted you to believe,' she told him, the smile fading.

'Paxton wasn't responsible for what happened between us.'

'No. I was. I created it and gave it life. I wrote it down and it happened. I wanted to prove to you that what I'd told you, what Cassano believed, was true.'

Birch began pacing back and forth. 'You still haven't answered my question,' he snapped. 'Did Paxton kill the others?'

'Every victim was found in a locked room with no signs of forced entry,' she said quietly. 'No one saw the killer come or go. That's right, isn't it?'

He stopped pacing and regarded her warily.

'In every case, the murderer got into the victim's room without a problem,' Megan continued. 'Entered, mutilated them, then left. Always unseen. Never leaving any clues other than the odd fingerprint. And, at every scene, there was a copy of John Paxton's latest book. Torn apart. Shredded.' She paused as if allowing her words to permeate Birch's mind. 'The reason no one ever saw the killer, the reason the victims were always taken by surprise, the reason the rooms were always locked from the inside, is because the killer was already in the room with the victims.'

'That's impossible,' Birch said dismissively. 'There's not a shred of evidence to suggest that.'

'What's your explanation for the wood pulp that was found on every body? For the torn-up copies of Paxton's books scattered about the scenes?'

'We haven't got an explanation.'

'The killer came from inside the book.'

For a moment, Birch didn't know whether to laugh or not. Instead he smiled humourlessly and shook his head.

'The person who murdered Frank Denton, Donald Corben and Sarah Rushworth lives inside a novel written by John Paxton? That killer periodically comes out of the book, slaughters someone, then escapes back into the novel? That's what you're telling me?'

Megan nodded.

'If that's the case,' Birch continued, 'if, for one minute, I forget everything I've learned over the years, if I ignore the fact that what you've just told me is insane, if I accept that three people are dead because some thirteenth-century Italian writer came up with a theory that practically got him wiped out of every history book ever written and if I accept that the world's most successful horror writer was responsible for the murders of three people, there's still one other problem. Who the fuck killed John Paxton?'

68

'The answer is in his books,' Megan told the policeman.

'Bullshit,' Birch snapped.

'I'm trying to help you, David,' she insisted. 'I'm right about the killings, aren't I? About all the rooms being locked? About there being very little trace of the murderer? About no one having seen him come or go?'

Birch nodded.

'Then why can't you accept what I'm telling you?' she demanded.

'That the killer came out of a book, murdered his victims, then disappeared back inside it again? No.'

'You believed what happened between you and me. Our lovemaking. That's why I scratched you, so you'd know it was more than a dream.' She moved closer to him, resting one hand on his thigh. 'When I climaxed, you told me to keep my eyes open. To look at you when I came. Remember?'

He tried to swallow but his throat was bone dry.

'That's true,' he admitted, putting one hand over hers and squeezing gently.

'All that can happen again,' she told him.

'What are you going to do? Write about us?'

She reached out and touched his face with her free hand, gazing deeply into his eyes.

'I don't need to write it,' she whispered.

'You were with Paxton tonight, weren't you?' he said, reaching up to grip her wrist. He lowered her hand gently from his face. 'At his hotel.'

'I didn't kill him,' she said, pulling away slightly.

'Then who did?'

'I've already told you, the answer is in his book. Read it, David. Then perhaps you'll understand.'

'I want you to tell me, Megan. You make me understand.'

'There's a character in four of his books, including the new one. He called it the Wrathchild. A being born from hatred.'

'And that's what killed Denton, Corben and Sarah Rushworth? This . . . Wrathchild?'

'It was summoned from the book, and used to kill them. Then it returned.'

'Returned to where?'

'In Paxton's novels, it lives in a huge deserted amusement park. That's why his new book is called *The Fairground Phantoms*. He said he was going to use the Wrathchild in one more novel and then kill it off. He told me that again tonight.'

'So did the Wrathchild kill Paxton too?'

'Yes.'

'But why would he summon his own creation to murder him?'

'He didn't. I did.'

'Why?'

'He knew about my illness. That I was dying.

As you know, I've managed to keep it a secret from nearly everyone. Paxton was threatening to go to the media and tell them about my cancer and about our affair.'

'But why would he do that?'

'Because he never accepted that it was over between us. He wanted us to become an item again. When I refused he tried to blackmail me by saying he'd tell the press about us and about my illness. I couldn't allow that, David. When my time comes I don't want to die surrounded by cameras. I don't want my friends and family grilled by the press on matters they know nothing about. Especially about the baby I had.'

'So you summoned the Wrathchild to kill Paxton?'

She nodded. 'Do you want to arrest me now, David?' she asked. 'Even if you manage to convince a court that I was responsible for Paxton's death, I'll be dead before I ever set foot inside a prison cell. I had a death sentence passed on me when I found out my tumour was inoperable.'

Birch ran a hand through his hair, his mind spinning.

'Jesus Christ,' he whispered.

'I appreciate the problems you'd have trying to get a jury to accept what I've just told you. I mean, look how hard it's been to convince you.'

'Why did Paxton want Denton, Corben and Sarah Rushworth dead? Why wait until now? If he's had this knowledge for ten years why not use it before?'

She merely smiled at him.

303

'You summoned the Wrathchild to kill the others as well, didn't you?' Birch stated. 'You. Not Paxton. It was always you, wasn't it? Right from the beginning. Why, Megan?'

'You know yourself that when someone discovers they're dying they go through those three recognisable states of mind. The denial. The anger. The acceptance.' She sucked in a deep breath. 'Well, there's another stage too. The bitterness.' Her tone hardened. 'When I was first told that I was going to die I felt cheated. As far as I was concerned there were other people who deserved to die more than I did. People like Donald Corben. A man who'd been so spiteful about my work and so many others' too. People like Corben don't serve any useful purpose. They only exist to destroy. They revel in causing distress to people who have no way of getting back at them. I felt as if I was tidying up loose ends. It's as simple as that.' She smiled weakly. 'There's nothing worse in a novel than to have loose ends and unresolved situations.'

'What about Frank Denton? Why have him killed?'

'He read my first novel. He told me that it was promising but that it needed work. That we should meet over dinner one evening and discuss it. I was naive. Stupid. So I agreed. He said that if I slept with him he'd make sure my novel was accepted.' She gazed into space. 'I believed him. So, I slept with him. I was that desperate for success. That was the price I was willing to pay in those days.' Megan smiled at the detective but there was no humour in the expression, only a

304

kind of sadness. 'It's even more ironic that he then turned my novel down. It was accepted by another publisher eventually.'

'And Sarah Rushworth? What did she do to you? Were you jealous because Paxton had an affair with her?'

'He had an affair with her less than a month after I'd given birth to his child.'

'But she didn't know about that. You said no one knew about the baby or about you and Paxton.'

'She betrayed me. Whether she did it knowingly or not doesn't change things.'

'So you had her killed?'

'Paxton caught something from her,' Megan said flatly. 'A sexually transmitted disease. He passed it on to me. She gave it to him and he gave it to me. She infected me, David.'

'Paxton infected you. He was the one fucking around.'

'He caught the infection from that slut. As I said, David, I was just tying up loose ends. I'm leaving this world soon. I just wanted to make sure that others less . . . deserving didn't enjoy the life that I was going to be denied.'

'How many more have got to die before you're satisfied, Megan?' he wanted to know. 'How many more people in your life have pissed you off so much you want to see them dead? Who else has stuck it to you so bad you want to take them with you?' He held her gaze challengingly. 'And what about me? I know all your secrets now. How long before you summon the Wrathchild to kill me?'

69

'I don't wish you any harm, David,' she told him. 'You haven't done anything to me.'

'I could arrest you on the spot. What you've just told me amounts to a confession. You might not have held the knife, Megan, but you're directly responsible for the murders of four people.'

'So take me in, detective,' she said, grinning, both arms extended before her. 'Put the handcuffs on.' She laughed and the sound raised the hairs on the back of the DI's neck. 'I can't wait to hear what you put in your report. And do you honestly think that anyone other than you is going to believe my confession? Think about it, David. It's taken me long enough to convince you of the truth. Do you think you could be as persuasive with your colleagues or with a jury?'

'What do you expect me to do? Just walk away from here? Pretend I've heard none of it? You said you were with Paxton tonight. I'm guessing that my forensics guys can place you in his hotel room close enough to the time of death for me to pull you in for questioning.'

'And after the questioning?'

Birch looked irritably at her. 'Where the hell is this thing now?' he demanded. 'The Wrathchild. Where is it?'

'Back where it belongs.'

'Until you summon it again to carve up some

other poor fucker that's crossed you in the past?'

She looked defiantly at him.

'Have you got any more scores to settle while you still can, Megan?'

'It doesn't need me any more, David,' she said quietly.

'What the hell are you talking about?'

'The Wrathchild. It isn't dependent upon me summoning it for it to leave its home.'

'What the fuck are you trying to say? That it can come out of Paxton's book any time it feels like it?'

'Any time. Anywhere.'

'Bollocks. You said it had to be summoned. Controlled by you or by Paxton when he was alive.'

'I never told you that. I said that we could control it. Not that it was reliant on us. All I did was guide it, David. It possesses the freedom to come and go between our world and the one created for it. Between truth and reality. It's the ultimate illustration of Cassano's theory that imagination and thought could become tangible. Burn every copy of every book Paxton's ever written and the Wrathchild will still exist in the place created for it. Even after I'm dead it'll live on. It's able to emerge when and where it likes. Free to kill whoever it chooses. Anyone with a copy of one of Paxton's books in their home is a potential victim.'

'Was that what you wanted? You're going to die so fuck everyone else? Let them die too?'

'I never intended it to happen,' she told him.

'For it to be free to move between our world and its own.'

'So who the fuck gave it that freedom?' he rasped.

'Paxton, obviously.'

'Why would he do that?'

'I don't know.' Her tone was almost apologetic.

'It'll be killing his fans if what you say is true. Surely he wouldn't have wanted that.'

'Then you've got to stop it.'

He looked angrily at her. 'How am I supposed to do that? What are you going to do? Summon it from one of the books and let me arrest the fucking thing?'

'No. I'll send you into the book to find the Wrathchild.'

70

For what seemed like an eternity, Birch didn't speak. He merely held Megan's gaze.

'There's no other way,' she told him.

Still he didn't utter a word. Thoughts tumbled over and over inside his head.

'Why can't you summon it?' he said, finally. 'Bring it to me.'

Can you hear yourself? Do you know how fucking crazy you sound? She's going to write you into a book. Do me a favour. Which madhouse would you like to reserve your room in?

'It'll kill you, David,' she told him.

'Not if I'm waiting for it with an Armed Response Unit. As soon as the fucking thing shows its face, it's dead.'

'It'll be ready for that. It isn't stupid.'

'But you can write its death. If you control it then you can manipulate its movements.'

'I told you before. It doesn't need me any more. It moves freely. It may not even respond if it's summoned.'

He ran a hand through his hair.

There you go. Now you know. Some fictional creature might decide not to pop its head out of a fucking novel to have the shit blown out of it. Simple as that.

Birch sucked in a deep breath.

'You're going to send me into a book,' he

murmured, even managing a smile. 'I still find it hard to believe, Megan. In spite of everything you've told me.'

She wandered across the hotel room to the desk where her laptop was waiting.

'Then let me prove it to you again,' she said, sitting down at the keyboard. 'You believe those scars on your shoulder. You believe we made love. Let me send you somewhere that'll prove to you once and for all that what I've said is true.'

He raised his hands in a supplicatory gesture. 'What do I have to do?' he asked. 'Turn round three times and count to five?'

'Just sit down.'

She rested her fingers gently on the keys of the laptop as Birch did as he was instructed.

'What was your first wife's name?' she wanted to know.

'Why?'

'Just tell me.'

'Claire,' he said softly.

Megan began to type, her fingers moving swiftly over the keys. Birch watched, listening to the clicking sound, watching words appear on the screen before her that were too small for him to read properly. He rubbed his eyes, suddenly tired.

'What was she wearing the last time you saw her?' Megan asked, her fingers still skipping rapidly over the keyboard.

Birch told her, his eyelids now feeling as if someone had attached weights to them.

He was aware of Megan's voice but it seemed to be coming from a great distance away. The words were barely audible now. He tried to focus on her but her image swam before him. He tried to speak her name but it was as if someone had sewn his lips shut.

He heard music, and for a moment he thought he was imagining it. Soft, soothing music that seemed as if it was being piped directly into his skull.

Then he saw the coffin before him.

71

Apart from the music, the only sound Birch could hear was his own breathing. He looked round the room in which he stood, noticing the heavy, red velvet curtains that covered the wall behind the coffin. The carpet inside the chapel of rest was thick and muffled his footsteps as he moved towards the casket.

The box itself was open.

The woman inside was dressed in a black jacket and a white blouse. Her make-up had been freshly applied but sparingly as she had used it in life. In fact, if he hadn't known better he would have thought that she still lived. At any moment he expected her eyes to open. Expected her to gaze up at him and smile. Birch gritted his teeth.

He looked down at her and felt his heart beating faster.

There was a tiny silver crucifix round her neck, glinting in the subdued lights of the room.

He had bought it for her on the occasion of their first wedding anniversary and he still remembered her horror when the chain had broken and the piece of jewellery had, they thought, been lost in the garden one Sunday afternoon.

How she had loved that garden. Tending it. Caring for the flowers and plants with infinite care. A single red rose, cut by Birch himself the previous day, lay on the plinth where the coffin rested.

He almost smiled as he recalled how they had both been out in the garden until late that Sunday night, searching in the dark earth for the crucifix. She had found it eventually, glinting in the beam of the torch she'd used to aid their quest to recover that most prized, loved and valued possession. It seemed a century ago. Just like the last time he had felt true happiness.

Now he reached down gently and touched her cheek.

Her flesh felt so smooth, as it always had done, and Birch was overwhelmed by the desire to lift her up in his arms and hold her for the last time. The following day was the funeral, when he would stand at her graveside and watch as the box was lowered into its final resting place.

More than once he had wondered if he would have the courage to endure that. He had questioned his own ability to even appear at the service. The thought of listening to the priest droning on about the woman he would never see again and yet still loved so deeply was almost intolerable.

Birch unconsciously touched his wedding ring, turning the gold circlet on his finger.

He felt tears forming in his eyes and, when he spoke her name softly, it was all he could do to maintain control over his emotions.

'I love you,' he murmured, touching her cheek once more.

The undertaker had told him that he could stay with her for as long as he liked, but Birch had decided that he had to leave. To look at her lying there before him was more than he could bear, knowing that she would never reach out for him again. He sucked in a deep breath and it smelled of polished wood and her make-up.

He hesitated a moment longer, then reached out and gripped the crucifix in one hand.

He pulled sharply and the thin silver chain that held it in place round her neck snapped easily.

Birch looked at the cross then closed his hand round it, turned and headed for the door.

The music was still playing, but, again, it was as if the melodies were inside his head, trapped there like wasps in a jar.

He felt dizzy, and for a moment he thought he was going to faint. There were chairs outside in the corridor. He knew he had to get to one, had to rest for a moment.

He sat down heavily, his fists still clenched, beads of perspiration on his brow.

'David.'

He heard his voice being spoken quietly and he blinked hard to clear his vision.

'David.'

He looked up, expecting to see his wife standing close to him.

He raised his head slowly.

Megan Hunter was looking at him.

'David,' she said again.

Birch moved to stand up but she shook her head.

'Sit still.'

He was struggling to get his breathing under control. When he tried to speak his throat was dry. He coughed, eyeing the glass of water that she pushed towards him.

As he prepared to reach for it he was aware that both his fists were still clenched and he slowly opened them.

Something fell from one.

He looked down and saw what it was.

Megan too was gazing at the object lying at his feet.

Birch reached down and picked up the tiny silver crucifix, cradling it in his palm.

'I saw Claire,' he said quietly.

'In the chapel of rest,' Megan added. 'The last place you ever saw her.'

He nodded slowly. 'You put me there and brought me out again.' He looked down at his clothes. 'Where's the wood pulp? The torn paper? Like we found on all the victims?'

'The Wrathchild came out of books that had already been printed on paper. What I just wrote is only here on the screen.' She turned the laptop so he could read what she'd typed. 'Look.'

'Detective Inspector Birch stood next to the coffin looking at his wife, Claire.'

He read the words aloud.

'He reached in and pulled the crucifix from round her neck.'

'But she was buried wearing that cross,' Birch protested, gripping the crucifix between his thumb and forefinger.

Megan hit the 'Delete' button on the keyboard

and the words on the screen began to disappear one by one.

'She still is,' Megan told him.

Birch looked down at his hand.

The crucifix was gone.

72

Detective Sergeant Stephen Johnson hadn't uttered a word for close to half an hour.

At first because he'd been listening so avidly to what his superior had been saying that there was no need to respond, but then, as Birch had continued, the younger man had found silence preferable because he simply could not find words to express what he wanted to say and certainly none appropriate to describe what he'd heard.

The two men sat opposite each other in the deserted Riverside Restaurant of the Savoy, the first light of dawn crawling meekly across the sky.

Uniformed and plain clothes police officers were still coming and going through the foyer of the hotel, watched by the members of staff unfortunate enough to be working at such an early hour.

No guests had yet ventured down from their rooms, something the staff were grateful for. More than one of them had already tried to imagine the kind of publicity the night's comings and goings were going to generate.

Birch took another drag on his cigarette and looked at his colleague.

'If you don't want to do this,' he said quietly, 'I'll understand.'

Johnson could only shrug. 'It's not that,' he

breathed. Again he found it difficult to force out the right words. He felt as if he'd suddenly been robbed of the power of speech.

'I know what you're thinking, Steve. I was the same to begin with. But I'm telling you now, I believe what Megan Hunter said last night.'

'Who else have you told?' Johnson muttered.

'No one.' The DI managed a smile. 'Do you blame me?'

Johnson shook his head slowly.

'We've worked together for a long time now,' Birch reminded him. 'Have I ever steered you wrong on anything? Ever lied to you or stitched you up?'

Again the younger man shook his head.

'And I'm not going to start now,' the DI said. 'Like I said, if you don't want to do this, I understand. But someone's got to and if I have to do it alone then I will.'

'The whole thing . . . ' Johnson couldn't even complete the sentence.

'Is fucking crazy,' Birch finished for him. 'I know that. But like I said to you earlier, if you look at all the facts there is no other explanation for these murders. Even forensics haven't been able to help much or give us anything worthwhile to go on. I believe what Megan Hunter told me because there's nothing else to believe.' He glanced at his watch. 'I want a five-man Armed Response Unit here in two hours. I'll go and pick up Megan Hunter myself.'

'And then?'

'We close this fucking case once and for all.'

'What are you going to tell the ARU guys?'

318

'As little as I can get away with. The same goes for the Commissioner when all this is over. Now all I need to know from you, Steve, is are you in or out?'

Johnson sat forward in his seat, exhaling deeply, his mind still spinning.

Birch took a final drag on his cigarette then ground it out in a nearby ashtray.

'When I sign out our weapons what do I say?' the younger man asked, finally, looking at his superior.

'Tell them we're in pursuit of an armed and highly dangerous suspect.' Birch smiled. 'You won't be lying.'

Johnson nodded and both men got to their feet.

'Back here in two hours?' he asked.

'Five men and the two of us.' Birch nodded, preparing to leave with his companion.

'Can you trust Megan Hunter, guv?' the younger man said falteringly.

'I told you, I believe what she said and what she showed me,' Birch answered. 'And besides, what choice have we got?'

73

Birch thumbed the last of the fourteen 9mm hollow-point bullets into the magazine of the .459 Smith and Wesson automatic then slammed the clip into the butt of the pistol. He worked the slide, chambering a round, and pushed the weapon into the shoulder holster he wore. He looked at Johnson and nodded. The younger man pulled aside his own jacket to reveal the Glock 9mm he wore beneath his left arm.

Both the detectives were wearing Kevlar body armour over their shirts. Birch tapped the chest and stomach area of his with one fist and looked around the room at the five other policemen who were standing watching him.

Like the two detectives, they wore Kevlar. It was strapped over their uniforms in much the same way a medieval knight would sport a breastplate.

Birch looked along the line at the men's faces and, more pointedly, at the weapons they carried. In addition to the Glock pistols strapped to their hips, each one was also equipped with a Heckler and Koch MP5K sub-machine gun, only an inch or so longer than the pistols the detectives themselves carried. Each MP5K held a thirty-round magazine of 9mm ammunition, capable, should any of the men need the option, of spewing out six hundred and fifty rounds a minute.

The room smelled of sweat and gun oil.

However, as Birch turned, an altogether more pleasing scent filled his nostrils, all the more strangely incongruous when compared to the other odours.

It was the aroma of Megan Hunter's perfume. She looked at the other men in the room, then at Birch.

'Is there anything else I should know?' he asked quietly. 'Other than what you've already told me?'

Megan shook her head. 'I told you everything.'

A brief and uncomfortable silence fell, broken by Megan.

'How am I going to know when it's over?' she enquired.

'You mean when we've killed it?' He shrugged and glanced at his watch. 'Give us three hours from now. Then bring us out. If we've got it by that time then great, if not, send us in again.'

Megan checked her own timepiece. 'Three hours,' she repeated.

Birch sucked in a deep breath, watching as her fingers rested gently on the keyboard of the laptop, and then he walked back across the hotel room to where the other men waited.

'Keep in radio contact at all times,' he said, looking at the armed officers and brandishing his own two-way like a weapon before him. 'Just remember, this bastard's already killed four people that we know of. I'm not banking on bringing him in alive and, to be honest, that doesn't bother me. Challenge him if you think it's worth it. If he wants to give up then that's terrific but I wouldn't hold your breath. If you get a clear shot, take it. Is that understood?'

The men nodded.

Birch turned to Megan. 'All right,' he said.

'Three hours,' she confirmed.

Birch nodded.

The clicking sound seemed to fill the room as Megan's fingers began to move with dizzying speed over the keyboard.

74

Birch rubbed his eyes, desperate to clear his vision as shapes began to swim into focus before him.

To his right, Johnson nearly stumbled as he tried to take a step forward but he recovered his balance and swayed uncertainly for a moment, also peering around him, blinking myopically.

The first of the ARU men dropped slowly to one knee, a hand feeling the ground beneath him like a blind man searching for his dropped cane. His companions stood motionless, wondering why it felt as if someone had stuffed their heads with cotton wool and hoping that the feeling would pass quickly. When it did, one of them sucked in a deep breath and gazed around, his jaw falling open slightly.

'Where the fuck are we?' he breathed.

'Where we need to be,' Birch told him, glad that his own vision had finally cleared fully. He glanced up quickly at the blazing sun then around at this new environment.

Another of the ARU men merely stood shaking his head, completely baffled as to both where he was and how he'd just arrived.

'What happened?' he asked.

Even if he'd been able to explain, Birch had neither the time nor the inclination to supply a satisfactory answer. Instead, he pulled the two-way from his pocket and flicked it on.

There was a loud hiss of static and he lowered the volume.

'All of you check your equipment,' he said, glancing around once more.

Johnson was shaking his head slowly, shielding his eyes occasionally against the dazzling rays of the sun. 'I didn't think it was possible,' he said.

Birch didn't answer, but merely watched as the ARU checked their radios, each satisfying himself that his was working. Two of them also flicked off the safety catches of their sub-machine guns.

Standing in a line, the seven men regarded what lay before them with a combination of awe and disbelief.

The fairground was vast.

Roughly rectangular in shape, it was surrounded on all four sides by a black painted brick wall that Birch guessed must be at least fifteen feet high. The twisting coils of rusted razor wire that ran along the top of it made it an even more formidable obstacle.

Behind them, two massive iron gates were padlocked together, sealing the men inside.

The fairground was concrete. Birch could feel the heat through the soles of his shoes. However, in many places, grass and weeds had forced their way up through the cracked surface and the splits in the uneven ground looked like gangrenous gashes. A warm breeze blew across the open area before them and a battered and sun-faded drink carton rolled into view like some kind of bizarre tumbleweed.

To both right and left, Birch could see

amusement arcades.

Slots of Fun, one of the signs boasted. *Las Vegas Strip*, the other declared. Many of the light bulbs that made up the letters were either missing or broken. The interiors of both buildings stretched back into darkness, away from the blistering rays of the sun.

Also to the right, Birch could see a public toilet and what had once been a doughnut stand. To his left was the source of the rancid stench that assaulted their nostrils. It was a child's ride — or had been at one time. Small boats floated on algae-choked water that was a vile green in colour.

Straight ahead was a large carousel, the paint peeling from the wooden horses that populated it. A number of the carved animals hung precariously from the rusted metal poles that skewered them to the canopy of the ride.

Beyond that he could see more rides and more disused food stalls. At the far end of the fairground, at least eight hundred yards away Birch guessed, the entire landscape was dominated by a massive roller coaster that towered over the rest of the amusement park. He could see three empty carts perched high on the most precipitous of the ride's peaks.

If anyone's watching us from up there, they'll see wherever we go.

Birch shielded his eyes against the sun, sweat already running down his face, and regarded the distant roller coaster warily.

Were they already being watched? And

possibly from a lot closer than that distant monolith?

'Right, let's do this,' the DI said, looking round at his companions. 'We're going to have to split up to cover the area fully but use your radios. Keep in contact at all times. If possible, keep each other in sight. I want every inch of this place searched.'

'But there's a hundred places to hide here,' one of the men said.

'Well check every one,' Birch told him. 'If anybody finds anything, call it in straight away.'

'Like what?' the tallest of the men asked.

'Any sign of life,' Birch said quietly. 'Any indication that there is someone living here.'

'And if we find the suspect?' another enquired.

'Like I said earlier, he's butchered four people already. Don't take any chances. If you can take him alive that's great. If not then that's fine too. Just watch yourselves. We're on his territory now. He'll know this place like the back of his hand. The best places to hide and, if he has to, to fight.' He looked at his watch. 'It's ten minutes past eleven. We'll do the first sweep now. Every stall, every ride, every room. I want this fucker found and I don't care how long it takes. We'll meet up in front of that roller coaster at two p.m.' He motioned away into the distance. Then he gestured to his left. 'Three of you take that side of the fairground. Two of you move straight down the middle. DS Johnson and myself will take the buildings on the right.'

Birch looked once more at the men before him. 'Let's go,' he said.

75

The stench was appalling.

Birch tried to breathe through his nose to diminish the stink as he approached the first of the cubicles in the toilet nearest the fairground's main entrance. The heat was making the atmosphere even more fetid. The thick dust around his feet, he noted, was undisturbed. It seemed unlikely that anyone had been inside recently. Even so, he had to check.

He slipped his right hand into his jacket, his fingers touching the butt of the .459, then he drew back one foot and kicked open the cubicle door.

It swung back on its hinges.

Empty.

So was the second. And the third.

The fourth was also unoccupied. He glanced in just long enough to see that the cracked and filthy porcelain was smeared with excreta that looked as though it had been baked on to the once shiny surface. There was no water in any of the toilets. Just several crumpled and empty crisp bags stuffed down there.

If this had all been created by John Paxton then he'd gone to town on details.

Birch shook his head and backed out of the toilet into the brilliant, baking sunlight.

Off to his left he could see two of the armed policemen moving slowly into the amusement arcade closest to them while a third headed towards the stall next to it. It was one of those 'hit a playing card with a dart and win a cuddly toy' jobs, Birch noted. He saw the third man vault the counter and sweep several dusty teddy bears and stuffed monkeys from the shelves.

Up ahead, two more ARU men were walking over the carousel of wooden horses. One of them said something to his companion then jumped down and advanced towards what had been a sweet stall just ahead. He too clambered over the counter to look inside.

Birch moved on to join Detective Sergeant Johnson, who was pulling at the doors of *Slots of Fun*.

They opened with a creak of unoiled hinges and dust billowed up like a noxious cloud, causing both detectives to pause for a moment.

Johnson reached into his jacket pocket and pulled out the small torch he carried, flicking it on and allowing the beam to penetrate the darkness within.

Birch followed him in a couple of steps, then moved back out into the sunshine again, heading on to another of the arcades next door. The entrance was partially blocked by a mound of rubbish that appeared to have spilled from an overturned waste bin but the detective merely stepped over the refuse and into the arcade, waiting a moment until his eyes adjusted to the gloom. It was a startling contrast to the unremittingly fierce glare of the sun.

He moved slowly through the arcade, heading for the rear of the building, past an air hockey table, a line of fruit machines and a roll-a-penny machine.

He could hear movement from next door. Johnson wandering about. Searching.

Birch reached for his radio.

'Steve, it's me,' he said. 'Anything? Over.'

His own radio crackled then he heard a hiss, followed by Johnson's voice.

'Nothing so far, guv,' the DS told him. 'Not a trace. Not even a footprint. Over.'

'Keep your eyes peeled. Out,' Birch said, pausing beside a bank of old-fashioned one-armed bandits.

He smiled to himself, then slipped his hand into his trouser pocket and pulled out a two-pence piece that he slipped into the requisite slot. Still smiling, he pulled the lever, watching as the reels spun.

One by one they thudded to a halt.

Three cherries.

The machine promptly coughed out six more two pence pieces and Birch scooped them up gleefully.

Grinning, he turned back towards the sunlight that marked the way out of the arcade.

It was as he did so that he noticed the door to his right.

★ ★ ★

'Building clear.'

The words came over the two-way and the tallest of the ARU men emerged into the sunlight nodding. He gestured to one of his companions who was peering distastefully into a waste bin, prodding the contents with the barrel of his sub-machine gun.

'I'm moving on to what looks like it was some kind of fish and chip place,' the tall man advised his colleagues, one of whom was clambering up on to the caterpillar ride towards the centre of the fairground. 'It looks like it was a snack bar or something. There's a door at the back of the deep fat fryers. Probably leads up to the first floor. Out.'

Beyond that was a ride, shaped like an Elizabethan galleon suspended high in the air on two hydraulic pistons, and still further ahead was the large arena that housed the dodgems.

The tallest of the men pushed the door of the fish and chip bar and stepped inside.

He clambered over the counter and made straight for the door he'd spotted from outside.

It was locked.

He took a step back, drove one booted foot hard against the door and looked up the dark and narrow flight of stairs that rose before him.

'This is unit one. I'm going up to the first floor,' he said into his radio, levelling the MP5K before him.

★　★　★

Birch put his hand on the cold metal of the doorknob and twisted.

It was locked.

He stepped back slightly, hand still gripping the knob, then, gritting his teeth, he slammed his weight against it, hearing the wood creak and groan under the impact.

The door remained stuck fast.

'Fuck this,' the detective murmured under his breath. He stepped further back, put a couple of paces between himself and the recalcitrant obstacle, then advanced rapidly and kicked it as hard as he could.

The metal knob came away and the door swung back on its hinges, slamming into the wall on the far side with a resounding crash.

Birch stumbled a little as he passed through, struggling to retain his balance and focus on what lay before him.

He blinked hard, and as his vision cleared he realised the rifle that was pointing at him was aimed directly at his head.

76

Moving purely on instinct, Birch's right hand shot inside his jacket, fingers closing over the butt of the .459.

As he pulled the pistol from its shoulder holster he knew that the figure facing him would have ample time to get off at least one shot before he himself even had time to swing the automatic into a firing position.

In that split second, many feelings spilled through the policeman's mind. Fear. Anger. Even shame.

What a stupid fucking way to die. Unprepared. Looking your killer in the eye.

The figure facing him didn't fire.

Birch had the 9mm up and aimed at the man now.

Why hadn't the man fired? What the hell was he waiting for?

The detective's breath was rasping in his throat as he stood only a foot from his opponent.

Birch looked at the man who faced him. At the jeans and thick checked shirt that he wore. At the dark, almost wax-like sheen of his skin. At the thick growth of beard he sported. At the hands that gripped the rifle. The index finger of the left hand was broken off at the second joint. The little finger was missing completely.

The detective lowered his pistol and took a step closer to the figure.

As he did so, he became more aware of the other figures and objects around him.

The wagon wheels. The straw on the ground. The arrows embedded in the barrel that the figure stood behind.

The figure of the red Indian warrior who was standing behind the bearded one brandishing a tomahawk.

Birch looked behind him and saw several targets set up along the shelves of a Western saloon. There were more on the red Indian, the barrel and the waxwork with the rifle.

It was then that he realised he was standing in the middle of a shooting range. A line of air rifles lay on the counter at the front of the stall.

'Jesus,' he breathed, prodding the figure before him. It swayed slightly.

His radio crackled and he reached for it with his free hand.

'Come in,' he said into the two-way.

There was nothing but static on the other end. Birch waited a moment then dropped the radio back into his pocket. The .459 he kept in his right hand. He pressed it to the head of the bearded cowboy and thumbed back the hammer.

'Draw,' Birch murmured. 'I want you out of town by sunset.' He smiled to himself, eased the hammer back down, then slid the automatic back into its holster.

He moved on.

★ ★ ★

The staircase was barely wide enough for one person to climb easily, let alone a man as broadly built and heavily armed as the ARU man who began the ascent.

He lowered the MP5K, holding it in one hand as he moved slowly up the wooden steps.

They creaked loudly under his weight and he cursed them for that. If there was anyone in the room above him they would be alerted to his approach.

Halfway up he stopped, his heart thudding hard against his ribs. Ears alert for any sounds of movement from above.

Nothing.

He continued up the stairs until he reached another door. He swallowed, then pushed it.

The door swung open and he walked in, trying to adjust to the gloom.

There was a light switch on the wall to his left and he slapped at it but the fluorescents in the ceiling failed to burst into life.

The room was large and completely empty. Not a stick of furniture. No sign that anyone had ever walked its wooden floor.

He reached for his torch and shone it around, dust motes swirling in the beam. He guided the light over the floor but saw no footprints. Nothing to suggest that anyone had ever been inside this place. There were neither windows nor doors other than the one by which he had entered.

He turned, lowered his sub-machine gun and made his way back down the stairs. It was as he reached the bottom that his radio crackled.

★ ★ ★

'This is unit one. We've got something.'

Birch heard the words on his own two-way.

'Unit one, this is Birch. Where are you? Over.'

'Above the dodgems, sir,' the metallic voice replied. 'We're in some kind of control room. It looks as if it controls the electrics for the whole fairground. There are switches everywhere. Over.'

'Stay there,' Birch instructed, hurrying over the hot concrete towards the location he'd been given.

Up ahead of Birch, Detective Sergeant Johnson was waiting outside the entrance to the House of Fun.

Birch saw his companion glancing up at the gaudily painted exterior of the building. Clown faces, some contorted in monstrous grimaces, gaped at him from the walls. In a large glass case, perched above the entrance to the attraction, the figure of a sailor was slumped, its false eyes gazing blindly out over the rest of the fairground.

The DI beckoned for his colleague to join him, and the two detectives vaulted the low fence round the dodgem arena and headed towards the flight of steps that led up to the room above.

'Paxton certainly had a hell of an imagination, didn't he?' Johnson noted, looking round at the disused dodgems, pushed together in one corner of the rink, paint peeling from their rusting metal hulks.

Birch didn't answer. Instead, he began to climb the stairs.

335

77

The control room was huge.

Fully one hundred feet long and half that again in width, it took up the entire roof space above the dodgems. As he entered, Birch saw that the wall to his left was a patchwork of switches, levers and panels. There were two dozen television monitors that he guessed must be used in conjunction with the CCTV cameras that dotted the fairground from end to end.

The three ARU men stood in the darkened room, torches moving slowly and evenly over the electrical array as Birch walked from one end of it to the other.

Behind him, Johnson was examining numerous maps and schematics pinned to the other wall. They showed every single detail of every ride in the amusement park.

'Why did Paxton need to put so much detail into a book?' the DS asked, regarding the plans by the light of his own torch.

Birch ignored the question, his gaze still travelling over the myriad controls before him.

'If we're really inside a book he wrote . . . ' Johnson continued, the words tailing off.

'There must be a generator somewhere,' Birch put in. 'A way of switching on the power in the park.'

'According to this,' Johnson said, tapping the map, 'it's about fifty yards away from here.

Behind some kids' ride between the funhouse and the Hall of Mirrors.'

'Find it,' Birch said to two of the ARU men. 'Get the generator working if you can. We'll turn the power on.'

'Why?' Johnson wanted to know.

'If we can get these CCTV monitors working then we can leave a man up here to watch the fairground while we carry on searching it. If anything moves he'll see it.' Birch nodded towards the third of the armed policemen.

The other two uniformed men were still hesitating at the door.

'Get that generator working,' Birch insisted.

The two men left, their footfalls thudding on the steps as they descended.

Birch reached into his pocket and took out a cigarette. He lit it and took a deep drag.

'What if Megan Hunter was lying?'

The question hung on the dust-choked air and, at first, Birch didn't acknowledge it.

'Guv, I said — '

'I heard you,' the DI snapped, still running his gaze over the switches and panels before him. 'Lying about what, Steve? Does this look like a fucking lie to you? Does this look imaginary?' He banged the back of the chair in front of him hard, sending more dust billowing upwards.

'We haven't found any evidence that anyone's here and we've already searched half the place.'

'Are you doubting the evidence of your own sense now?' Birch challenged. 'You can see this place, smell it. Touch it.'

As if to reinforce that realisation, Johnson

reached out and flicked one of the switches near to him.

'Can we communicate with the outside world from here?' the younger man wanted to know.

'Try,' Birch suggested.

Johnson reached into his pocket for his mobile. It was dead. Birch examined his own and found that it too wasn't working.

There was a long silence, finally broken by Johnson.

'When this is over, guv,' he said falteringly, 'when we've got the killer, we're relying on Megan Hunter to get us out of here again, right?'

Birch nodded.

'What if she can't do it?' the younger man persisted.

Birch regarded his colleague evenly for a moment, groping for the words he wanted but not sure where to find them.

The crackle of the radio lanced through the silence.

'This is unit one,' the metallic voice hissed, all but drowned by a violent hiss of static.

'Go ahead,' snapped Birch into his own two-way. 'What have you got? Over.'

' . . . found the generator . . . it . . . though . . . working . . . '

'Shit,' Birch rasped. 'Say that again,' he said loudly. 'You're breaking up.'

' . . . generator . . . to be . . . '

'Come on, for fuck's sake,' the DI snarled, glaring at the two-way as if that would cause it to work effectively again.

There was another savage blast of static, so

loud Birch momentarily held the radio away from his ear.

' . . . oil level . . . to be good . . . it . . . '

The interference was overwhelming now. Birch moved towards the door of the control room, hoping for a better reception.

'Unit one, come in,' he said into the two-way. 'Repeat what you said about the generator. Over.'

'The fuel level's high,' the voice at the other end of the radio told him with a clarity Birch welcomed. 'The generator looks as if it's been used recently.'

Birch turned briefly to glance at Johnson, who had followed him to the top of the stairs. The DS looked as puzzled as his superior.

'Switch it on,' the DI instructed. 'Got that? Switch on the generator.'

There was a rumbling sound both over the airwaves and also from a point up ahead of Birch.

'Generator on,' the voice at the other end of the radio informed him.

'Hit the switches, Steve,' Birch commanded. 'All of them.'

Johnson spun round, headed back into the control room and began pressing any button and switch he could lay his hands on. The fluorescents in the ceiling sputtered into life, bathing the control room in cold white light. When he pressed a red button beneath a bank of CCTV monitors the screens flickered and then, one by one, burst into life, each camera showing a different angle on the fairground.

'Unit one,' Birch said into the two-way. 'Carry on with your search now. Over.'

There was a steady hiss of static on the line but nothing else.

'Unit one, come in,' Birch persisted.

Only static.

Then something else.

A scream of pain and terror.

Birch looked at the radio as if it could show him the source of the high-pitched ululation.

'Unit one, come in,' he shouted into the two-way.

Another scream. It was a sound that froze his blood.

A short burst of gunfire.

' . . . Christ . . . out of here.' The noises coming from the radio were terrible. As if someone had just connected him directly to a nightmare. 'Please . . . fucking run . . . No . . . No . . . Oh God . . . '

'Stay here,' Birch shouted to his companion as he bolted for the stairs. His hand was already reaching inside his jacket for the automatic.

78

Birch covered the ground from the control room to the building that housed the generator in less than a dozen frantic strides.

Those lights that weren't broken were now blazing brightly on a ride called *Jungle Adventure*.

Small plastic wild animals, the paint peeling from them, were lined up on a narrow track that began to move just as Birch reached it. The procession of creatures, just large enough to accommodate the children they'd been designed to carry, trundled past him and the detective leaped onto the wooden centre of the ride and onwards towards the door at the rear of it. Painted to blend in with the rest of the backdrop, the entryway was almost invisible at first glance but Birch found the handle and tore at it, the .459 raised in readiness for what lay on the other side.

He swallowed hard then entered.

A narrow corridor about twelve feet long led down towards another door.

Birch hesitated a moment then advanced, the rumble of the generator beyond now complemented by a combination of recordings of jungle noises and the sound of machinery coming from the ride behind him.

The detective could feel his heart thudding hard against his ribs as he drew nearer the door of the generator room, the gun gripped tightly in his fist. Back pressed against one wall of the corridor, he moved closer until he was within touching distance of the door.

On the other side, he could hear the loud puttering of the generator but nothing else.

He steadied himself then kicked the door open, swinging the 9mm up into a firing position.

The room that housed the generator was about fifteen feet square, dominated by the machine itself.

It stank of oil and petrol, but now other odours too assaulted Birch's nostrils: those of blood and excrement. He could also smell the unmistakably pungent stench of cordite. There were a dozen bullet holes in one wall.

The gunfire we heard on the two-way.

'Fuck,' he rasped through clenched teeth.

Both of the ARU men who had entered the room were dead. One of them lay face down on the ground, arms stretched out on either side of him. From the amount of blood around the body, Birch guessed that his throat had been cut.

The detective knelt quickly beside the body and lifted the man's head gently by the hair to check.

As he did so, the few tendrils of flesh that still connected the head to the neck tore and the entire thing came free. For interminable seconds, Birch found himself staring into the bloodied face, the eyes of which were still open and staring wide.

The detective dropped the head and moved away, glancing over at the other ARU man who was slumped against the wall.

Two blows from an incredibly sharp instrument had killed him. Both had been to the top of the skull and each one delivered with such incredible force that they had practically split the head in two. Large portions of pinkish-grey brain matter had bulged from the savage gashes, and some had spilled into the dead man's lap.

Birch didn't even bother to check for a pulse.

The room was like a slaughterhouse.

His gaze darted quickly around, ensuring that the killer wasn't still in the room. He wondered how the one he sought had entered and left this place of death.

When he felt something warm and wet drip on to his hand he realised he had his answer.

There was a wooden hatch in the ceiling, blood smeared thickly round the edges, in places so thickly that it was dripping to the floor. Birch aimed his gun up at the hatch and stood there like that for a moment. Then, eyes still fixed on the ceiling, he reached for his two-way.

'Steve, come in, it's me,' he said, forced to raise his voice over the noise of the generator.

'Yes, guv,' Johnson answered.

'They're both dead.' Birch eyed the corpses closely, his eyes narrowing slightly. 'He's taken their weapons and their radios too. Chances are he's listening in to this now.' Birch held the two-way so tightly it seemed he would snap it in two. 'Can you hear me, you cunt?' he snarled. 'I'm going to kill you, you fucking piece of shit. Got that?' He continued glaring at the two-way for a moment longer, the knot of muscles at

343

the side of his jaw throbbing angrily. He had to struggle to control his breathing. 'Steve, I'm coming back. I think I know how he managed to take them both by surprise. I think I know how he's moving around.' The DI backed slowly towards the door, eyes still fixed on the hatch in the ceiling. Reaching the threshold, he glanced once more at the two dead bodies, then edged out of the room, pulling the door shut behind him.

Inside, the generator continued to rumble.

Birch looked at his radio. Then, with a grunt of fury, he hurled it at the door.

It hit the partition and broke.

Birch turned, the .459 still at the ready. He looked out at the fairground, checking that the way back to the control room was clear.

As long as the bastard's not watching you. Ready to pick you off with one of the sub-machine guns he's taken off those poor bastards he slaughtered.

The jungle noises coming from the ride rang in his ears. The painted animals continued to trundle around.

Birch sprinted back towards the control room.

Even as he ran, he waited for the burst of automatic fire to cut him down.

He heard deep, rumbling laughter and glanced up to his left.

The figure of the sailor in the glass case above the entrance to the House of Fun had been activated when the power was switched on.

It was that mocking laughter the detective could hear.

79

'There must be a walkway that leads over some of the rides,' Birch declared, tapping the schematic with one index finger and tracing the digit along the plan. 'That's how he's moving around without us seeing him and that's how he managed to take the two ARU guys in the generator room by surprise. By the time they realised what was happening it was too late. He used the hatch to get into and out of there.' The detective drew on his cigarette. 'He doesn't even need to come out in the open if he doesn't want to. Not unless he has to cross from one side of the fairground to the other.'

Birch regarded the CCTV monitors carefully, watching for any signs of movement. He saw none.

'What about the others?' he wanted to know.

'Still looking,' Johnson told him.

'Moving up the middle, sir,' the ARU man announced, scanning the diagram. 'They've got two more amusement arcades, a couple of what were games stalls and the ghost train to search before they reach the roller coaster.' He looked at Birch.

'The ghost train,' Birch observed. 'Plenty of places to hide in there.'

'And that walkway runs above it too,' Johnson added, indicating the schematic.

345

Birch nodded and glanced round at the banks of CCTV monitors.

He saw two dark figures clearly visible on one of them.

'Looks like they're just going in now,' he said, watching as the duo of ARU officers paused before the facade of the ghost train. It was dominated by a huge, green-painted dragon's head shaped from plastic or resin. The mouth was open to display a number of sharp teeth. The two men hesitated a moment longer then advanced towards the narrow metal track that led to the entrance.

'What about us?' Johnson said. 'Where do we go?'

'The House of Fun and then the Hall of Mirrors,' Birch said, taking a final drag on his cigarette. 'After that, there's another toilet block and then we're at the roller coaster.'

Both men moved towards the stairs that would take them out of the control room. The DI paused, jabbing a finger towards the ARU man.

'You keep your eye on those screens,' he said tersely. 'You see anything, you let us know. My radio got broken, but Detective Sergeant Johnson's is still working.'

On the television monitors, another shape moved quickly and sure-footedly into view.

By the time the uniformed policeman had turned back to face the screens, the shape was gone.

★ ★ ★

Abandon hope all ye who enter here.

The two ARU men stood looking up at the yellow and red painted letters that decorated the entrance to the ghost train.

There were two swing doors, decorated with a painting of the devil's face. A huge, goat-like, half-human head that also had its mouth open to welcome them. Its red eyes were blinking courtesy of the two crimson light bulbs that flashed intermittently in the painting.

On the metal track behind them were six small metal carts, each decorated with gaudy paintings of demons, skulls and other horrors.

The first man nodded to his companion and pushed the double doors.

They stepped through to find themselves confronted by a length of track that bent to the right and another set of double doors.

There was a sudden explosion of sound that startled both men: a clap of artificial thunder that sounded more like a gunshot. It was accompanied by a blinding flash of white light.

'Welcome to hell,' said a deep, thick bass voice that echoed from speakers mounted on the wall to their right and left.

'Fuck off,' rasped the first of the uniformed men, irritated with himself for having been taken unawares by the sudden eruption of sound.

'If the power's on, don't step on the rails,' said his companion, also a little shaken. 'I think they're electrified.'

'There's not enough current running through them to do us any damage,' the first man said dismissively. 'It's not the fucking Underground, is it?'

Even so, as he advanced towards the second set of double doors he made sure that he walked on the sleepers between the rails.

He nudged the doors open with the barrel of his submachine gun and entered.

There was another deafening blast of fake thunder and lightning, this time accompanied by a series of screams. Despite themselves, both men again felt a jolt of fear.

The track sloped rapidly down, the incline causing them to walk a little faster than they liked just to maintain their footing. It finally levelled out, turning to the right.

A scream reverberated in their ears.

It was pitch black inside the ghost train and the leading man pulled the torch from his pocket and attached it to the top of his MP5K. The beam picked out thick black curtains on both sides of the track. Speakers were set into the walls and, every few yards, they could see small red lights blazing at track level.

'Electric eye,' said the first man, indicating the pinprick of glowing crimson. 'It must trigger something when the beam's broken.'

He advanced slowly towards it. As he reached it there was a faint buzzing sound, and a skeleton swung into view from his left, plastic arms and legs rattling, mouth agape. Its appearance was accompanied by a high-pitched, cackling laugh.

'Thought so,' the first uniformed man said, watching as the mechanical device was pulled

348

back towards the wall by a short hydraulic piston.

The second of the two ARU men stepped over the electric eye, ensuring that the skeleton remained firmly hidden behind the black curtains from which it had appeared.

'No service doors to the rides,' the first man noted. 'Not like a real fairground.'

'It looks real enough to me,' the second man commented.

He glanced up at the ceiling. It was thick with cobwebs. Some were fake. He swallowed hard as he wondered momentarily how large the spiders must be that had made the others.

A woman was crying softly, the sound coming from the speakers. As the two men neared another bend in the track, the sound turned from crying to sobs of terror. Then there was another ear-splitting scream.

They walked on.

80

Birch paused to wipe sweat from his forehead.

The Kevlar was beginning to feel heavy; the straps were rubbing against his shoulders. He glanced at Johnson and saw that the younger man was also sweating profusely.

The corridor along which they were moving was barely six feet wide and the enclosed space intensified the heat inside the House of Fun. The walls were bright yellow. Cracked and peeling. The colour of rancid pus.

Speeded-up piano music was blasting from wall-mounted speakers. The same tunes over and over again.

Birch turned a corner.

This corridor was painted green and there was a handrail on either side. He paused for a moment and looked down at the floor.

A section of it was moving quickly from one side to the other. It was too large to jump. He realised that he and his companion would have to walk across it. Gripping the handrail, the DI began to traverse the moving panel. It jerked violently beneath his feet and he almost over-balanced.

The piano music seemed to speed up even more, and now it was joined by high-pitched laughter.

There were framed pictures on the wall of the corridor, each one of a poorly painted face, the features contorted by laughter.

'Ha fucking ha,' Birch muttered as he continued across the rapidly shifting section of floor. Johnson followed him, almost losing his footing at one point.

The DI jumped the last three feet from the moving platform, finally reaching the stability of the corridor floor once again. He put out a hand to help his companion across the last few feet and Johnson staggered over to join his superior.

The corridor turned sharply to the right again and both men saw that there was a narrow flight of steps leading up to a higher level. The walls here were painted bright pink, and on both sides of the stairwell there were more of the painted, laughing faces.

Birch took the lead, heading up the stairs cautiously, his eyes fixed on the top.

He didn't realise that the fifth step had retracted into the wall until he stumbled on it.

Behind him, Johnson also shot out a hand to support himself as the step he was standing on shot back from beneath his feet.

Birch, cursing under his breath, continued upwards, his attention now fixed on the stairs that were sliding in and out with alarming speed. He gripped the handrail and hauled himself up.

The piano music continued, as did the laughter.

Johnson grunted something and fell, cracking one knee painfully against a step as he tumbled back down. Massaging the throbbing joint, he started up the steps once more, this time making it halfway before his footing was again

351

threatened by the disappearing stairs. He shot out a hand, gripped the rail, and steadied himself before hurrying up behind Birch, who was almost at the top.

The DI swung himself on to firm ground again and once more offered a helping hand to his colleague, dragging him up to the walkway on which he himself now stood.

Both men stood gasping for a moment, soaked with sweat from their efforts.

Birch walked cautiously forward and felt a warm breeze on his skin. It took him only a second to realise that the next stretch of the walkway passed across an open section of the front of the funhouse behind the laughing sailor in the glass case. The deep rumbling laughter from the motley-looking figure joined the more high-pitched chuckling that was still rattling in the detective's ears. Another section of moving floor, this one shifting rapidly back and forth, had to be crossed to reach the other side of the walkway.

The DI realised that, ordinarily, anyone crossing this stretch would be clearly seen by whoever was watching from below.

Yeah, very humorous. Paxton had thought of everything, hadn't he?

Birch steadied himself then ran across the shifting section of floorboards, stumbling as he reached the far side. He slammed into the wall and turned to Johnson, waving him across.

The younger man followed, almost crashing into Birch as he left the moving floor.

Again the corridor turned to the right.

'Are we going in circles?' Johnson said, forced to raise his voice to make himself heard above the incessant piano music and laughter. 'There must be an easier way of searching this place.'

Birch shook his head, noticing with trepidation that there was another flight of steps leading back down from the walkway.

He hesitated.

What happens this time? Do the whole fucking lot just give way? Turn into a slide and send you tumbling to the bottom?

He put his foot on the top step, half expecting it to collapse beneath his weight.

When it didn't, he moved down to the next. Then the next.

He was halfway down when the smell struck him.

A pungent, cloying odour that clogged his nostrils and made him cough.

Birch recognised it.

He made it to the bottom of the steps and turned to his right. A few seconds later Johnson joined him.

There was a thin, dusty, black curtain at the end of the red-painted corridor. Through it Birch could see wildly flashing strobe lights.

The smell was becoming stronger.

Johnson put one hand over his nose, so vile was the stench. The heat inside the building only served to make it worse.

Birch slid his hand inside his jacket and pulled the automatic free, nodding to his companion to follow his example. Johnson hefted his own pistol before him as both men advanced towards the curtain and what lay beyond it.

The smell was almost intolerable by now and Johnson felt his stomach contract. He clamped his jaws together. It was all he could do not to vomit.

Birch had one hand on the curtain, preparing to pull it aside.

The music and laughter grew in volume. The flashing lights in the room beyond flared and died with ever increasing rapidity.

And, all the time, that infernal, fetid odour seemed to fill the men's noses and lungs.

Birch looked at his companion and nodded.

He pulled the curtain aside, practically ripping it from the rail that held it in place above the entrance to the next part of the funhouse.

Both detectives stepped through, weapons levelled, eyes darting round the room.

The space they were in looked vast compared to the cramped corridors they'd been traversing. A circular area with distorting mirrors all around them, the glass twisting and mutating their reflections into something unnatural and bizarre. The strobe lights bouncing off the surfaces made it seem as if there were ten times as many of the blazing white orbs.

But it wasn't the lights or the mirrors, or even the putrescent smell that drew the detectives' attention.

It was what hung from the ceiling in the centre of the room that transfixed them. Suspended on a length of thick chain, it was held, arms outstretched in a Christ-like pose, by the two meat hooks that secured it in position ten feet above the ground.

The two men looked up at the body of Frank Denton.

81

The screaming had been replaced by incessant maniacal laughter by the time the two ARU men reached what they guessed was the centre of the ghost train.

The leading man stopped, wiping his face and looking around.

His companion also slowed his pace, gazing at the setting they now found themselves in before checking behind the thick, heavy black curtains that lined the walls.

The track wound its way through what was meant to be a graveyard. A bright white beam, disguised as a full moon, shone down from the painted sky like a spotlight, flashing erratically. It plunged the men from cold luminescence into impenetrable blackness and back again every few seconds. And now the maniacal laughter was joined by the hooting of an owl and the loud howling of wolves.

The second man scanned the tableau on either side, his breathing laboured. It wasn't helped by the thick dust that swirled in the air like noxious fog.

To his right there were several gravestones, constructed, like the coffin that lay close to the track, from wood and crudely painted.

A ghoulish figure sprang into view behind the headstones every time the electric eye on the track was tripped, as did a shrouded figure in the coffin that sat bolt upright seconds later.

To the left there were two more waxwork figures dressed in Victorian garb, dragging a corpse away from the graves towards another figure that looked like Frankenstein's monster.

The second man allowed his foot to break the red beam of the electric eye and the ghoul popped up from behind the gravestones, all sharp teeth, spiky hair and huge yellow eyes. The body in the coffin sat up sharply then lay down again, while the eyes of the Frankenstein monster glowed red and it raised its arms.

The ARU man grinned. His companion didn't find the tableau so amusing.

'What the fuck are you doing?' he snapped irritably. 'Let's just get out of this bloody place. Stop pissing about.'

'All right, take it easy,' the second man urged, tripping the electric eye again. He grinned as the figures performed their movements once more. 'It's clever the way it's been done, isn't it?'

The first man merely shook his head, wiping more sweat from his face. He was about to move on when he raised a hand in his companion's direction.

'Did you feel that?' he asked.

The second man looked vague.

There was a deafening clap of fake thunder from the speakers, followed by more wolves' howling.

The leading ARU man looked down at his feet.

'The track's vibrating,' he said, raising his

voice to make himself heard above the unholy cacophony.

The second man dropped to one knee and put his hand on the nearest sleeper.

'Feel it?' his companion asked.

'One of the carriages must be moving,' the second man said slowly.

From somewhere behind them, the two men heard a loud bang and a scream.

Beneath their feet, the track shuddered more violently.

'It's getting closer,' the first man said agitatedly.

They were plunged into darkness as the light went out once more. Only their torch beams offered illumination.

'Get off the track,' the first man warned.

His companion needed no prompting and the uniformed men took up position among the wax exhibits, the first man standing behind the figure of Frankenstein's monster while the second man used the gravestones to hide himself. In the darkness, he could feel the ghoul figure close to him. The rags it had been dressed in stank of neglect. The entire scene smelled fusty, like damp clothes. But, for now, his attention was focused on the curve in the track twenty yards away.

It was at the top of a gentle slope. A curtain of fake spider webs dangled from the ceiling, designed to brush the faces of any passengers.

The carriage would appear at the top of that slope very soon.

The rumbling that signalled its approach was

now audible even through the wolf howls, screams and laughter.

The lights went out again, plunging the men into blackness so total it was impossible to see a hand in front of them.

There was a bright blue flash from the top of the incline. Some kind of electrical short as the carriage drew nearer.

The two ARU men gripped their sub-machine guns more tightly and waited.

The darkness was rent by the cold brilliance of the light and, in that moment of brightness, the second ARU man could see his companion raising his MP5K into a firing position, training it in the direction of the track.

Another second or two and the carriage would swing into view.

82

The two detectives looked fixedly at the corpse of Frank Denton hanging above them.

Both struggled to control their breathing as the fetor clogged their nostrils.

'Megan Hunter said the Wrathchild took the body,' Birch murmured, glancing up again at the corpse then swiftly swinging his pistol round to cover the strobe-lit room, wondering if whoever had put Denton on the meat hooks was present now.

'Why bring him here?' Johnson wanted to know.

Birch could only shake his head. 'Come on,' he said. 'Let's keep moving.'

'Are we just going to leave Denton here?'

'What the fuck do you want to do with him, Steve? Carry him around with us?' He sucked in a tainted breath. 'Perhaps he's been put there as a warning. Maybe the Wrathchild wants us to know what he's got in store for us.'

Johnson was still looking at the body when his superior moved away towards another narrow corridor off to the right.

'Come on,' the DI called, beckoning his companion to follow.

★ ★ ★

The graveyard was in total blackness when the carriage swung round the bend in the track.

The two ARU men waited for the flash of white light to illuminate the area and, sure enough, it came.

There were three carriages moving down the slope towards them and, in that blinding explosion of brilliance, both men saw that the last of the three had a passenger.

The speakers spewed out their wolf howls and their screams. The track rumbled as the three carriages trundled down the slope. And then another sound eclipsed everything else.

The staccato rattle of automatic fire seemed to fill the building. The blinding white light of a muzzle flash illuminated everything as the first ARU officer, driven by fear, opened fire on the carriages and their occupant.

His companion joined him immediately and 9mm rounds tore into the train, blasting lumps from it or drilling into the wood.

The figure in the rear carriage was struck dozens of times, bullets hammering into the face, chest and stomach.

By the light of their blazing guns, the two ARU men could see the body jerking wildly as each round hit home. As the hammer slammed down on an empty chamber, the leading officer reloaded then sprinted forward towards the carriage, weapon still lowered, ready to empty another magazine into the passenger if necessary.

The light in the ceiling flashed on.

'No,' roared the ARU man, eyes bulging madly.

His companion rose from behind the gravestone where he'd been sheltering, the stink of cordite strong in his nostrils.

He too saw what his colleague saw.

The figure in the last carriage, most of the upper body shredded by the fusillade of 9mm rounds, was one of their fellow ARU officers.

The uniformed man's throat had been slashed from ear to ear, almost severing his head. There were two more stab wounds in his face, one of which had penetrated his left eye, bursting the orb like a slimy balloon. Blood and vitreous liquid had spilled down his cheek. The other had pierced the base of his skull, the blade having been driven in with such force that it had erupted from his mouth, slicing his bottom lip in half and knocking out several teeth. The bloodied weapon was still embedded in his head, the point protruding a good five inches from his mouth like some lethal metallic tongue.

Both men looked on helplessly as the small train reached the bottom of the slope, turned left and headed off towards another set of double doors.

As the leading carriage passed the electric eye the ghoul rose from behind the gravestone and the body sat up in its coffin.

The second ARU man stood motionless, smoke from his own and his colleague's weapons drifting like fog through the air.

In the dazzling light, the uniformed men looked blankly at each other, then in the direction of the disappearing carriage.

The first man turned and sprinted after it. His colleague lowered his weapon, his breathing harsh and laboured.

The lights went out again and he felt the ghoul figure drop back down into position on his right-hand side.

What he wasn't expecting was the touch of cold metal against his left temple.

He couldn't move. Paralysed for a second by the realisation that there was someone now standing next to him in the impenetrable blackness. He could smell their breath, feel it warm against his cheek. Time seemed to have frozen. The only other fact that registered in his mind was that the cold object pressed to his temple was the barrel of a gun.

He heard the hammer being pulled back, then a thunderous explosion.

Then nothing else mattered.

83

'We're never going to find him, are we?'

Birch stood gazing up at the front of the House of Fun, sucking on a cigarette.

'Guv,' Johnson said, taking a step towards his superior. 'I said — '

'I heard what you said,' Birch cut across him, his gaze moving towards the Hall of Mirrors.

There were several sheets of old newspaper blowing about near the entrance. The main door was open.

An invitation? A challenge?

'I'm not leaving here until that fucking thing's dead,' Birch said, through clenched teeth. 'But you're right, we could look all day and all night and never find it. And, in the meantime, it just picks us off when it likes.'

'So what do we do?'

Birch fumbled in his jacket pocket and pulled out his lighter, his gaze drawn again to the sheets of newspaper outside the Hall of Mirrors.

He flicked the Zippo open and struck a flame.

'We burn this whole fucking place to the ground,' he said quietly. 'If the Wrathchild's hiding somewhere it'll burn. If it gets out, it has to come into the open and we'll be waiting for it.' He looked into the lighter flame once again, then at Johnson. 'Burn it.'

* * *

The first ARU man caught up with the ghost train easily. He swung himself into the middle carriage, turning to look at the bullet-riddled body of his colleague slumped in the last one.

The train turned another corner into a long tunnel barely wide enough to accommodate it. It trundled along the tracks, the inside of the tunnel now lit by a hellish red light.

On each side of him, the ARU man could see that there were perspex-covered windows that, as the carriage drew level with each one, lit up to expose a monstrous head within.

He guessed that these too were moulded from wax and they all looked uncomfortably real.

Vampires, werewolves, zombies and other monstrous creations peered at him from both sides of the tunnel. The deafening clanking of chains reverberated in his ears, echoing off the tunnel walls until he felt that his head would explode.

He gripped the sub-machine gun in shaking hands, his eyes bulging with fear.

'Come on then,' he roared defiantly. 'Come out, you bastard. I'll kill you.'

The three carriages rumbled on towards the end of the tunnel, past the decaying head of an Egyptian mummy.

'Where are you?' the ARU man shouted once more, standing up in the carriage as it passed the burned visage of a masked creature resembling the Phantom of the Opera.

He fired a short burst into the ceiling, pieces of wood and plaster falling around him as the bullets blasted lumps from the tunnel.

'Too fucking scared to show yourself?' he bellowed furiously. 'Cunt. I'll kill you.'

The train was almost at the end of the tunnel now.

As it drew level with the last window it stopped. The ARU man looked wildly to his left, wondering why the transport had come to a halt. He saw the head of Satan gazing at him with blank eyes. He turned to his right to inspect the head there.

For a split second he froze as he stared at it.

That instant was long enough.

As he remained transfixed by the head that stared back at him, a figure stepped on to the track in front of the motionless train.

The ARU man finally managed to tear his gaze from the head to his right and he looked directly at the shape that confronted him.

He experienced a moment of devastating clarity in which he seemed aware of everything. Especially the fact that the figure before him was carrying a gun identical to the one he himself held.

The MP5K was pointed directly at him. The ARU officer opened his mouth to shout something but the figure before him was too quick.

The barrel of the sub-machine gun flamed, rounds erupting from the muzzle. Moving at a speed in excess of one thousand feet a second, the bullets drilled into the ARU man, some striking the Kevlar and flattening uselessly but enough hitting areas above and below the body armour.

One blasted away his testicles as two others scythed through one of his femoral arteries and sent an arc of blood fully six feet into the rancid air. More of the bullets caught him in the face and neck, pulverising his larynx, ripping part of an ear off and smashing into his forehead and open mouth. Several erupted from the back of his skull, carrying splintered bone and gobbets of brain matter with them.

The ARU man pitched backwards in the carriage, then fell sideways against the tunnel wall.

His killer advanced towards him and squeezed the trigger again, but the gun was empty.

It wasn't a problem. The figure merely reached, instead, for the knife it carried.

84

'There isn't enough fuel to burn the whole place,' panted Johnson.

He set down another of the plastic containers he and Birch had fetched from the generator room and watched as his superior continued to splash the petrol over the wooden steps that led up to the roller coaster entrance.

Birch seemed oblivious of anything but the task in hand. He had stuffed rolled-up pieces of the newspaper they'd found lying discarded around the fairground into the doorway of the Hall of Mirrors and also spread it over the front of the House of Fun. Now he continued to empty petrol over everything in front of him, finally hurling the empty container on to the track of the roller coaster. Then he spun round and snatched up another, and started to unscrew the cap.

'There isn't enough to burn it all,' Johnson rasped, grabbing his superior by the arm. 'Are you listening to me? Think about this. What happens to us when it goes up?'

'The fucking place is wood,' Birch snarled, pulling loose. 'It's dry. Once one of the buildings or rides starts to burn the others'll go too. The fire'll spread round the whole fucking fairground.' He glared at his companion for a moment then continued hurling petrol on to anything within range.

'I'm going to burn that bastard.'

'And what about the other ARU guys?' Johnson protested, watching as the DI began to edge backwards, pouring a trail of petrol on to the cracked concrete as he backed up. 'If they're inside one of the buildings when it catches fire they'll — '

'Then they'll have the sense to get out, won't they?' Birch interrupted, glaring at him.

Johnson held his superior's gaze and saw something beyond fury in his expression. Something that couldn't be reasoned with.

Birch waited a moment, his breath coming in gasps, then he hurled the empty can in the direction of the roller coaster. 'It isn't going to matter to the poor bastards he's already killed, is it?'

The DI looked around him and snatched up another piece of the newspaper that littered the fairground. He rolled it rapidly into a funnel shape and held it before him, glancing up at the roller coaster with a twisted smile on his face. He looked down at the trail of petrol that led to the towering edifice, knowing that the slick fluid would act like a fuse once he lit it.

He reached for his lighter.

'We'll move back to the control room,' he said. 'Let this fucking thing burn for a while, watch what happens on the CCTV monitors. See if the bastard comes out into the open.'

'And if he doesn't?'

Birch merely flicked his lighter, waiting for the flame. He gritted his teeth and watched as tiny sparks appeared, then, finally, a flame. He lit the piece of newspaper he held, brandishing it as if it was the Olympic torch.

Birch smiled as he and Johnson backed away.

Both men were gazing fixedly at what lay before them. Birch could feel the heat from the flame on his face.

Neither saw the figure behind them.

It stood motionless, the sub-machine gun it held lowered and aimed at the two detectives.

Birch was preparing to light the petrol trail when the figure opened fire.

The bullets struck the ground around the two men, fragments of concrete spinning into the air as bullets cracked it and the high-pitched whine of ricochets filled their ears.

Birch dropped the burning paper and rolled over, grabbing for the .459, trying to pull it free of its holster so that he could defend himself.

Johnson managed to grab the Glock from beneath his left arm and he got off two rounds as he scrambled to his feet and began to run towards the Hall of Mirrors, seeking cover from the sudden attack.

Another burst of fire raked the ground near his feet, several of the bullets cutting into his lower legs. One round shattered his left ankle. Another sliced effortlessly through his right calf, exploding the muscles. A third bullet pulverised his right shin bone. Another blew one of his toes off.

He screamed in pain and hit the concrete hard, the Glock spinning from his grasp. He lay there in agony, feeling as if someone had dipped his legs in molten lead. The pain was unbearable and he had to fight to remain conscious. Blood spread out in a dark pool round his legs.

Birch was still rolling, attempting to make himself more difficult to hit as he finally tore the automatic free and succeeded in squeezing off two shots in the direction of his attacker.

Both bullets cut through empty air.

There was another short burst from the sub-machine gun, bullets chewing up the concrete close to the DI. Three bullets hit him in the chest, and despite the protection of the Kevlar the pain of the impact was intense. He yelled in agony, the wind almost knocked from him when one slug struck him in the solar plexus. However, to his horror, one of the bullets slammed into his left elbow, obliterating the bone and sending white hot agony lancing up his arm.

He roared his pain and frustration and squeezed off another round from the .459, but he couldn't steady the weapon and again the shot ripped harmlessly through the air.

Both detectives lay still, both in severe pain, both of them gazing at their attacker who took a couple of steps forward, the MP5K still levelled. Birch saw the figure step purposefully on the burning paper, grinding out the flame.

Johnson was barely conscious now. He moaned through gritted teeth as he looked down and saw that part of his shattered shin bone was protruding not only through the flesh of his leg but actually through the material of his trousers. It gleamed whitely in the sunlight, dark marrow dribbling from the centre of the splintered bone.

Birch still clutched the .459 in his right hand.

If you can just get off one shot . . .

But his whole body was shaking. The pain from his smashed elbow was excruciating. And yet, even through that haze of pain, he felt something else as the figure approached him and stood over him, pressing down hard with the heel of one foot on his outstretched right wrist until he finally allowed the automatic to drop from his fingers. The figure kicked it away and the weapon skittered out of reach across the concrete.

A combination of rage, fear and disbelief flowed through Birch's veins like iced water.

He peered up at his captor.

Megan Hunter looked impassively down at him.

85

Birch tried to sit up.

Megan kicked him hard in the face, slamming his head back against the concrete. For fleeting seconds, the detective feared he was going to black out. Her image swam before him.

'Bitch,' he hissed, grabbing for her leg.

She stamped down hard on his outstretched hand.

The heel of her boot descended with such incredible force that the thin heel pierced his palm, tearing the flesh with ease, crushing several metacarpal bones.

Birch shouted in pain and eyed her malevolently. She kept her weight on his hand for a second longer then stepped back slightly, the barrel of the sub-machine gun aimed at his head.

'I'm no expert with this, David,' she said quietly. 'But from this range even I can't miss.'

'You twisted fucking bitch,' he rasped through clenched teeth. 'Did you kill the ARU guys too?'

'One of them.'

'Why did you do it?' he wanted to know.

'I couldn't let you kill it. Couldn't let you destroy this.' She gestured around her at the fairground.

'But you led me to the Wrathchild,' the DI grunted. 'Why? No one need ever have known about it.'

'I knew that once you came here it would all

be over,' she told him. 'You'd be inside the book. You'd be gone. No one would know where. With you gone, the investigation would be over. No one would ever be able to find this place or the Wrathchild.'

'You set me up.' He winced. 'I don't understand why.'

'I just told you, David. So the investigation would be closed. You were the only one who knew about this place, about what Paxton and I had done. About the killings and how they'd been committed. With you dead, the Wrathchild would be safe for ever. If you'd lived you would have carried on looking.'

'Why the fuck do you want it safe?'

'Paxton asked me the same thing.'

'Paxton invented the Wrathchild,' Birch protested. 'Imagined it. Dreamed it up. He created it, not you.'

She shook her head. 'He didn't imagine it,' she said. 'No one did. You see, David, the Wrathchild isn't the product of John Paxton's imagination. Or mine. It's real. It's alive. Flesh and blood just like you and me.'

'Bullshit,' Birch grunted.

'Do you want proof? I know your cynicism requires it.' She smiled coldly.

Johnson was lying silently on his side, watching and listening, his body racked with pain but his mind focused enough to realise that the pistol he had dropped was less than a foot away from the tips of his fingers.

If he could stretch those few inches and close his hand round the weapon, he could catch her unawares. The DS began to move his shaking fingers towards the Glock, feeling the hot concrete beneath him.

'Are the others dead?' Birch asked.

Megan nodded.

'So now what?' he continued. 'You kill us too and that's it? What then, Megan?'

'They'll look for you, David, but they'll never find you. You know that. Not you or him.' She nodded in Johnson's direction. 'Or the other five men. It's all over.'

'And you go back to the real world and wait for that fucking tumour to kill you,' spat Birch.

'Unfortunately, yes,' Megan conceded.

Johnson's fingertips were less than nine inches from the butt of the dropped Glock and stretching closer.

'Who else are you going to get the Wrathchild to kill for you?' the DI demanded.

Johnson's straining fingers were within six inches of the pistol.

'There's no one left,' Megan said. 'I told you that before.'

Three inches and Johnson would be able to touch the weapon. He gritted his teeth against the incredible pain that had engulfed his lower body. Part of the protruding shin bone actually scraped the concrete and it was all he could do to prevent himself from shrieking in renewed agony but, instead, he strained those last few inches to reach the Glock, his fingers brushing the metal.

'If you're going to kill us then get it over with,' Birch snapped defiantly.

Johnson pulled the gun towards him.

The metal scraped on the concrete.

Megan turned towards him and raised the MP5K, a look of anger on her face. The look faded rapidly.

Birch wondered why she was smiling.

He glanced in the direction of his colleague. Johnson had the Glock in his hand, ready to fire at Megan. Birch's eyes gaped wide. He tried to shout a warning.

Megan was still smiling.

The Wrathchild was standing behind Johnson, looking down at him.

The sun glinted on the huge curved blade it held.

86

'Steve!'

Johnson heard his name roared by his superior and, in that split second, he rolled over to see why both Birch and Megan Hunter were looking past him.

The Wrathchild chose that moment to strike.

It brought the blade down with incredible power, catching Johnson across the bridge of the nose.

The blow was delivered with such ferocity that the curved weapon shattered the bridge of the detective's nose with an audible crack then ploughed on through the skull, pulverising the bones of his temple and hacking through his brain before exploding from the rear of his cranium. The upper portion of the head came away as neatly as the top of a boiled egg, blood and brain matter spilling on to the hot concrete.

Johnson's muscles spasmed and his index finger tightened around the trigger of the Glock, a single shot coming from the barrel and cutting harmlessly through the air. He rolled on to his back, his body twitching as the soft hissing of his collapsing sphincter could clearly be heard.

The Wrathchild bent close to the body as if looking for any signs of life. It dug the blade deeply into the throat of the dead man, then kicked the corpse, so that it rolled forward before lying still in a rapidly widening pool of blood.

Megan smiled again, standing motionless as the figure walked across to join her.

'You see, David,' she said, touching the arm of the Wrathchild.

'What the fuck is it?' Birch breathed, his gaze riveted to the newcomer.

The Wrathchild was over six feet tall, its powerful arms hanging at its sides like those of an ape, one huge hand gripping the handle of the curved blade. Birch studied that hand and saw that the index and middle fingers were joined at the base, forming one thick, elongated digit.

Syndactylic fingers.

The fingers on the other hand were short and thick, like half-smoked cigars.

Brachydactylic fingers. No wonder forensics had thought there were two killers.

It was broad across the chest and shoulders. Powerful. But it was the face that Birch found himself staring at, albeit unwillingly.

There was downy hair round the otherwise bald crown but it lacked eyebrows and eyelashes. The mouth was little more than a twisted crimson slash across the milk-white skin. The eyes were bulging in the sockets, the whites of one orb criss-crossed so thickly by blood vessels that the eye looked red. The nose was pig-like, the nostrils too wide apart. There was thick mucus dripping from them. When the Wrathchild licked its lips, saliva hung from the end of its swollen tongue. It craned its neck to look down at Birch.

'Paxton was afraid of him too,' Megan said quietly. 'Right from the beginning.' She reached out and touched the Wrathchild's cheek.

It made a vile mewling sound deep in its throat and looked at her with those bulging eyes.

'But I understood what had to be done,' Megan continued. 'I told Paxton to put him here. To leave him here, where he wouldn't be troubled by others. Where he could grow.'

'So Paxton wrote that fucking thing into a book,' Birch sneered, looking disgustedly at the Wrathchild.

'Ten years ago.' She looked challengingly at the detective, who frowned slightly.

Again the Wrathchild made a gurgling sound. Bubbles of thick mucus formed at one of its nostrils. Its breathing was laboured.

'For ten years he's been here,' Megan persisted. 'Growing. The disease caused the abnormally accelerated growth and the physical deformities.'

'Cushing's syndrome,' Birch said flatly. 'Like the kid you had that died when it was a year old.'

Megan smiled.

'But it didn't die, did it?' Birch murmured.

'No, David,' she said softly, pulling the Wrathchild towards her. 'He didn't die.' She kissed the creature on the lips, some of its sputum dribbling on to her chin. 'This is my son.'

87

'They'd never seen such a rare case of Cushing's disease,' she said venomously. 'The doctors, the nurses. They couldn't believe the extent of it. How virulent it was. Paxton wanted him to die. My son. His son. But I wouldn't allow it. He was my child. He still is and he'll live on after me.'

'That fucking retarded piece of shit is your legacy, is it, Megan?' Birch said disdainfully. 'You must be really proud.'

She kicked him hard between the legs.

Birch doubled up in pain. 'It's a fucking freak,' he gasped. 'No wonder you wanted it shut away.'

Again she kicked him, this time in the face, splitting his bottom lip. He rolled over on to his back and she advanced on him, the Wrathchild keeping its distance, a little bewildered by what it was seeing.

'It's going to die, just like you are,' Birch reminded her.

She stamped hard on his injured elbow and he shrieked madly.

'Like it should have died ten years ago,' he bellowed, rolling over again.

The .459 was less than three yards away. He could see the metal glinting in the sunlight.

'But you wanted it to live,' he taunted. 'If you'd cared about the fucking thing you'd have let it die when you first shat it out.'

Again she kicked him in the face, opening a

cut above his right eye that sent blood flowing warmly down his cheek. He rolled over again, the gun even closer.

'Whose genes were fucked up, then?' he grunted. 'Yours or Paxton's? One of you must have been to produce something like that.' He hawked and spat in the direction of the Wrathchild. The creature advanced towards him and leaned close, pressing the point of the blade to his throat, but Megan held out a hand to keep it back.

'Let the fucking thing kill me,' Birch gasped. 'It does whatever you tell it, doesn't it?'

Again she kicked him and again he rolled over.

It was only the pain now that was keeping him awake. Every muscle in his body ached; the pain from his wounds was appalling. He thought how wonderful it would be to just surrender to the oblivion of unconsciousness that was waiting for him.

A yard from the automatic now.

'Is that why you never had another child, Megan?' he said. 'Afraid you'd push out another fucking mongrel that looked like that cunt?' He nodded in the direction of the Wrathchild.

She swung the MP5K into position, her finger hovering close to the trigger.

'Do it, you sick bitch,' Birch growled, pushing himself backwards a little further by digging his heels against the concrete. He was only a foot from the .459 now. 'Finish it. Killing me isn't going to keep you or that fucking thing alive for much longer.'

She lowered the weapon slightly and leaned closer to him.

'I'm not going to kill you, David,' she told him. 'My son is.'

Birch took his chance. He made a grab for the dropped pistol, rolling clumsily but effectively, forced to endure fresh agony when he landed on his shattered elbow. But with his other hand he grabbed the weapon and swung it up, his index finger finding the trigger.

The Wrathchild roared something incomprehensible and ran at the policeman, the huge curved blade held above its head.

Megan also screamed, realising that she couldn't use the gun without hitting her own offspring.

Ignoring the incredible pain from his punctured and broken right hand, Birch pumped the trigger.

The first shot missed. The second hit the Wrathchild in the left shoulder, tearing through bone and muscles and exploding from its back. As it screamed like a wounded animal, the third 9mm slug tore into its stomach and bent it double. The fourth shot grazed its right cheek, leaving a bright red bloody furrow in its white flesh.

Megan was screaming, tears welling up in her eyes as she watched.

The Wrathchild struggled closer, swinging the blade down with as much power as it could muster.

The cutting edge hacked easily into Birch's left calf, tearing the muscle open and sending more blood spurting into the air. The metal clanged against the concrete beneath and the Wrathchild tried to swing at the detective again but Birch kept on firing, the automatic slamming back against the heel of his hand, empty shell cases spinning into the air.

Another shot hit the Wrathchild in the chest and punctured a lung. The next thudded into the hollow of its throat and sent it reeling backwards, a fountain of blood spraying out behind it.

Tears were pouring down Megan's cheeks now and her lips were moving but Birch couldn't hear what she said because of the thunderous reports from the pistol.

He was crouching as he fired the final two shots. The first one cut through the air close to the creature, the second caught it squarely between the eyes, tore through bone and brain and exploded from the back of the skull, carrying a reeking flux of cranial matter and pulverised bone.

The Wrathchild dropped to its knees, then fell forward on to what was left of its face.

Birch turned the automatic on Megan Hunter.

She had the sub-machine gun levelled at him.

They fired simultaneously.

88

The staccato rattle of the MP5K was matched by the roar of the .459.

Birch felt several bullets hit his body and, even with the Kevlar for protection, he felt as if he'd been hit with a hammer. The breath was torn from him but he remained in his crouching position, still pumping the trigger of the automatic.

Another slug ripped through the top of his left arm and he shouted in pain.

Megan Hunter was hit in the chest and stomach.

She fell backwards, dropping the sub-machine gun.

Birch grunted and fell forward, his clothes soaked in blood and sweat, his body racked with intolerable agony. Deafened by the sustained gunfire, half blinded by the muzzle flashes and the sun that still blazed overhead, he crawled slowly towards the body of Megan Hunter.

Only then did he hear her laboured breathing and a sound that reminded him of air escaping from ruptured bellows. The sound came every time she breathed and he realised that one of his bullets had torn a hole in her lung. The sound he could hear was of a sucking wound. Air rushed into the bullet hole every time she tried to inhale.

She lay motionless on her back, eyes open and still full of tears.

'It's over, Megan,' he said, through gritted teeth.

'You'll never get out of here,' she gasped without looking at him. She coughed and bright red blood spilled over her lips and ran down her face. 'Not without my help.'

'You put me here,' he breathed. 'You knew that from the beginning. You never wanted me to get out.'

He looked behind him at the body of the Wrathchild, then back at Megan. She was slipping rapidly into unconsciousness.

'You'll die here,' she whispered. 'You've lost.'

'I stopped the killings,' he told her. 'That's all that matters. Case closed.'

He lay down beside her, listening to the breath rasping in her lung wound.

Gradually the sound grew fainter until, finally, it ceased altogether.

Birch assumed she was dead. He was close enough to her to have reached out and felt for a pulse but he saw no point. He rolled on to his back, the pain from his many injuries tormenting him.

Above him, the sun still blazed, warming his face. He felt an overpowering urge to close his eyes but feared that if he did he would not open them again.

He badly wanted a cigarette, but when he fumbled in his jacket pocket for one he could barely feel his fingers and the pain from his broken right hand was too great.

Birch lay back again, another sound drifting to him. One that seemed to stand out from the others.

It sounded like laughter.

It took him a moment or two to identify the source of the sound.

He was lying fifty yards from the main entrance of the House of Fun. The waxwork sailor in the glass case over the door was moving shakily back and forth in his transparent prison. The deep bass sounds of merriment were coming from there.

'Fuck you too,' Birch murmured, finally allowing himself to slide towards oblivion.

The laughter echoed across the fairground.

Birch closed his eyes.

'Let them perish through their own imaginations.'

Psalms 5:11